OTHER COUNTRIES

OTHER COUNTRIES

Jo Bannister

Severn House Large Print
London & New York

This first large print edition published 2017
in Great Britain and the USA by
SEVERN HOUSE PUBLISHERS LTD of
Eardley House, 4 Uxbridge Street, London W8 7SY.
First world regular print edition published 2017 by
Severn House Publishers Ltd.

British Library Cataloguing in Publication Data
A CIP catalogue record for this title is available from the British Library.

ISBN-13: 9780727893178

Severn House Publishers support the Forest Stewardship Council™
[FSC™], the leading international forest certification organisation. All
our titles that are printed on FSC certified paper carry the FSC logo.

Typeset by Palimpsest Book Production Ltd.,
Falkirk, Stirlingshire, Scotland.
Printed and bound in Great Britain by
T J International, Padstow, Cornwall.

'Thou hast committed—'
'Fornication? But that was in another
country; and besides, the wench is dead.'

Christopher Marlowe (1564–1593)

One

They won't let you on an aeroplane with a flame-thrower. Rachid Iqbal didn't know much about the world, but he knew that much.

He also knew that he needed papers that would pass serious examination. He was an Arab man travelling to Britain from Turkey, the front line between prosperous, self-protective Europe and the turmoil of the Middle East. The immigration officials who would happily nod through all the tourists and businessmen would hold their rubber stamps in abeyance until they'd taken a really good look at Rachid's documentation. His passport would be subject to close scrutiny. He would be asked the reason for his visit, and you didn't need to be a seasoned traveller to know that Murder wouldn't be a good answer to give.

Most things, including top-class travel documents, can be bought by a man with bottomless pockets. Rachid Iqbal's pockets were not bottomless, and he wasn't even a legal citizen of Turkey. But he had friends, and his friends had friends, and between them they'd supplied him with a passport and visa, and with letters and receipts from a college in London which had enrolled him for a four-week course in the English language for business users. There were other things – the address where he would be staying, the money with which he would meet his expenses, the names and phone-numbers of people who would vouch for him – and all these had cost more than Rachid would ever be able to repay. Even if he'd had any expectation of coming back.

People he knew, people who had travelled by plane, told him what the officials at passport control would be watching for. First, they said, the dark skin; and after that, someone who was nervous. Someone who, though he was plainly accustomed to a warmer climate than England in September, was sweating, and fidgeting with his wristwatch, and looking uneasily about him.

Do a crossword, they'd said. All Englishmen do the crosswords in their newspapers when they have time to kill. (Time to kill! Rachid liked the sound of the words.) It followed that anyone doing a newspaper crossword was already halfway to acceptability. It wouldn't matter that he didn't know any of the answers, or even that he didn't understand the clues. If he had a news-paper, and a pen, and looked thoughtful and occasionally made a mark in one of the little white boxes, no one watching for terrorists and illegal immigrants would give him a second glance. Rachid had spent almost the last of his money – his own money, not that provided for him – buying an exorbitantly expensive copy of *The Times* in the departure lounge at Istanbul.

The one thing he didn't have was a flame-thrower. But that didn't matter, because he knew how to make one.

Two

Grace Maybourne picked at her breakfast, unable to ignore the fluttering of unease in her stomach. Her mother watched, covertly over the cornflakes, unsure whether sympathy or a pep-talk would be a better response.

'It's only first-day nerves,' she said at last. 'You won't be the new girl for long.'

Grace made the effort to smile. She was, and had always been, a dutiful daughter. 'I know.' She pushed away the golden sludge that cornflakes, dowsed in milk but then untouched, invariably turn to. 'I just wish . . .'

'What? That today was over? It will be, before you know it.'

Grace considered. 'Maybe this wasn't such a good idea.'

Definitely not sympathy, thought Mrs Maybourne. No-nonsense briskness. 'Of course it was. You'll like it once you find your way around.'

'Maybe.' Grace thought some more. Finally her fears came spilling out. 'What if I don't? What if they all hate me?'

Mrs Maybourne laughed. 'Gracie! Why on earth would they hate you?'

'Because they all know one another, and I'm the outsider! Because they'll all have their little enmities and allegiances, and I'll say the wrong things to the wrong people because I don't know

3

what they are! Because they'll think I'm intruding, and they'll want to cut me down to size right away to save themselves the trouble of doing it later.

'Because they'll hate my smart new uniform, and the way I do my hair, and my stupid cut-glass accent that's *your* fault for sending me to elocution lessons! Oh Mum,' she wailed, 'I don't want to go! Will you phone in and tell them I'm sick?'

Mrs Maybourne, half laughing still, half crying, reached out plump arms and gathered her daughter to her breast. 'No, of course I won't. You'll be just fine. You'll march in there as if you owned the place, and anything that needs dealing with, you'll do it. This time tomorrow, all this will be forgotten.'

Grace hoped she was right. Still she gave it one last try. 'I don't have to go if I don't want to.'

'Yes,' said Mrs Maybourne firmly, 'you do.'

'Why?' Grace peered out rebelliously from under the freshly trimmed fringe.

Her mother sighed. 'Because, dear, you're the new superintendent of police in Norbold, and they can't ask the last one to come back because somebody shot him.'

That was this morning. Now it was afternoon, and it hadn't been as grim as Grace had feared. There were a couple of decent sergeants at Meadowvale Police Station, and the head of CID seemed to know what he was doing, and now it turned out she wasn't even the only new girl starting today.

4

Superintendent Maybourne glanced at the note on her pad. Constable Hazel Best: not exactly new, but back from extended sick leave. Why did that ring a bell? Ah – yes. She was *that* one. The one they'd told her about. The reason Norbold had needed a new superintendent in the first place. She gave a pensive frown. Did that mean she owed her promotion to Constable Best? And if so, should she be grateful or not?

For now, all she needed to be was courteous and professional. She sent word to the front desk that Constable Best should report to her as soon as she was free. Three minutes later the girl was in her office.

In fact, Hazel Best wasn't a girl. She was twenty-seven, which didn't make her a grey-haired old granny but did make her a little long in the tooth for a probationary constable. This was her second career: she'd been a teacher before joining the thin blue line. She'd done well in college, done well in basic training, was doing well in her first posting . . . and then it had all gone pear-shaped.

Superintendent Maybourne smiled encouragingly. 'Do you want to tell me what happened?'

'I'm happy to tell you what happened, ma'am,' Hazel said carefully. She was still standing at attention, hands behind her back, a tall, well-built young woman with a mass of fair curls that she forced into a bun for work but allowed the freedom of a rough ponytail when she was off duty. 'I'm equally happy for you to hear it from someone else. The facts are a matter of record.

5

In fact . . .' She heard herself straying onto dangerous ground and stopped.

'In fact?' echoed the superintendent, encouragingly. She was twenty years older than the constable, and infinitely more experienced, but her manner, though non-committal, was polite. When women first started reaching the upper echelons of the police service, it seemed that the best way to achieve advancement was to be like their male colleagues: if they weren't hard, brash and abrasive, they pretended to be. By the time Grace Maybourne was making her presence felt, though, there was a recognition that good women officers brought different qualities to the table. There was nothing mannish about her. But no one ever looked into her cool blue eyes and thought she represented an easy option.

Hazel took a deep breath. She had known this interview was coming; she hadn't expected it to be easy; but she was damned if she was going to apologise for things that weren't her fault. 'In fact,' she went on determinedly, 'I imagine you've already read the report. It exonerated me of any wrong-doing. Bad things happened in this police station, but I wasn't responsible for any of them. And I didn't shoot Superintendent Fountain. That was his old friend and co-conspirator, Mickey Argyle.'

'But you *did* shoot *him*.' It was a comment rather than an accusation.

'Yes, I did. He had a gun, he'd already shot Mr Fountain, he was going to shoot others, including me. I had a gun too. I stopped him.'

And though the official report had been

substantial enough to deforest a small area of Sweden, that, really, was all that needed to be said. Meadowvale's senior officer had forgotten his duty. One of its newest recruits had remembered hers.

'You've been on leave for, what, four months?'

'A little over,' said Hazel.

'Long enough?'

'Quite long enough.'

'The medical board agrees, on the whole. With the proviso that you should work yourself in gently. No more shoot-ups and fisticuffs, at least for a while.'

'I have no problem with that.' It was true. Hazel didn't go looking for trouble. Somehow, trouble seemed to come looking for her.

'I don't doubt we can find something useful for you to do while you're getting back up to speed.'

This had been inevitable. Hazel was resigned to manning a desk for a while. 'I'm good on a computer. I used to teach IT.'

Grace Maybourne smiled again. This time, Hazel noticed, it was a little impish round the edges. 'That's certainly a useful accomplishment. But actually, I had something else in mind . . .'

Hazel went home early. Another idea of the medical board's: a week of short days. She changed, bailed her hair on its own recognisance, and went out again.

Gabriel Ash was doing housework. The big stone house in Highfield Road looked cleaner and brighter for his efforts, but not necessarily more cheerful. He lacked an eye for homeliness. Hazel made a mental note to take him shopping soon, and stock up on things that weren't brown.

His dog Patience was staying out of the way. She rolled her toffee-coloured eyes in despair as Hazel passed her in the hall.

Ash stopped when he saw his visitor and put the vacuum away under the stairs. 'How was your day?'

'Could have been worse,' Hazel said pensively. 'Most of the guys seem to have forgiven me for being right. And I liked the new superintendent.'

'Was this the first time you'd met him?'

'Her,' said Hazel deliberately. 'Yes. She came down from Birmingham.'

'What's she like?'

'Refreshingly normal. A bit smaller than me; mid-forties, light brown hair, blue eyes . . .' She heard herself describing a suspect and broke off with a wry chuckle. 'Normal. Talks to you like a human being rather than a faintly disgusting sub-species.'

She moved the duster from where Ash had left it on the leather sofa – cushions, she thought, green and yellow, something to bring a bit of sunshine in – and sank into it. 'What about you? Why the sudden interest in domestic science?'

He didn't understand. When he was at school, the boys did woodwork while the girls were doing domestic science. He hadn't understood the woodwork either.

Hazel waved an airy hand at the results of his labours. 'The tidying-up. The dusting. Hell's bells, I can even smell polish!'

And in that moment, with the words barely out of her mouth, she knew exactly what had prompted it. She should have realised before, and not joked about it. Ash would forgive her, because they were friends and he knew she would never deliberately hurt him; still Hazel wished the words unsaid. 'Have you had the social workers round?'

'Tomorrow.' He took the broad-bosomed chair beside the stove. 'I thought I'd try to make a good impression.'

'Well, yes,' Hazel agreed, 'it can't do any harm. But don't let anyone suggest that a bit of dog-hair on the carpet means you're not a good father. You *are* a good father. You're a good man.'

Ash accepted the compliment with a rueful sniff. 'I *want* to be a good father. I'm not sure I know how.'

'I think most parents worry that they're not up to the job.' Hazel wasn't speaking from personal experience. 'The better the parent, the more they seem to worry. You've just got out of the way of it. You'll do fine.' She glanced round the kitchen and listened for a moment. 'Where are the boys?'

'After-school club. Their head teacher thought it would be a good idea: help them to make new friends. They're not actually that far behind their year-groups. Cathy had them in a little private school in Cambridge: a bit 1950s, but they've got the basics in place. What they've mostly missed is the social side: doing things with boys their own age. For obvious reasons, they weren't encouraged to make friends.'

Well no, thought Hazel, since they were supposed to be under armed guard in Somalia, Ash's wife wouldn't want them making the kind of friends you trade confidences with. 'Our name didn't used to be Anderson. It was Ash, but Mummy said we had to change it. We're not supposed to tell *anybody*!'

'They'll get the hang of it soon enough,' she said.

Ash grinned. 'Guy, of course, loves being part of a gang. He doesn't care what they're doing as long as there's a bunch of them doing it. Gilbert is more reserved. But then, I was no good at that sort of thing when I was eight. His reticence may have more to do with genetics than social deprivation.'

Hazel sighed. 'Gabriel – you're *still* no good at that sort of thing.'

As if aware that the housework had been abandoned for now, the white lurcher came padding back into the kitchen, assessed the seating arrangements and headed for the sofa. Hazel shuffled up obligingly.

'They've got me on restricted duties for a couple of weeks. Guess what they want me to do.'

Gabriel Ash was supremely good at logic. He could take a shedload of apparently unconnected facts, mentally weigh the probabilities and extrapolate to conclusions that would have seemed mere flights of fancy but for his track-record of being right. It was a skill he had learned in the insurance industry and honed as a government security analyst. In spite of that, or perhaps because of it, he had no talent for guessing. 'Er . . .'

Hazel shook her head. 'You never will, so I'll tell you. They want me to nurse-maid a visiting celebrity. Oliver Ford.' Seeing his puzzlement, she explained, as she would have had to for almost no one else she knew. 'The historian? Fronts a whole load of television programmes. Was short-listed for a BAFTA for his series on Richard the Lionheart last summer.'

Still Ash had the attentive, blank expression of a sniffer dog with a head cold – willing but unable to help.

'Okay,' said Hazel resignedly, 'let's take it a step at a time. You know how a television works?'

'By picking up a signal transmitted . . .?'

'No, no,' said Hazel. 'I mean, you turn it on at the wall and then you press the button. And a lot of the time a little man comes out and talks to you about stuff. Well, quite often, if the stuff has anything to do with history, the little man is going to be Oliver Ford.'

Ash was nodding slowly. Her teasing didn't offend him. He'd been out of circulation for a while. It was only thanks to Hazel's efforts that he was slowly gaining on the twenty-first century. 'What's he doing in Norbold? A series on the treasures of the Black Country?'

'Hardly,' chuckled Hazel. 'There's a new museum opening at Wittering. Britain's role in the Crusades or something. That's his period.'

'I thought the Crusaders were rather frowned on these days,' Ash commented mildly. 'All that

11

riding over other people's countries, and poking the residents with sharp sticks to make them believe in the goodness of the Christian God.'

Hazel shrugged. Her interest in history had come to an end when she left school. 'Maybe it's not that helpful to judge people who lived almost a thousand years ago by the standards of today. Plus, even today common sense goes out the window when religion marches in by the door. Christian Europe thought it was important to keep the infidels away from the Holy Places around Jerusalem. Funnily enough, the Saracens thought pretty much the same thing. At least while they were fighting one another they weren't persecuting anyone else.'

It wasn't exactly an in-depth analysis of three hundred years of political, military and economic upheaval spread across half the then-known world. But it served.

'All the same,' said Ash doubtfully, 'I can't see people forming a queue outside a museum set up to glorify the Crusaders.'

'They will if Oliver Ford's involved. This is what he does – takes a subject nobody's interested in and makes it required viewing. He's a bit of a charmer. He's the eye-candy that makes people – well, all right, women – who've never given any thought to the Crusades before want to know more about Richard and Saladin and whose turn it was to hold Jerusalem. It's not a bad way to drip-feed the general populace a bit of extra learning – give them someone pretty and witty to look at.'

'And that's what makes Oliver Ford a celebrity

instead of just an historian.' Ash considered. 'I mean, David Sperrin is an historian – at least, he's an archaeologist – but no one ever suggested he needed police protection.'

Hazel couldn't decide which was more unlikely: that their bad-tempered friend might be deemed in need of protection as he knelt in his muddy holes groping for bits of broken pot, or that he might accept it if offered. She shook the image from her head. 'David isn't famous.'

'Oliver Ford can't be that famous either. *I'd* never heard of him.'

Hazel let that pass without comment. '*Everyone* on the TV is famous. If only for being famous, which is pretty much what being a celebrity is.'

'And celebrities need police protection?'

'Apparently. There's a big film crew in tow, a lot of vehicles, so a police presence is required. To control the hordes of salivating middle-aged women who might want to throw their corsets at Mr Ford. To make sure that, in order to film him in the most flattering light, the crew don't close all six lanes of the motorway. That kind of thing. Someone has to liaise, and this time it's me.'

'Well, it should be interesting.'

Hazel rocked a non-committal hand. 'I thought they'd want me to hang out with Melvin the computer geek for a fortnight. Tidying up the networks, backing up the files, playing *Warriors of Wolfworld* when no one's around. I was looking forward to getting all the gossip I've missed over the last four months. It never occurred to me they'd actually have a job for me to do.'

'It doesn't sound like a very *demanding* job,' ventured Ash.

'Keeping a television hot-shot and his retinue from turning the district upside down? Of course not,' she said sourly. 'I'm so lucky that none of the people heading up the queue for plum jobs was available, so the task was delegated down the line until it reached the station trouble-maker just back from a psychiatric break!'

Three

Oliver Ford was not quite as tall as he looked on television. He was also a little older and a little heavier, and right now a lot more harassed. His trailer had taken a wrong turn outside Nuneaton and he hadn't seen it since. The producer kept assuring him she was in contact with the driver, Ford's home-from-home would be at the shoot by the time he needed it, but he couldn't help worrying. Everything that made filming bearable was packed into that trailer. Fresh clothes, his favourite tipple, reading matter – scholarly tomes for when the cameras might stray his way, a paperback thriller for when he was alone – and the cosmetics that made him look human under the powerful lighting. He laughed and called it 'My slap', and aloud bemoaned the fact that television makes normal people look like startled zombies. Privately, though, he'd noticed that life was starting to have the same effect.

Now this blonde girl was trying to attract his attention. He didn't even recognise her. Surely they weren't letting the groupies in yet! He inclined his head – where *was* that damned hairdresser? – slightly in her direction. 'Listen, sweetie, I'm a little busy right now. Why don't you have a word with the PR guy? – Justin, that's him over there. I'll try and catch you later.'

'Mr Ford' – and that surprised him, right there, because mostly they called him Oliver and occasionally Ollie – 'my instructions are to stay with you. To protect you from over-enthusiastic fans. You can call me Hazel or Constable Best, but not Sweetie unless you're sure your insurance is up to date.'

That got his full attention. He swivelled and stared at her, the only fixed point in a river of bustling bodies. She smiled back amiably, as if she hadn't just threatened him. As if he must have misheard, or misunderstood. 'Hazel?'

'Or Constable Best. I'm your police liaison officer while you're in Norbold.'

'Norbold.' Ford looked around vaguely. 'Is that where we are?'

'More or less. This is Wittering: Norbold's about four miles that way.' She pointed. 'This is the new Museum of the Crusades.' The historian continued to look blank. Hazel went on, pointedly, 'Today is Wednesday, the opening ceremony is in a couple of hours, and you're doing the honours. Afterwards you're doing some filming here. For your new series?'

Finally that seemed to ring a bell. 'Oh – yes. Quite. Sorry, I'm a bit jet-lagged – I only got into Heathrow last night. Interesting period, the Crusades,' he said, warming to his subject. 'Nearly as interesting as the way twenty-first-century political correctness has tried to airbrush it out of history. That whole era between 1096 and 1453, that involved pretty well everyone of consequence in much of Europe and the Middle East, that laid the foundations of alliances and rivalries whose ripples spread up to the present day – we're supposed to pretend it never happened.'

Ford shook his head bemusedly; the thick conker-coloured hair, cut just a shade too carefully, danced in his eyes. 'You know what they say about history: that those who don't remember it are condemned to repeat it. It's my job to present people with the facts: what they make of those facts is up to them. Love them or hate them, the Crusaders were important in their own time and have been consistently misunderstood ever since. I hope this new series will set the record straight.'

Hazel was pretty sure he'd already forgotten who she was. He was giving her the sound-bite he'd prepared for the reporters covering the opening ceremony. 'Jolly good,' she said encouragingly.

Ford blinked velvety chocolate-brown eyes. Apparently that wasn't the response he was expecting. 'And you're from – where, again?'

'Meadowvale Police Station, Norbold.'

The historian frowned then as another thought struck him. 'You're not in uniform. Are you a detective?'

16

Hazel shook her head. Her hair was down, gathered in the nape of her neck by an elastic band. 'Just trying to blend in, Mr Ford. No need to make people nervous. The Crusaders aren't the only ones who're consistently misunderstood.'

A tall, angular woman with a clipboard bustled by. 'Oh good, you two have met. Heather's going to keep you out of trouble, Oliver.' She snorted a laugh. 'Rather her than me! Anything you need, Heather, just give me a shout.' She bustled away without waiting for a reply.

'Hazel,' Hazel murmured to her departing back.

'Or Constable Best,' added Oliver Ford; and they traded a grin.

Rachid Iqbal had learned English at school in Istanbul. He had thought himself fairly proficient – had once won a prize for it. At Rachid's school, prizes were always books, and you were allowed to choose your own. Rachid had chosen a book in English – *Pride and Prejudice* by Miss Jane Austen – immediately earning himself points towards the next year's prize.

Now he was here, though, he seemed to be rather less proficient in English than he'd thought. Either that, or the inhabitants of that broad area around Birmingham known variously as The Midlands or The Black Country spoke a local patois only loosely related to the language he'd studied. In the general store, spending some of the English pounds his friends had gathered up for him, they tried to sell him hair gel and cigarettes rather than

17

what he was – quite clearly, he thought – asking for.

Finally, with a sigh of relief and his modest purchases in a plastic bag, he left the store and began looking for the bus station. Again, the unfamiliarity of the local inhabitants with their own language proved an obstacle. They directed him variously to the train station and the police station, before somebody eventually understood that he wanted to take a bus.

At the bus station, at last he got lucky. There was a picture of where he was heading pinned to the booking office wall. Abandoning all attempts to communicate in English, he pointed and proffered his money. The clerk took almost all of it. But that didn't matter. Rachid had only to get there. He wouldn't need money after that.

Museums weren't really Hazel's cup of tea. She was the wrong age: neither an enthusiastic pre-teen nor a serious grown-up. Given a wet enough weekend, she had been known to wander into the Birmingham Museums & Art Gallery to marvel at their Pre-Raphaelite collection, but she doubted if it could ever be wet enough to drive her into a military museum. Because that's what this was, even if the wars it commemorated were long enough ago to have acquired a kind of glamour. Although she was a soldier's daughter, she didn't thrill to the colours and the bands. In fact she harboured an instinctive suspicion that the more panoply an army required, the less confident it was in the rightness of its cause.

She'd been the only girl in her class to side

18

with Cromwell and the Roundheads when they'd studied the English Civil War. There was no denying that the Cavaliers had all the best hats; but the principle at issue – the Divine Right of Kings versus the primacy of Parliament – seemed unarguable to her. If the king and his champions hadn't been allowed to wear lace and plumes but had had to debate their case instead, she reckoned the whole thing would have been over in a fortnight.

On the subject of panoply, Oliver Ford was being prepared for his close-ups: primped and painted to even out the flaws the television cameras would otherwise home in on ruthlessly. It was a little like getting a house ready to sell, thought Hazel – repointing the mortar and painting the down-spouts.

The official opening of the Museum of the Crusades was still an hour away, but there was work to be done before Ford would cut the ribbon with a twinkle of the eye and some charmingly provocative banter. The producer, whose name was Emerald, was setting up the to-camera pieces she wanted to shoot inside the museum for the forthcoming series, on the grounds that the place would never be tidier, the glass never better polished, than today, before the public were admitted. So two sets of activities were converging in both time and space, and the scene was one of mounting chaos as people in museum blazers laid out rows of chairs in the little stone-walled courtyard outside the foyer, and other people in jeans and T-shirts moved them because they were in the way of the cameras.

Amidst all this busyness, Hazel felt surplus to requirements. If any liaising needed doing, it wasn't here and now, and there was nothing to protect the celebrity from except the excesses of his own make-up artist. She wandered round the museum, being careful not to leave fingerprints on the glass cases, but there's only so much pleasure to be had from seeing model soldiers fighting in a sandpit, however splendid their tiny flags.

At least she wasn't the only one watching from the sidelines, isolated from the mounting activity. When she first saw the boy wandering along the edge of the scrum, plainly looking for someone, she thought he was Ford's hairdresser. But he wasn't just too young, he was too ordinary, entirely lacking the flamboyance of person, dress and gesture which are part of the stock-in-trade. He was a gopher, the can of hairspray in his hand the missing necessity he'd been sent in search of. Now he'd found the hairspray, he'd lost the person who wanted it, and he was verging on panic.

Hazel tapped him on the shoulder. 'Mr Ford's trailer is over there. They're doing his make-up right now.'

The boy cast her a grateful look, and a quick nod, and hurried away.

Emerald stalked by, tapping her clipboard with her pen in an irritable, staccato rhythm. 'What do you *mean*, we can't get the swords out of the case? I want to film Oliver handling them – wielding them! Otherwise there's no sense of scale. They're steel, for pity's sake, what harm's it going to do? He'll put his gloves on. I never have this problem at the V&A . . .' The tide of activity carried her, and the small but incredibly dogged-looking museum director she was arguing with, out of earshot.

Hazel was left in an improbable hiatus, like the eye of a storm, all the bustle circling around her, with nothing to do but perch on a low stone wall and watch the activity, and wonder if the few minutes of coverage that the museum's opening would get on the television news tonight could possibly be worth all this effort.

And think.

There's a lot to learn as a new police officer. More than anyone applying for the job ever expects. There's the law, and the role of the police in upholding the law, and the procedures hammered out to protect both the officer and the public. There are the respective roles of all the other statutory authorities, and how they should dovetail, and how to manage the fall-out when they inevitably fail to. There's even what is often called the feel for the job, which is an amalgam of all the things that can't be written down, tested for and marked, but without which no police officer will be successful: an instinct for when the public good will be best served by coming down hard on transgressors, and when more will be achieved by offering advice and support. In short, when to help little old ladies cross the road, and when to book them for jay-walking.

Hazel had been well taught, but she also had good instincts. She had never wanted to judge her performance by the number of arrests she

21

made. Arrests meant crimes, the commission of which transformed some citizens into criminals and some into victims. It had to be better, she reasoned, if good attentive policing could prevent the commission of crime in the first place. Also, she was a kindly young woman. She would rather keep people out of trouble than make them pay.

Closely allied to this feel for tactful versus muscular policing was the sixth sense for when a situation was inherently dangerous and when it was merely boisterous. The invisible line between a rowdy party and an incipient riot. You can't teach that, either. Mostly, people learn it by experience or they don't learn it at all. Hazel was beginning to learn it.

Now she found, sitting on her wall out of the surge of activity, that she was experiencing that sense of heightened alertness – the pricking of the hairs on her arms, the sharpening of her eyes and ears – that signalled something wrong. She might have looked around, seen nothing amiss, been unable to think what *might* go amiss at a museum – unless the exasperated director finally stabbed Emerald with one of his precious swords – and dismissed her edginess as an aberration. She didn't do that. She scanned the scene carefully, and interrogated her memory, and though she still couldn't pinpoint the reason for her unease, she was never tempted to dismiss it. Something had provoked it, even if she didn't know what. She kept looking, kept thinking.

The door of the trailer opposite opened and Oliver Ford emerged, as carefully groomed as a finalist at Crufts, thick hair swept back theatrically over his left temple, talking over his shoulder to the make-up artist as he came down the steps.

His hair. His thick dark chestnut hair was perfect. It needed another can of hairspray like a lily needs gilding. *So what was that boy with the lost expression actually doing?*

Hazel was on her feet now, scanning the sea of heads for the out-of-place one. If he hadn't been sent for hairspray, what was he doing wandering round with it? *Hiding in plain sight, that's what.*

He might have been nothing more than an enterprising autograph-hunter. But Hazel didn't think so. She *knew* that something was wrong, had known even before she focused in on the boy. She moved purposefully towards him, shouldering indignant camera crew out of her way. At the same time the boy was moving towards Ford, and Ford was moving towards the little podium in front of the entrance, still symbolically sealed with blue ribbon.

They were all going to come together in the thickest part of the crowd.

Hazel knew what to do as if she'd been dealing with such situations all her life. She didn't even have to think about it: she knew. She went from purposeful march to Usain Bolt in a split second, driven through the crowd by strong muscles and the certain knowledge that she had only moments to prevent a disaster. A yell of warning preceded her.

That had the desired effect. No one knew what she was shouting about, but every head turned her way. The smarter among them realised there was some danger, even though they couldn't work out where or what it was. The very smartest headed for the car park without even trying to.

Hazel was almost fast enough. She reached Oliver Ford with an outstretched arm as the boy pointed the spray can in the historian's face and thumbed down hard on the button, simultaneously flicking the cigarette lighter in his other hand.

She couldn't reach the boy to wrest the components of his homemade flame-thrower from him. Instead she piled into Oliver Ford with enough force to throw him out of the belching flame, the fiery tongue that swept everything within a metre like a dragon's breath.

Ford was in the blast zone for less than a second. But in projecting him out of range, Hazel took his place. She just had time to think, with a kind of desperate self-recrimination, 'Oh bugger!' Then the world blew up.

Four

The rest of the day passed in a kind of fog, neither sleeping nor waking. Hazel was aware of unfamiliar sounds, of people fussing round her, and later of people she felt she ought to know sitting with her and talking quietly. But the painkillers stopped her worrying too much about what they were saying. She was content to lie in this comfortable if unfamiliar bed and snooze, and protest weakly when someone came to take her temperature or check her dressings.

Somewhere during the night she started feeling more in touch with the world again, as well as sorer. She moved her head cautiously on the pillow, trying to work out who the slumbering figure in the chair beside her was. 'Dad?'

Her voice wasn't much more than a breath in the dim room. But Fred Best had been twenty years a soldier: like a flamingo, he slept with only half of his brain at a time. He was immediately wide awake.

'I'm right here, Hazel. Everything's all right. You'll be fine in a few days. Are you in pain? I can get someone . . .'

She gave a minuscule shake of her head. A large dressing on her left cheek prevented her from moving far. ''M okay. What happened?'

'There was an – incident – at the museum. Some kid tried to blow it up. Politics, I guess. The bloke who was opening it was in the firing line. You shoved him out of the way, but you took some of the blast yourself.'

Now she nodded, slowly, remembering. 'Hairspray. And a cigarette lighter. And then . . .' She frowned. 'The roof fell in?'

Best gave a bleak chuckle. 'No, but I bet it sounded like it. The can exploded in his hand. You were about four feet away at the time.'

Hazel winced. 'Is he dead?'

'Not yet. He lost the hand, I'm told, and he's badly burned. They've got him under guard somewhere here in the hospital.'

25

Hazel was puzzled. 'Isn't a museum rather an odd thing to want to blow up? What was he hoping to achieve?'

'He's an Arab,' said Best simply. He hoped that didn't make him sound like a racist, but wasn't concerned enough to tiptoe around the facts.

'And Wittering is a Museum of the Crusades,' murmured Hazel. 'Still, eight hundred years is a long time to hold a grudge!'

'Who cares about his cause?' growled Best. 'You behave like a terrorist, you forfeit the right to be heard.'

Something he'd said earlier caught up on her. 'What did you mean,' asked Hazel, 'he's not dead *yet*?'

'I told you. There's a guard on his room. I haven't figured out how to get past them yet.'

Another visitor was Grace Maybourne. She considered Hazel pensively. 'I was told I should keep an eye on you.'

'It wasn't my fault!' insisted Hazel indignantly.

'Of course not. Neither was what happened before. It's just that, for good or ill, some people have the habit of being where the action is. You're one of those people. That's why I should keep an eye on you. Like watching a weather-vane.'

'My dad said he was an Arab. Is that really what it was all about? He wanted to avenge the Crusades?'

Maybourne shook her head wearily. 'Hardly credible, is it? All the trouble in the Middle East, and he's nothing better to worry about than which

26

bunch of religious maniacs held the keys to a desert city eight centuries ago. If people would just stop fixating on what happened to their ancestors and concentrate on what's going to become of their children . . .!'

She heard herself growing strident and stopped abruptly. After a moment she said, in a normal tone of voice, 'He's still in intensive care, he wouldn't make any sense even if we were allowed to interview him. When he's on the mend, I'll ask him if that's really the best excuse he has for fire-bombing some history buffs, a TV personality and one of my officers.'

'Will he live?'

'Yes. He'll need skin-grafts on his face, and they couldn't save his hand, but he'll live.'

'Is he local? I didn't recognise him.'

'You wouldn't. He flew in from Turkey on Monday.'

'He came fifteen hundred miles to do this?' What was left of Hazel's eyebrows climbed until they met bandage. 'What possible interest could a Turk have in a little museum in an English village? If he'd been an Iraqi or an Afghan, and it was a big London museum celebrating the modern British Army, maybe. But Wittering? I wouldn't have thought the average Turk had even heard of it.'

'We don't actually know that he's a Turk, only that Istanbul is where he boarded his flight. His passport was a forgery, so he could have come from anywhere.'

'Do we know his name?'

'Only the name on the documents we know to

27

be false.' Maybourne gave a troubled little smile. 'Hazel, I don't think you should spend too much time thinking about this man. He's an angry, misguided young man who thought he could change history by hurting people who never hurt, or wanted to hurt, him or anyone he ever met. There is no sense in what he did, and therefore no point in wondering who he is or why he did it. You don't need to know his name. He didn't ask yours before he tried to kill you.'

'To be fair,' said Hazel reasonably, 'it wasn't me he was trying to kill. It was the TV personality that everyone's heard of – that was how he was going to get the media coverage. And I want to know his name' – she frowned, trying to explain it to herself as much as to the superintendent – 'because he had some purpose in mind when he lit that spray-can. Who he is, where he came from, goes some way towards explaining what he did. I'd like to know what was going through his head when he burnt my fringe off!'

Maybourne was nodding as if something was becoming clear to her. Possibly it was nothing to do with the young man in intensive care. 'Actually, Hazel . . .'

'Mm?'

'From what they tell me . . .'

Now she was becoming alarmed. 'What?'

'Your fringe is the least of your problems.'

At the weekend Gabriel Ash brought his two sons in to see her. That still gave Hazel a little start. She couldn't get used to seeing two little boys where she was used to seeing the white lurcher.

28

Of course, they didn't let dogs visit you in hospital, although they would almost certainly be cleaner and less troublesome than little boys.

By now the dressings had been pared back so that she looked more like an Indian brave than an Indian maharajah. Looking in the mirror she'd insisted on having, she'd seen what Superintendent Maybourne had been referring to. Still wildly indignant, she made Ash look too. 'What am I supposed to do with that? One plait? Half a Mohican? Or just keep walking anticlockwise so people only ever see the side of my head with hair still on it?!!'

'I'm sure it'll grow back,' murmured Ash. 'Won't it?'

'It had bloody better!' snarled Hazel. 'But it'll take months. Years before both sides match again.'

'Cut the other side,' volunteered Gilbert.

He was the quieter, more intense, more intelligent of Ash's boys. When he thought something was worth saying, it was usually worth listening to him.

Hazel stared at him. Dark-eyed and moody, his father at eight years old, he stared back. 'You want me to shave both sides of my head? You really think that would be an improvement?'

'He has a point,' ventured Ash. 'Not shave it, but cut it short. It'll match up a lot quicker if you do.'

'Have you any idea how long it took me to grow it?' she demanded. 'How long it takes me every night to wash it, dry it and plait it up, because otherwise I can't get a comb through it

29

in the morning? You think I do that because when I stagger in from a late shift smelling of stale beer, fish and chips, and vomit, there's nothing I'd sooner be doing? I do it because . . . because . . .'

And there, hearing herself whining like a girl, she stopped. She shrugged and lay back on her pillows. 'You're right. Gilbert's right. Who needs all that anyway? I'll lop the rest off tomorrow.'

Five

Which is what she was doing, doggedly, refusing to think of it as a loss so much as a tidying-up of loose ends, when Oliver Ford arrived the next morning.

At first she couldn't see who it was. She appeared to be getting a visit from an enormous bunch of flowers and a pair of shoes. It was only when the flowers addressed her, somewhat hesitantly, as 'Constable Best?' that she recognised him.

She might still have had trouble recognising him, even without the flowers. When he put them down on the bedside table, Hazel saw that the improvised flame-thrower had left its mark on him too. One side of his face and neck was a deep bluey-red, with some of the gubbins her own injuries were painted with on top.

'Mr Ford! Have a seat.' Then she realised that the chair was covered with a sheet of newspaper and her discarded hair, and she tried to bundle them out of sight before she embarrassed him.

It was too late. He'd seen the hair, the straw-gold profusion piled sadly beside her, and that side of his face that could do, paled. To her astonishment he was blinking back tears. 'Oh Hazel . . .'

Somehow, his distress made her see her own for the self-indulgence it was. 'For heaven's sake,' she said briskly, 'nobody died. Hair grows back; even skin grows back. A month from now you won't know anything happened except that I had a haircut.'

'Of course I'll know,' he said in a low voice. 'I'll know you saved my life, and risked your own to do it.'

Hazel cleared the chair and patted it. 'That's pretty much part of the job description. It isn't a big part. You pick up a lot of drunks and take home a lot of nuisance kids, and stop a lot of bad drivers and you even give a lot of people the right time. But if push comes to shove, protecting the public is the highest priority. Higher than protecting yourself. Because that's what you're paid for, and they're the ones doing the paying.

'You don't find yourself in that position very often,' she assured him earnestly. 'You can go through an entire career without finding it necessary to put your life on the line. But if the circumstances arise where you have to, you hope to God you will. Because otherwise there's been an element of fraud in everything you've done. You've taken all the strawberry creams out of the chocolate box and left someone else with the jaw-breaker toffee.'

Ford laughed at that: an awkward, half-swallowed little laugh, because the last thing he wanted was for Hazel to think he was amused by her quaint, old-fashioned ideas about duty.

She put him at ease with a ready grin – a slightly lopsided grin, because one side of her face was swollen. 'So thank you for the flowers. They're beautiful. But they're not strictly necessary. I did what I was there to do. Any of my colleagues would have done the same. As for that' – she screwed up the newspaper and lobbed it into the waste-paper basket – 'it's time I tried a new hairstyle.'

Ford wasn't deceived by her cavalier manner. He was however impressed by it. 'When are you getting out of here?'

'Tomorrow, I think. There's nothing more to be done. Time and clean living will repair the damage.'

'When you feel up to it, I'd like to take you out to lunch.'

'That's very kind of you,' said Hazel. 'But like the flowers, it isn't . . .'

'. . . Strictly necessary. I know. But I'd enjoy it. Will you come? Nothing too formal – a country pub somewhere, if that's your pleasure. I can't repay what you did for me. But I can thank you.'

'Well . . . that would be very pleasant,' decided Hazel. 'If we can find somewhere that'll let us through the door looking like this.'

The idea that he might not be welcome

somewhere clearly surprised Oliver Ford. A dangerous light flickered in his eye. 'You choose where we're going,' he said, 'and if there are any problems, I'll *buy* the place.'

Hazel chuckled. Only when Ford failed to join in did she realise that he was entirely serious. 'I'll give it a bit of thought.' She scribbled out her number. 'Call me tomorrow and we'll find a day. How long are you going to be in the area, anyway?'

Ford gave an elegant shrug. 'I'm not sure. I've still got to open that museum. I never did cut the damned ribbon. Then there's filming for the series – but Emerald may want to wait until I look a bit more like my mug-shots again.'

They chatted inconsequentially for a few minutes, then Ford got up to leave. 'I'll call you tomorrow.' He got as far as the door, then hesitated. 'Time and clean living, you say?'

Hazel's smile broadened. 'They sort out most problems.'

He sighed. 'I may have to settle for what time alone will achieve.'

The burns specialist paid Hazel a last visit the following morning. 'Come back in three days and we'll check those dressings. Apart from that, all you need do is keep it dry, put your feet up and stay out of trouble. Finish the painkillers but I don't think you'll need any more. Take a couple of weeks off work, and be a bit careful with yourself for a month after that.'

Hazel scowled. 'I've only just got *back* to work.'

'And now you're off again,' he said, entirely without sympathy. 'A fortnight at least, longer if there are any signs of infection. Just be glad you don't need grafts – we'd be talking months then.'

There was one last thing Hazel needed to do before she left. Perhaps *needed* wasn't the right word, but it was more than casual curiosity. She'd come through the attack without permanent damage, yet she felt to have left something behind in that little stone-walled courtyard. One thread of her existence had become ravelled up in the desperate moment of the explosion, and though she had emerged essentially intact, it hadn't come with her. It was there still, tangled, waiting for resolution. There were two things she needed to do to make herself whole again. One was to return to the museum. The other was to understand *why*.

She found her way to intensive care. Constable Budgen was propped in a chair by the entrance to the ward, reading a magazine. It was called *Fancy Birds* and had a couple of cool chicks strutting their stuff on the front cover. Constable Budgen was a pigeon fancier.

'Hi, Wayne. So you drew the short straw. Anything happening?'

He had the magazine halfway to the floor before he saw who it was and retrieved it. 'Hi, Hazel. Yeah – Mr Gorman asked for volunteers to stand guard here, and everyone else took one step backwards.'

Hazel chuckled in sympathy. She had a fondness for Wayne Budgen. He was a decent,

34

well-meaning, unambitious young copper and though he would never make chief constable, she doubted if he'd ever do the dirty on anyone either, which was perhaps more important.

'No,' he went on, answering her last question, 'not a thing. He's well out of it. Poor little bugger.' Then he looked up, guiltily. 'Sorry, Hazel – I know he hurt you. I know he came here to hurt people. But you look at him lying in that bed, half his body covered in burns and a bloody great dressing where his hand ought to be, and he doesn't look old enough to be out alone. And you wonder who the hell made him hate us so much that this seemed like a good idea.'

Knowing she probably shouldn't, but also that right now – seared and cleansed and dosed with antibiotics – she was as aseptic as a human being ever wants to be, she edged into the ward, to where she could see him. Or as much of him as wasn't covered in gel and bandages. She'd had a good look at him at the museum and exchanged a few words, and she expected to recognise him now. But his own mother wouldn't have recognised him now. Wayne Budgen was right. He was just a poor little bugger who'd been conned into believing that someone else's death was more important than his life.

'Do we have a name for him yet?'

Budgen shook his head. 'False papers. He could be anybody.'

Hazel was still looking at the unconscious figure, horribly flat under the hospital sheet. 'He isn't, though,' she murmured. 'He has a name. He has a family, and friends, and there are things he cares

35

about and things he believes in. What in the name of God did he hope to achieve by fire-bombing an obscure little museum in the middle of England?'

'He's an Arab.'

Hazel went on waiting. She thought there was more coming. But there wasn't: that was it. 'So?'

'Well – they *do* hate us, don't they? In the name of God.'

'I think that's a bit sweeping,' frowned Hazel. 'But even if it is that simple, that he wanted to kill English people because of . . . whatever . . . why come all the way to Wittering? There aren't any English people in London, where his plane landed? There weren't any in Birmingham where he got off the train? What brought him all this way to do what he did?'

'The Crusader connection?' hazarded Budgen. 'He was striking a blow at British imperialism.'

'By fire-bombing a TV celebrity? How many Arabs have even heard of Oliver Ford? Hell, *Gabriel* hadn't heard of him. He might think he's universally famous, but he isn't.'

'Hazel,' said Constable Budgen sharply, 'you're doing it again. You're making a mystery out of something that's just sad and stupid and pathetic. Some bastard who wasn't prepared to do it himself persuaded that kid that his god or his ancestors or somebody wanted him to strike out against the British imperialists. He came here on spec, saw a flier advertising the museum and thought that would do. Well, he made the ten o'clock news and that's probably enough to get him a medal where he comes from. Only it's going to be twenty years before he can collect

36

it, and if they give him a home-coming present I hope it's not a digital watch.'

Hazel was surprised and rather touched. She'd never guessed Budgen was a philosopher. 'I'd still like to know his name. If you're here when he wakes up . . .'

'Go home,' said Budgen sternly. 'It'll all come out in the end. You'll know when everybody else knows. You don't need to know any sooner.'

He was probably right. Hazel nodded, rather dispiritedly. 'I suppose.' She headed for the exit. On an impulse, though, she paused. 'But I'm not doing it again.'

He didn't understand. 'What?'

'If I'm making a mystery where none exists, I'm not doing it again. When I did it before, there was an actual mystery. It was just that none of the rest of you had noticed.' Satisfied with her parting shot, Hazel left him to his vigil.

Six

Ash was waiting at the main entrance. It made a change, Hazel thought, Ash driving her home from hospital. In recent weeks he'd become quite proficient with his car again. Except that it was his mother's car, inherited along with her house, and nearly twenty years old. His sons had been agitating for something modern – red, shiny, with spoilers – but Ash had developed a fondness for the old bus and was stalling for time.

It was mid-morning, so Gilbert and Guy were at school. Patience was curled up on the back seat. She was refusing to wear her seatbelt again.

Hazel opened the back door. 'Up.' The dog sat up. 'Paw.' She lifted her right paw. Two deft moves and Hazel had her safely strapped in. The dog lay down again, with an audible sigh.

Ash had the grace to look ashamed. 'She won't do it for me.'

'She's a *dog*,' Hazel explained heavily. 'She'll *do* what she's made to do.'

Ash shrugged helplessly. 'That's the bit she seems not to understand.'

'Doing what she's told?'

'Being a dog.'

He drove to the little house in Railway Street. Hazel's lodger was out, so they had the living room to themselves. In deference to her status as the latest casualty, Ash made the coffee. 'Your father said he'd come round later.'

Hazel was taken aback. 'From Byrfield?'

'From my house. Sorry, didn't I say? He's been staying with me for a couple of days. He wanted to be handy until he was sure you were all right, and there's more room at my house. He said he'd pop in this afternoon, and drive back to Byrfield tonight.'

Hazel nodded. She'd appreciated him coming, but she was on the mend now and didn't need anyone fussing over her. 'How did you get on with the social workers?'

A little frown gathering over Ash's deep-set eyes had the effect of closing his face in. 'I'm not sure. They asked a lot of questions, but I

38

couldn't tell if they were satisfied with the answers. They were sympathetic, of course. They said how well I'd got my life back together again. But they didn't give any indication as to whether they thought I was a fit guardian for two young boys.'

'You're their father.' She was about to add: How fit do you need to be? – but stopped herself in time.

'Yes. And a patient in a mental institution rather more recently than they were comfortable with.'

It was a fact that couldn't be discounted. The details of his breakdown earned him more sympathy than trust. 'What happens next?'

'I don't know. They said they'd discuss the situation with the Family Support Team. They said I'd be invited to a meeting before anything was decided. They kept saying that all they wanted was what was best for Gilbert and Guy. And *I* kept saying I wanted that too.'

'Fair enough,' said Hazel evenly. 'We knew that, in all the circumstances, they'd want to keep an eye on things. You were ready for that. The boys have been with you for six weeks now, they're in school and they're doing well. Better than might have been expected after all the disruption. You're feeding them, you're keeping them clean, and you haven't sent them to school in their pyjamas. There'll be plenty of kids in that school whose parents aren't doing as well by them, but nobody will try to take them away. Why would Social Services want to take yours?'

'Gee, I don't know,' said Ash edgily. 'Maybe because I was in a padded cell for nine weeks?

39

Maybe because, for three years after that, I was pretty much a recluse, and after I got Patience I became famous as the man who wandered round town mumbling to his dog. The day we met you didn't know my name, only what they called me at Meadowvale. Rambles With Dogs. Don't try to deny it – my mind may be suspect but there's nothing wrong with my memory.'

It was true. It was also accurate and, in spite of his accusatory tone, Hazel didn't think it pained him much. She grinned. 'It *is* rather funny.'

'It is *not* funny,' said Ash severely, 'when you're trying to convince two earnest young social workers that you're perfectly normal and entirely reliable.'

'I can see that,' conceded Hazel. 'So maybe you shouldn't share with them that little gem of information you entrusted to me. Or were you hoping I'd forgotten? There's nothing wrong with my memory either, Gabriel.'

He frowned. 'What information?'

'You told me you didn't just talk to Patience. You told me she talked back.'

They regarded one another over the coffee-pot. Hazel said nothing more. She was genuinely interested to hear what he'd say next.

At length Ash blinked, and took his mug, and pushed his dog onto half of the sofa so he could sit down. 'That was a joke,' he said quietly.

'Gabriel – you don't make jokes!'

'I'm not very *good* at making jokes,' he corrected her. 'That's why you didn't recognise it as one.'

It was about the lamest excuse Hazel had ever

heard. 'If you say so.' She yawned, unexpectedly tired. 'I think I'll go to bed for a couple of hours. Tell Dad to pop in this afternoon.'

Ash said he would. He washed the pots, collected his dog and headed out to his car.

He looked at Patience. He held out the seatbelt he'd bought for her. 'Up. Paw.'

She looked at him as if he was mad.

He gave up and started the car. 'How come you'll do it for Hazel and you won't do it for me?'

How come you don't want people to know I can talk? countered Patience.

Whatever else she was, Hazel was a realist. She knew the cost of her thank-you lunch would come not out of Oliver Ford's pocket but the production company's publicity budget. She had no reservations, therefore, about nominating the smartest hostelry she knew.

Only afterwards did she wonder what kind of outfit would do the venue justice without clashing with her luminous face.

Ford said he'd pick her up at half-past ten. It was a week since they'd first met, although it felt much longer.

'It won't take us two hours to get there,' protested Hazel. 'The Royal Oak is in Whimbury – it's only about four miles out of Norbold.'

'There's something I want to do first. Humour me.'

She couldn't get him to explain what until they were approaching the Museum of the Crusades where they'd first met. The production vehicles, including his trailer, were still parked rather forlornly round the side.

'Oliver?'

He saw her looking at his trailer, heard the note of doubt and warning in her voice, and realised it was time to come clean. 'There's somebody waiting for us. Minnie Merchant is my hairdresser. She's incredible, she's worked in London and Hollywood, she's a real artist. And I thought . . .'

He'd thought that a professional hair-stylist trained by the demands of the film industry to think outside the box would be able to do something about Hazel's half-shorn head that would put even a good salon hairdresser to shame. And he was right. Ninety minutes later Hazel looked in Minnie Merchant's mirror and couldn't believe what she'd achieved.

It still looked outlandish. There was no way, short of a wig that she wouldn't wear, to disguise the fact that most of the hair on one side of her head was missing. But now it looked as if it was *meant* to look outlandish. That she'd paid serious money to a genuine artist to make it look outlandish. It was boldly modern, sharply cut and asymmetric, and Hazel found her eyes welling at the transformation. At Oliver Ford's sensitivity in realising that this, of all the gestures he could have made, was the one that meant most to her.

'I don't know what to say,' she mumbled.

'Say "Thank you, Minnie," and let's go eat.'

'Thank you, Minnie,' Hazel said obediently. 'Oliver, I—'

'Now, don't come over all girlie on me,' he said sternly. 'I treated you to a haircut, you saved my life.' He made a balancing gesture with both hands. 'Life, haircut – haircut, life. Do you know, I think I still owe you lunch.'

The Royal Oak was as good as she'd heard, and Oliver Ford was a practised host: attentive and entertaining. Hazel had to keep reminding herself that it was his field of expertise, even more than the Crusades. Being an historian was the easy part: anyone could have done it, given an interest in the subject and time to read enough books. Being a television personality required different, largely indefinable, skills. He had to be attractive, when there was no consensus as to what constitutes attractiveness; old enough to be taken seriously but still young enough to be personable; clearly intelligent yet not too intellectual. He needed a good speaking voice, but not so good as to sound affected; the piquancy of a slight regional accent was no barrier, although the need for subtitles would have been. He had to look good on camera, but any hint of prettiness would undermine his credibility. He needed to be unselfconscious but not brash, authoritative but not didactic. Perhaps most of all, he needed the ability to make whoever he was addressing – Hazel amended her first thought, which was 'performing to' – feel they were the only person in the room.

All these skills and abilities Oliver Ford had in spades. The accent was so subtle Hazel struggled to pin it down, finally settling on Yorkshire via private school. He could project like an actor, and occasionally did so, for comic effect, but otherwise his voice dropped to a level of friendly intimacy that even a street-wise policewoman found beguiling. And though he was undeniably handsome, and Hazel had never really trusted handsome, a lot of it was put on for the cameras. With no professional expectations to satisfy, he relaxed into a persona that was slightly more rumpled but also more youthful than she had supposed.

By the time their starters arrived, she was enjoying herself immensely.

She asked how he'd got into television.

Ford shrugged. 'Luck, mostly. Being available at the right time. One of the people at the production company had been a student of mine: when they couldn't get their first choice to present a documentary on the Saracens, he remembered my lectures and asked if I'd do it. I thought it would make a change from field work for a summer, and I'd be back at the university come October. In fact I never went back.'

'The Saracens? The guys we lost to?'

He gave a tolerant chuckle that only just avoided condescension. 'If by "we" you mean Christian Europe, we lost, and won, and lost, and won, and lost again. It was a score draw decided on penalties. The crucial factor was that the Saracens wanted to stay in Jerusalem, and most of the Crusaders wanted simply to collect souvenirs and head home. For them, Jerusalem wasn't so much a place as an idea. You can fight for an idea, but even if you win – especially if you win – what do you do next? As far as the Crusaders were concerned the answer was, Go back to their own lands and resume bickering among themselves the way they had for hundreds of years.'

Hazel had no interest in the subject: the fact that Ford was able to engage her attention, and explain succinctly the motives and limiting factors of a conflict almost a millennium old, was a tribute to his skills as a communicator. That was what he was paid, and feted, for. Every museum, school and university in the country has a department full of historians, and book-shelves laden with the work of many more. Mostly, they spoke only to one another. Many of them struggled to make themselves under-stood even by one another.

Ford's achievement was that he spoke to millions. He had the ability to condense and simplify history just enough to make it digestible for the mass market without stripping the essence out of it. Serious historians – and historians can be *very* serious – might sneer at television's teaching-by-soundbite, but the bottom line was that the nett national knowledge of the past was raised more by one affable, good-looking charmer like Oliver Ford than by a dozen grizzled peer-honoured professors.

'Why are you smiling?' he asked.

Hazel hadn't realised she was. 'It's always nice to see a professional at work.'

Ford wasn't sure if that was a compliment. He wasn't entirely sure how to take Hazel – when she was on the level, and when she was gently pulling his leg. He shrugged ruefully. 'Was I lecturing? I'm sorry. It's just, this is what I do. I'm television's tame historian. I'm a nursemaid, spoon-feeding dollops of easy-to-eat, one-pot television dinners to people with a minimal interest in history. It doesn't even have to be my period: I can talk about the Dark Ages or the English Civil War without making any greater demands on my audience's intellect.'

He sighed. 'It isn't what I had in mind when I studied history. I had a real passion for the subject then. But passion isn't what this job demands. It's history-lite for the masses; and I tell myself that it's better for people to know a little bit about something than nothing at all.'

'Of course it is,' said Hazel stoutly. 'We all struggle with attention span these days. The world moves quickly, and television is the only way most of us can keep up with it. What you do isn't less important because ordinary people like me can understand it.'

Ford dipped his head graciously. 'Thank you. Anyway, people find their own level and this is mine. I was never going to make my name as a serious historian. I found research too dry, archaeology too uncomfortable, which really only left teaching. I think I was a good lecturer, but television gives me a larger audience. I enjoy what I do, but it isn't in any real sense important. But then, what is?'

He answered his own question. 'Your job is. People who work in medicine. Those who grow food, and govern countries. The rest of us are mostly creating a demand for products that we

46

can then supply. I get people interested in history, and then I tell them about history. I'm the go-to guy for family-viewing old stuff.

'Producers hire me because they hired me before and people like to see a familiar face on TV. I don't even write the script most of the time. Someone who's a subject specialist does that, and I work it up into something our audience can relate to. The right balance of hard facts and pretty pictures. Serious enough that people with some prior knowledge won't feel patronised, light enough to appeal to the general viewer. At least this time we're working in my own field; but if it hadn't been for the interest sparked by the new museum, I could be talking equally engagingly about the agricultural revolution or the Bevin Boys.'

He gave a wry little smile then, and changed the subject. He asked about Hazel's career – what she did when she wasn't saving people from arsonists. A little uncomfortably, she was forced to admit that she hadn't done anything for a while, that this had been her first week back at work after four months out of commission.

She'd had his attention all along. Now she felt the power of his focus. 'You were injured in the course of duty?'

She could refuse to answer. She could lie, or dissemble. But Hazel had fought hard to establish the fact that, though the episode had been an embarrassment to Norbold police as a whole, she personally had nothing to be embarrassed about. She was damned if she wanted Oliver Ford to get a different impression. So she told him. She kept it short, and down-played the amount of danger involved, but there was no avoiding the conclusion.

'I had to shoot someone. Kill him. Division took me off line until they were sure I wasn't going to make a habit of it.'

She'd succeeded in shocking Oliver Ford. For a moment he didn't know what to say. History is full of people killing one another, but historians don't often find themselves talking to the killers over lunch. Finally he managed, 'I'm pretty sure that you wouldn't have been returned to duty if you hadn't been able to justify your actions.'

'That's true. Oh, everyone was very nice about it. They agreed that I'd had no choice, and that in a perfect world someone would have shot the guy years before. They were more concerned that at some point a sense of misplaced guilt would hit me like a ton of bricks and I'd curl up in a ball and start sucking my thumb.'

'And did it?'

'No.' She could have been hiding private pain behind a façade, but so far as Ford could tell it was an honest response. 'I never had any doubts about what happened. If I'd done anything different, a bad man would have lived and some good people would have died, and I'd have been one of them. I was trained to save lives. That's what I did.'

'And after four months they let you come back.' Hazel nodded. 'And sent you to liaise with a visiting celeb on the basis that even you couldn't get into trouble doing that.'

'It wasn't my fault,' protested Hazel. 'You know that. You were there.'

'I certainly was.' Ford's right hand advanced across the white linen napery and his long slim fingers stroked the inside of her left wrist. 'And it's only thanks to you that I'm still here. Don't forget that. Because I never will.'

As they left an hour later he said, 'We're having another go at opening the museum tomorrow afternoon. You will come, won't you?'

Seven

Hazel didn't share that particular detail with Ash when she saw him the next morning.

Thinking about it afterwards, she wasn't sure why not. Their friendship in no way precluded personal relationships with other people. When she first met him, Ash had been deeply wedded to the memory of a wife he believed was dead. Hazel herself had had a number of suitors, casual but hopeful, and saw no reason not to enjoy the company of men who interested her when the opportunity arose.

So it was unclear to her why she didn't want Ash to know about Oliver Ford. Because she feared his disapproval? It wasn't for Ash to approve or otherwise of any friendship she might care to make; and she didn't think he thought it was. Ford was older than her, but twelve years isn't that much between adults. He was a celebrity – but that wasn't what attracted her to him, and Ash knew her too well to think it might have been.

Finally she decided it would just give too much importance to a casual acquaintance to talk about it, even with a good friend. When he finally managed to cut his ribbon, and his latest series was in the can, Oliver Ford would go back to London or wherever his next project took him, and she might get a postcard but she might very well not. She imagined a man like Ford made a lot of these temporary friendships as he travelled round: pleasant companionship for a drink or a meal but never intended to last. A month from now he would struggle to remember her face.

And that was fine too. Hazel had no claim on him, was happy to enjoy his company for a few days and then wave him off back to his work. But she didn't want to find herself explaining to Ash, or to anyone, that she was not a jilted lover. Much better to say nothing. She stopped thinking about it and paid attention to what Ash was saying to her.

Only to find that he'd finished and was waiting patiently for a reply.

'Sorry, I wandered off there,' she admitted. 'What were you saying?'

Ash was ironing. Hazel had shown him how to do it: how tackling a shirt in the right order – collar first, then yoke, cuffs, sleeves, front and back – meant you weren't constantly having to go back and iron out the creases you'd just ironed in. He'd never done ironing before the boys came home. First he'd had a mother, then a wife, then

50

the kind of clothes that didn't need ironing because nobody cared what he looked like, not even him. He was making an effort now as part of his drive to appear thoroughly normal.

He said patiently, 'I was asking if you'd pick the boys up from school. Since you're not going in to work.' He managed not to add, *Again*, but Hazel heard it just the same.

'Today?'

Ash nodded. 'I've got a meeting in town with the social workers. I think they deliberately arranged it for three o'clock to see what I'd do when I needed a bit of help.'

For five months, any time he'd needed any kind of help, Hazel had been his first port of call. He hoped he hadn't imposed on her too much, although he suspected he had. But Hazel had never objected. She'd taken him under her wing initially as a charity case, but then a friendship had developed that had enriched both their lives. And, at times, made them much more complicated.

'Gabriel, I can't,' she said. 'You'll have to ask someone else.'

'Oh.' He was as taken aback as if it had been settled weeks ago. 'Er . . .'

She explained about the second attempt to open the Wittering museum, only coming to feel halfway through that no explanation had been necessary.

'Surely Meadowvale can send someone who *is* deemed fit for duty.' He heard the note of criticism in his own voice and winced. It was one thing to ask, another to argue when she refused.

51

'They are doing. Oliver wants me there as his guest. He thinks it'll be good for both of us. Like getting back on the horse that threw you.'

'Oliver?' *Shut up,* he told himself. *Just shut your mouth and stop making things worse!*

'Oliver Ford,' she said evenly. 'The man I saved from the mad arsonist. The man who treated me to the sharp new haircut. Which, incidentally, you haven't yet said you like.'

Ash put the iron down. A moment later he snatched it up again and put it down, correctly, on the heatproof plate rather than the back of his best shirt. 'Of course I like it. I'm sorry, I'm a bit distracted. You look terrific. The haircut, the singed eyebrow, the red cheek – the lot. You look like a hero. I am immensely proud of you.'

At which her other cheek grew red, too.

'What time will you be finished?'

He wasn't sure. 'Five o'clock, maybe?'

'Saturday could pick the boys up before he goes to work.'

'*Saturday?*' If she'd suggested that Sweeney Todd, or King Herod, could baby-sit his sons, Ash could hardly have sounded more horrified.

'Certainly Saturday,' said Hazel firmly. 'Why not? He's put his neck on the line for both of us before now. You think he can't keep your boys out of trouble for a couple of hours?'

That was exactly what Ash thought. But she was right. When they first knew the youth they called Saturday – his name was Saul Desmond – he was a homeless criminal-fringe sixteen-year-old with no family, no friends, no possessions, no future.

But his life had changed as much in the last five months as Ash's had. He was seventeen now, had a regular job, had a room in Hazel's little house and paid his rent religiously every Thursday night. He looked after himself, stayed the right side of the law – so far as Hazel could ascertain, and she didn't just take his word for it – and made occasional forays into housework. He was better with an iron than Ash was.

'I don't want to make him late for work,' Ash said lamely, looking for an excuse.

'He doesn't leave till seven-thirty. I'll be home before that – if you're going to be late, call me and I'll take over.'

Saturday was another of Hazel's little projects, and Ash could see no way of refusing that wouldn't offend her. He accepted with as much grace as he could manage. 'Unless, of course, he has other plans.'

'If he has other plans he can rearrange them,' said Hazel briskly. 'Leave it to me.'

Saturday had no other plans. Still he received his orders with as much enthusiasm as any other teenager tasked with minding a couple of undertens. 'What am I supposed to do with them?'

'Take them to the park,' suggested Hazel. 'You'll have Patience too, she'll keep them amused. Then take them home and make them beans on toast. It's only a couple of hours, Saturday – Gabriel will be home around five.'

'Do I get paid?'

'Of course you do,' said Hazel, although she wasn't sure whether Ash had yet realised baby-sitting was a service you had to pay for. 'So you'll do it.' It wasn't really a question.

'I suppose so.'

'Don't blow this, Saturday,' she warned him. 'If anything happens to those boys, Gabriel will have your guts for garters. And you don't even want to know what part of your anatomy I'll be coming after.'

The youth snorted a little laugh, his humour restored. It always amused him when Hazel Best talked like one of the Sopranos.

Oliver Ford picked her up at noon. They had lunch at The Royal Oak again before driving on to Wittering.

He took his eyes off his meal long enough to steal a sideways glance at her. 'Are you nervous about this?'

'Of course not,' she said; but it wasn't entirely true. She hadn't been. She hadn't even asked herself if she was going to be until they were on their way. Over the soup, though, she started to feel the quiver of anxiety.

'*I* am,' Ford said honestly. 'I thought it was only to be expected. Now you're making me feel like a wimp.'

Hazel chuckled. 'All right, then – yes. But it's stupid. It was incredibly unlikely that anyone would try to fire-bomb the opening ceremony of a little local museum the first time. What are the odds that anything similar will happen again?'

Ford nodded, reassured. 'Like taking your own bomb on an aeroplane.'

'*What?*'

54

Straight-faced, he explained. 'The odds of boarding an aeroplane with a bomb on it are a million to one. The odds of boarding a plane with *two* bombs on it, carried by people with no knowledge of one another, are a billion to one. So the moral is, Always carry your own bomb.'

He topped up her wine, dutifully refraining himself. Then he reached into his pocket and put a little cardboard box on the table between them. It was so small, and so plain, it had to contain something valuable.

'I want you to have this.' His voice had dropped to where only she could hear him. 'You're going to tell me it isn't necessary. I know it isn't necessary. But just saying Thanks isn't enough. I need you to know how very grateful I am for what you did. It was way beyond the call of duty. I won't be around forever, but I want you to know that wherever I am, I will always know how much I owe you. This is a very small token of that. Open it.'

Astonished, Hazel went on looking at the little box and made no move towards it.

'Hazel, open it.'

So she did.

If she'd thought to wonder, she'd have guessed his taste ran to statement jewellery. Big pieces that glittered and gleamed and said *Guess how much I cost*. This wasn't like that. It was tiny, a little golden bird on a fine gold chain. It had chips of ruby for eyes. She held it up close. The detail was remarkable, making up in the skill of its execution what it lacked in size. Even so she was puzzled.

'A chicken?'

Oliver Ford laughed out loud, a bell of a sound. All around the restaurant, heads turned. There were murmurs of recognition. 'It's a phoenix. You know – rising from the ashes?'

She understood. She blushed and returned her gaze to the little pendant.

Ford was vastly amused. 'I thought it was perfect. I pestered jewellers up and down the country looking for one. And you thought it was a chicken!'

Hazel put it back in the box. 'I can't accept this.'

The laughter fell off his face as if a tap had been turned. 'Why not?'

'I was doing my job,' Hazel said simply. 'I get paid for it. I can't take private rewards as well.'

Ford appeared genuinely nonplussed. As if he had never considered the possibility that she might refuse his gift. 'You think this is a *bribe*? You think other people will think there's something dishonourable about it?'

She realised she'd hurt him, and for that she was sorry. 'Of course not, Oliver. It's just . . . there are rules. We can't be seen doing anything that might raise questions of fear or favour.'

'Hazel – you saved me from a mad bomber! Damn right I'm in favour of that! And I can't see that I'm doing anything very terrible by showing my gratitude. It's a trinket, not a villa in the Algarve!'

'You're doing nothing wrong,' she assured him. 'It was a generous thought. But I'd be doing something wrong if I accepted it.'

56

He sat back, astonished and displeased. After a moment he returned the box to his pocket. 'All right. Well, perhaps it's time we were moving.' He signalled the waiter. 'Unless you'd like to pay? You know, so no one can think I'm corrupting you.'

The sudden change of mood, the unexpected sourness of his tone, left Hazel floundering for a moment. Then she said, 'As a matter of fact, I would. You bought lunch yesterday, I'll buy it today. This is, after all, the twenty-first century,' she added lightly. 'Equality that doesn't cut both ways can hardly be described as equality.'

She expected him to argue, even to fight her for access to the card machine. Instead he sat quiet and aloof while she settled the bill. But he made a point of holding the door for her as they left.

Eight

Despite his objections, Saturday embarked on his task full of good intentions. It took ten minutes to walk from Railway Street to the Norbold Quays Junior School where the Ash boys were now pupils. He allowed an extra five minutes to present himself at the principal's office and have the children formally delivered into his care. No one was taking any risks with Ash's sons. They might not have been kidnapped before, but that was no reason to tempt fate.

Being paranoid doesn't mean they *aren't* out to get you.

The three of them were not strangers. But it was still too early in their acquaintance for them to claim to be, or perhaps even want to be, friends. The boys were still getting to know their father; their father's friend's friend was, for now, a bridge too far.

It hardly mattered. Saturday didn't need them to like him. He just needed them to stay out of trouble for a couple of hours. How difficult could it be?

Patience led the way to the park. Where they crossed the road she waited until her small flock – or perhaps she saw them as a litter of unruly puppies – were gathered together before escorting them through the traffic. Locals who were used to seeing the white dog walking her owner were amused to see her transfer her shepherding skills to his family.

'What do you want to do?' asked Saturday. 'Swings?'

'Swings!' agreed Guy happily.

Gilbert invested the same word with a wealth of scorn. 'Swings?' Ash's sons approached the business of living from diametrically different directions.

Saturday shrugged. 'Slide, then. Or the round-about. I'll push.'

Gilbert looked down his nose at the teenager. Since Saturday, no giant himself, was significantly taller than an eight-year-old, this involved tipping his head backwards. 'Nobody,' he declared with hauteur, 'is actually called Saturday.'

This kind of non sequitur is familiar to anyone with young children. But Saturday had no experience of anyone younger than himself, and was momentarily floored. 'Er – I am.'

'No,' said Gilbert, shaking his head decisively. 'You don't call people after days of the week.'

'What about Man Friday?'

Robinson Crusoe is no longer required reading for young boys. Gilbert looked at him as if he'd made it up. 'Who?'

They were at the swings. Guy clambered up. 'Push me!'

'I'm pushing, I'm pushing.'

'Push harder! I want to go over the top!'

'And I want to see my eighteenth birthday,' growled Saturday. 'This is high enough for anyone.'

'I've been over the top,' declared Gilbert, an untruth so obvious – and so obviously designed to stir up trouble – that Saturday felt a surge of dislike.

'Yeah? Well, when your dad's here you can do it again.'

Gilbert shrugged and turned his back. 'Swings are for little kids, anyway.'

Saturday gritted his teeth and kept pushing. 'So what do you want to do?'

'Football.' This was almost certainly another lie. Gilbert, like his father at his age, and since, had minimal interest in ball games.

'Fine. Then we'll play football next.' A slow suspicion grew to certainty. 'Did you bring a ball?'

'No,' said Gilbert in quiet triumph.

Patience had brought her ball. Toys were a new departure for her: she had never shown much interest in running after things – except rabbits: she was after all a lurcher – until she'd had the boys to keep amused. But recently she had discovered the charms of Fetch, and now she presented her soft-spiked, jelly-pink ball hopefully to Gilbert. After a moment's consideration he shied it down the park, and Patience hared off in pursuit, jaws wide, ears flying in the slipstream. But by the time she'd brought it back he'd lost interest and was kicking the iron frame of the swings as if determined to wear out his shoes before he outgrew them.

Saturday looked at the dog and the dog looked at Saturday. He could have sworn she rolled her eyes.

'All right,' decided Saturday. 'You' – he stabbed a finger at Ash's first-born – 'push your brother. For five minutes. Then we'll do something else. I'll throw the ball for Patience.'

Reluctantly, Gilbert did as he was told. 'You're supposed to be entertaining *us*,' he complained.

'No, I'm supposed to be keeping you safe. And I am,' insisted Saturday. 'I'm restraining myself from kicking your tiresome little arse round the swings, round the cricket pitch and halfway across the arboretum. Now push. And don't even *think* of pushing your little brother over the top.'

Gilbert grunted. The swing creaked. Saturday threw the ball. Patience raced after it and brought it back. Guy giggled happily. The swing creaked.

Saturday threw the ball. Patience raced after it and brought it back. The swing creaked.

Saturday threw the ball. Patience made no attempt to chase it. She was staring at the swings. With a sick surge of foreboding, Saturday turned to see why.

The swing was creaking back and forth of its own accord. The boy who should have been riding it and the one who should have been pushing were nowhere in sight.

By the time Hazel got there, fear had rendered Ash incapable of rational thought. He was prowling the playground like a cage-crazy tiger, shouting his sons' names in a voice worn hoarse. Anxiety had carved deep trenches down each side of his face, and filled them with tears. Hazel thought he was unaware of this. He had ripped off the tie he'd donned specially for his meeting and was wringing it savagely between his hands.

'Gabriel. Gabriel!' She tugged his sleeve until he stopped prowling long enough to look at her. 'Calm down. Tell me what happened.'

'It's happened again! They're gone! Someone's taken them . . .'

'That isn't what happened before,' she reminded him firmly. 'They were with Cathy. They were always safe.'

'Cathy? You think *Cathy* has them?'

'I didn't say that . . .' But he wasn't listening – seemed incapable of listening, his attention span reduced to seconds by the shock. Hazel turned to Saturday. 'What really happened?'

White and visibly shaking, the youth told her everything he knew. It didn't take long. 'When I couldn't find them, I called Gabriel. I couldn't think what else to do. He called the police.'

Superintendent Maybourne had responded with no fewer than three cars and a dozen officers, and was on the scene herself, organising the search.

Ash's dog was lying at Saturday's feet, washing her paws.

Hazel chewed thoughtfully on the inside of her lip. After a moment she walked over to join her colleagues. 'Gabriel thinks his sons have been kidnapped. I know why he thinks that, but I don't think it's the most likely thing to have happened.'

She had the superintendent's full attention. Conscious that she could be making a mistake, Hazel pressed on. 'Those boys haven't been in Norbold very long. They know Highfield Road, and the park, and the way to school, and that's probably about it. Has anyone checked Gabriel's house?'

Grace Maybourne was obscurely disappointed. She'd hoped for something more creative from the problematic Constable Best. 'Of course we have. The house is locked – if they'd found their way home, they'd have been waiting in the garden. They weren't.'

'Has anyone checked for two little boys who don't want to be found?'

Superintendent Maybourne blinked. 'You think they're *hiding*?'

'I don't know,' Hazel said quickly. 'But I do

know the older one is quick to take offence, easily bored, and calls the shots. If he took offence at being dumped on Saturday, he might very well decide to teach his father a lesson.'

'By running off?'

Hazel nodded. 'But since they don't know this town very well, they'd probably end up going home. They'd know they were in trouble – if a police car came to their house, there's a good chance they'd stay out of sight until it left.'

If she was wrong, she might delay the start of a thorough search. If Ash's sons were really in trouble, that could be disastrous. But dragging the lake and throwing a cordon around the ring road wouldn't find them if they were actually hiding in the shrubbery behind their own house.

'Tell you what,' she offered, 'I'll take Saturday and Patience, and we'll check out Highfield Road. If they're not there, maybe something *has* happened to them.'

'All right,' agreed Maybourne. 'Do you want a car?'

'Please.' Hazel had left Oliver Ford at the museum and taken a taxi back to Norbold as soon as Ash called her.

Only as the younger woman turned purposefully towards the area car did the superintendent give way to a puzzled frown. 'Who's Patience?'

Hazel had the area car stop at the corner of the road. She pushed Saturday out onto the pavement and followed with the dog, whose lead she immediately removed. 'Okay, girl, time to shine. Find the boys. Where are they?'

Patience, still carrying her ball, headed for home at a steady jog. Perhaps, thought Hazel, the animal actually understood what was required of her. Or perhaps she was aware, with that uncanny sense dogs have, that it was time for her dinner.

In any event, she turned in at Ash's driveway and – tucking her long legs under her and arching her slender back – hurdled the side gate that was supposed to keep her in the back garden. Hazel followed at half a run, though she paused long enough to open the gate.

The garden was empty. Hazel tried the back door in passing, but it was indeed locked. Patience was trotting down the path to the garage. When Hazel tried the side access, the door opened under her hand.

Hazel went inside. 'Okay, guys, fun's over. Your dad's having kittens and my boss is about to issue an All-Points Bulletin. Let's get our heads together and come up with an explanation that leaves you looking thoughtless rather than cruel.'

Saturday was looking at her as if she was mad. But Patience was gazing up into the rafters, where old bicycles and half-rotted tents and a small canoe were lashed to the timbers, reached by a wooden ladder.

After a moment, two small, pale, anxious faces appeared among the cobwebs.

Nine

Hazel had decided against putting her uniform on. She was on sick leave and not available for duty, so while she would have appreciated the authority it gave her, it seemed a little impertinent to use it just for that. She opted for smart civvies, did what she could with her hair and presented herself at Superintendent Maybourne's door at 8.15 a.m. precisely.

She could not tell, either from the other woman's expression or her tone, how much trouble she was in. Partly because they hadn't known one another for very long, but also because the superintendent didn't give very much away. She was invariably quiet, polite and precise, and if Hazel had been summoned here to receive her dismissal, she was confident it would be delivered in a quiet, polite and precise manner.

She was not invited to sit so remained standing, hands behind her back, at attention despite the absent uniform.

Maybourne regarded her with a curious mixture of amusement, exasperation, and what Hazel dared to think might almost be tolerance. She gave the quietest, politest sigh imaginable. 'Constable Best – you're one of them, aren't you?'

Hazel was completely wrong-footed. She had

no idea which *them* the superintendent was referring to, and therefore whether she should be offended or agree enthusiastically. 'Ma'am?'

'People to whom things happen which could happen to anyone, but don't.'

It took Hazel a moment to work through the syntax. When she had, she found herself unable to disagree. 'I can see why you'd think that, ma'am.'

'Was it always so?' Superintendent Maybourne seemed genuinely interested. 'When you were a little girl, were you the one that stray dogs followed home? The one who happened to be passing when the fire alarm went off unexpectedly? Do you find yourself in lifts when there's a power-cut, or living under the flat where someone habitually lets the bath overflow? In short, Constable Best, if a tornado were to rip through Norbold, would you lay odds on it picking up your car?'

Hazel decided there was nothing to be lost by being honest. If she was going to get the sack, she'd find out soon enough. 'It would pick up my car,' she agreed, deadpan, 'and use it to demolish my house.'

A tiny smile played momentarily around Maybourne's lips. She hid it quickly, but Hazel knew she hadn't imagined it. 'How is Mr Ash now?'

'I haven't seen him since yesterday. It took him a couple of hours to calm down, but then the shock started giving way to embarrassment. He was very sorry for the trouble he'd given you.'

'I know. He phoned me yesterday evening.'

Maybourne gave a graceful shrug. 'I told him, and I hope you'll tell him, there's nothing to be embarrassed about. That nobody's more relieved than us when missing children turn up in their own garage.'

'I *did* tell him that. I'm not sure he believed me. He was very conscious of wasting police time. He just couldn't think, in the heat of the moment, what else to do.'

'He did the right thing,' said Maybourne. 'Even if it had occurred to him that his sons might be playing a trick on him, he couldn't risk doing nothing. If they had been abducted, the twenty minutes it would have taken him to go home and *not* find them would have been enough to get them out of Norbold and on their way to anywhere at all.'

'Of course,' ventured Hazel, 'Gabriel's children are no more likely to be abducted than anybody else's children. And that's very unlikely indeed.'

'But after everything that happened, that won't be how it feels to him. And in fact, with their mother being sought in connection with a criminal conspiracy, the risk that she might try to take them from him isn't insignificant. No, constable, I think we have to forgive Mr Ash for being over-sensitive. In all the circumstances.'

'That's very generous, ma'am,' said Hazel. 'May I tell him you said that?'

'Certainly. I said as much to him myself, but I'm not sure he really took it in. He's still' – she hesitated, looking for the right word – 'quite troubled, isn't he?'

'It's not the sort of thing you put behind you in a few weeks. His wife conspired with her lover to convince Gabriel that she and their sons had been kidnapped. He believed that for four years. Then he learned the truth. Perhaps "troubled" is the best we should expect for a while.'

Hazel waited. But the superintendent seemed to have nothing to add. Hazel began to hope that maybe, since forgiveness was in the air, some of it might come her way. 'Will that be all, ma'am?'

'Not quite.' Maybourne opened the top drawer of her desk, took out a padded envelope. 'I have been asked to pass this on to you. You may open it now, if you like.'

Perplexed, Hazel did as she was bid. The first thing out of the envelope was a letter bearing the badge of Divisional Headquarters. So *this* was how they sacked you . . .

Except that it wasn't. She read what was written. Then she read it again. Then she took out the plain little cardboard box she'd seen before, and out of the box she took the tiny gold phoenix with the ruby-chip eyes. She looked at the superintendent. 'I don't understand.'

Maybourne smiled coolly. 'Of course you do, Hazel. Mr Ford wanted to give you that to thank you for protecting him. Very properly, you said you couldn't accept. Mr Ford sought permission from the chief constable to offer it again. That is written confirmation that the chief constable considers it entirely appropriate for you to accept, in view of the service rendered, the comparatively modest value of the item to a person like

Oliver Ford, and the fact that since the *Norbold News* will be carrying a photograph, no one can claim there was anything underhand about it. Mr Ford will be in touch shortly. Do us all a favour: take the bloody necklace.'

Ash didn't blame Saturday for what had happened. He knew who was responsible, but actually he didn't blame Gilbert either. He blamed himself. For panicking when he should have been thinking. For involving the police instead of assessing the situation logically, the way Hazel had done. For letting his emotions swamp his common sense. He knew better. He'd made a good career of seeing to the truth of things. He didn't understand why that acuity seemed to fly out of the window when it would have been most valuable to him.

Now, because of his over-reaction to the mischief of an eight-year-old boy, both he and Hazel could lose the things that mattered to them most.

He'd been tempted to keep the boys off school – let them start the weekend a day early. But that would have been a mistake. Nothing had happened. Nothing had *nearly* happened, only a fairly routine bit of family drama, and keeping the boys at home would invest the affair with more importance than it warranted. It might be understandable that he'd behaved like a neurotic mother-hen. But it was important that he shouldn't make a habit of it.

So he walked them to school as he did every weekday morning. There was little conversation.

69

Guy, largely oblivious of the strained atmosphere, chatted intermittently with Patience, trotting on her lead beside them, but Ash and his first-born exchanged nothing but terse necessities.

At the school gates Gilbert hesitated. 'I *am* sorry,' he said again. It wasn't the first apology he'd offered, although it was the first one that sounded genuine.

'I know,' Ash said quietly. 'Me too. Neither of us distinguished ourselves. I just hope . . .' He let the sentence peter out. The boy was only eight years old, too young to share the burden of possible consequences. That was for Ash to carry alone.

But this was Ash's son. More than that: Gilbert was his father at eight years old. Given three or four words, and a certain tone of voice, and a certain expression, he was entirely capable of inferring the comment Ash had thought better of airing. 'You think the ladies from the council will think you're a bad father?'

Ash gave a little snort, half of surprise, half amusement. 'Well, they might. They might even have a point.'

'It wasn't your fault.'

'It was my responsibility to see that you were safe – that you'd be safe with whoever I asked to look after you. And you weren't.'

'Yes, we were. Nothing happened.'

'You were missing for over an hour. I *thought* something had happened to you. I called the police. If I'd had the number, I'd have called in the army.'

'We weren't missing,' insisted Gilbert. '*I* knew where we were.'

70

Ash had no answer to such perfect logic. He let his sons head in to school. But he watched until the door closed behind them.

When he finally turned away, he saw that he too was being watched: by Hazel Best, leaning against her parked car. He nodded a greeting. He didn't much feel like smiling.

'I've just come from The Presence,' said Hazel. 'I thought she was going to sack me.'

Ash was alarmed. 'Did she?'

'No, she gave me a necklace.' Hazel still looked bemused. 'Never mind that. Everything's fine. What happened was a false alarm. The police *like* false alarms. They're much easier to deal with than genuine emergencies.'

'Superintendent Maybourne told you that?'

'In as many words. Gabriel, stop beating your-self up over this. It really wasn't that big a deal. The boys gave Saturday the slip. If you over-reacted, everyone understands why. It's early days. It'll get easier as you get used to the job. It'll never get *so* easy that they won't cost you sleep from time to time.'

Ash hesitated, then voiced the fear that was tormenting him. 'I'm going to lose them, Hazel. They're going to take them away from me. They're going to use this as an excuse to take them away.'

Hazel's eyes flared wide in astonishment. 'The Child Protection people? They said that?'

'No. But it's what they're thinking. They think I'm barely competent to look after myself, let alone two under-tens. Let alone *those* two under-tens, who've hardly had the most normal upbringing to date and desperately need some

71

stability in their lives. They think the boys would be better off living with a proper family, or in care, and I could take them out for tea every Sunday as long as I got them home by six.'

The grief in his voice was like an open wound. What was almost worse than the fear of losing his sons was the belief Hazel could hear in his tone that a decision to remove them might be justified. She felt her heart lurch with compassion. After everything he'd been through . . .

She forced herself to speak calmly. 'I'm sure nobody's thinking any such thing. Gabriel, you didn't do anything wrong! You left them with a responsible adult when you couldn't be there yourself.'

'Well no, I didn't,' he retorted, 'I left them with Saturday. Possibly the only person in Norbold worse qualified to look after them than I am!'

Hazel shot to her lodger's defence. 'Hey, don't blame Saturday for not having eyes in the back of his head! He did what you asked him to do. He met them from school and took them to the park. It's not his fault the little brats thought it would be clever to run off and hide.'

'They've never done it when they were with me. And I don't believe they'd have done it if they'd been with you.'

'So now it's *my* fault?' Hazel heard her voice soaring and didn't care. 'For wanting a social life that doesn't revolve exclusively around you and your brood? You wanted to be a parent, Gabriel – well, guess what, this is what it's like! Juggling your time. Trying to be in two places at once. Having to pick up the pieces when you fail. But it's what you wanted, so good luck with it. Only, don't expect me to hold your hand while you do it. I have my own life to get on with. I'm happy to help, when I can. But I am not your own personal Nanny McPhee!'

Most people would have understood the allusion. But Ash hadn't had a television in his house until his sons came home; and now he had a television, he hadn't time to watch it. He stared at her angrily. 'Nanny who?'

'McPhee!' snapped Hazel.

They glared at one another from a range of inches, each feeling ill-used and resisting the suspicion that they weren't behaving well either. Ash straightened up with dignity. 'My sons are *not* brats.'

'No? Well, they do a pretty good impression of it sometimes. They were angry that you had something to do besides meeting them from school, and they took it out on Saturday. He did the best he could. If you want someone better qualified to look after them when you can't, you'll have to employ someone. No one will be more relieved than Saturday.'

'All right, I will.' Ash sniffed, childishly. 'I rather thought it was the sort of thing friends did for one another.'

Hazel wanted to slap him. 'It is. And when *I* have some ill-mannered little brats that need taking care of, I'll be sure to let you know.'

Fuming, she got back into her car and slammed the door. But before she drove off she was aware that she hadn't handled the situation well. Ash had made so much progress in the last few months: it wasn't reasonable for her to be impatient that there were still hangovers from the bad times. Like Saturday, he was doing his best. If she hadn't wanted him to rely on her so much, perhaps she shouldn't have made her shoulder quite so available to lean on.

She felt eyes on her and looked round, ready to apologise, only to meet a steady golden gaze. Ash had turned for home but Patience lingered outside the school and was regarding her with gentle disappointment.

Hazel scowled. 'What are you looking at?' she demanded. The dog blinked, and Hazel drove away.

Ten

Ford's car was parked in front of the little house in Railway Street. As Hazel pulled in behind it, Ford got out. But he stood beside it, leaving the door open, as if he might have to beat a hasty retreat.

'You're in my parking spot,' Hazel said by way of greeting.

Ford looked uncertainly at the kerb. 'Shall I move it?'

'Don't be silly.' She locked her own car. Her fingers picked out the house key automatically. 'Are you coming in?'

'May I?'

'No, let's stand on the pavement and trade

recriminations,' said Hazel shortly. 'Of course you can come in. Saturday would have let you in if he'd known you were waiting.'

'He went out,' said Ford. 'Just as I arrived. And I'm not here to argue. I'm here to apologise.'

The sparser of Hazel's eyebrows climbed just enough to express surprise. Nothing she had seen of Oliver Ford suggested he apologised very often. 'Really?' she said coolly. 'Then you definitely need to come inside. I shall want to sit down.'

If Jack the Ripper had called round, she'd have felt constitutionally compelled to offer him coffee. It stemmed from her upbringing, and her mother's views on hospitality. By the time the kettle was boiling, some of the awkwardness had gone out of the atmosphere.

'I so wanted you to have a nice day,' said Ford ruefully. 'After what happened the first time we tried to open the damned museum. I let my good intentions get the better of me. I was . . . Well, I was upset when it went pear-shaped again. But I behaved badly, and I'm sorry.'

'All right,' said Hazel. She passed him a mug. (She'd thought about using the good cups and saucers, decided he hadn't earned them.) 'Your apology is accepted.'

Clearly expecting something more fulsome, he floundered slightly. 'I – er – I should have brought you back to town when you asked.'

'Yes, you should. Never mind, I managed.'

'Yes,' Ford said softly. 'You always do, don't you?'

'Well, being let down is a great way to learn self-reliance.'

'That's a bit harsh . . .!'

'Is it?' She rounded on him, not in anger – though she had felt anger enough at the time – but in a kind of calm savagery. If he'd come here for platitudes, he was in for a surprise. 'Of course you let me down. Big time. I was your guest. I was miles from home, without my car, when I got word that my friend's children had gone missing. And you wouldn't leave your bean-feast to drive me back. Well, don't worry about it because there's always another way. Nobody's indispensable, Oliver, not even you.'

'I was there to work,' he protested. 'I wasn't free to leave early.'

'Then what are you apologising for?'

She'd wrong-footed him again. She gave him no time to recover. 'And another thing. I don't care if you play golf with the chief constable three times a week. I don't care if he thinks the sun shines out of your left ear. You don't go behind my back and have my boss order me to take something I wouldn't take from you.' She took the plain little box out of her pocket, and the little gold pendant out of the box, and quite slowly and deliberately dropped it in his coffee.

Their eyes met. Then, quite slowly and deliberately, Ford drained his cup.

Hazel was still waiting for him to spit the thing out when he started to choke.

For a moment she simply watched, deeply sceptical, expecting him to give a sheepish little grin and let it slip out of his sleeve. But he didn't. He bent almost double, his chest heaving, a strangled cough bubbling in his throat. Then he stood

76

up, his eyes wild, his face red with effort, reaching for her with a desperate claw-like hand.

That was the point at which it went from a bad joke to deadly reality for Hazel. And she knew exactly what to do. Had been taught exactly what to do. She crossed the living room in two swift steps, evaded his clutching hand and positioned herself behind him. Her left hand, fisted tight, went *here*, and her right hand gripped it *here*, and it didn't matter a damn if she broke his ribs because they would heal but he'd be dead in three minutes if she didn't . . .

A split second before the considerable power of her strong young body drove all the air out of his system, hopefully dislodging the obstruction in his gullet, she felt a tap on her wrist. She looked down over Ford's shoulder and saw the forefinger of his left hand politely attracting her attention. When he had it, he pointed to his right hand. Which went to his right ear and appeared to pull out, slowly, a length of slim gold chain.

Hazel became aware that she hadn't taken a breath for nearly as long as Ford. She let go of him and took a step back, breathing heavily; and he, breathing heavily, turned towards her, the gold phoenix in his hand and an expression of sly humour on his face, waiting to see what she would do.

He may have expected tears, he may have expected laughter. He probably didn't expect a swinging right hook to catch him on the jaw and spill him, startled, onto the sofa.

Hazel made no attempt whatever to help him up. She felt more inclined to hit him again. She couldn't remember the last time she'd felt quite so angry.

Ford clambered to his feet, unsteady from the blow and perhaps more so from the shock. He felt his jawline, wincing at the pain, and checked his teeth – not vital, perhaps, to an historian but indispensable to a TV personality. Finally he looked at her. 'If you'd seen the trick before,' he mumbled thickly, 'you only had to say so.'

'I thought you were dying.' Her own teeth were clenched hard.

'So you hit me?'

Hazel regarded him, silently, with such fierce ambivalence that he began to realise she might not have finished yet. When, abruptly, she grabbed for him, he flinched.

Still, he could hardly have been as surprised as she was when, instead of round-housing him again, she kissed him.

Some people believed Gabriel Ash to be a highly intelligent man. Many people believed him to be an idiot. Ash himself suspected that the truth lay not in a comfortable median, but in an awkward combination of extremes. That he was a stupid man whose flashes of insight gave the impression of intelligence.

He had one of those flashes now.

As so often before, it was something Hazel had said which triggered it. He went to the computer and did a bit of googling. (A part of his mind not needed by his fingers reflected on the fact that a single new word, which hadn't existed even as a concept when he was growing

78

up, could define a whole social era. Googling. Hoovering.) He made copious notes, read them over, wrote them out again in a different order, then made some phone calls.

When he was finished he found Patience looking at him expectantly.

'I suppose you're going to tell me it's a bad idea.'

The lurcher did nothing of the sort.

'I need some help,' he explained. 'And I can't keep relying on Hazel. She has her own life to lead. I need someone whose services I have the right to call on, any time I need to. Who's paid to do what I want.'

He flushed then, as if he'd heard what he just said through the filter of someone else's understanding. 'Not like *that*,' he assured the dog quickly. 'I mean a nanny. I've been calling nanny agencies. I need a professional nanny to help look after the boys. Then those well-meaning busy-bodies from Family Support can go and worry about someone else.'

The Darling family had a Newfoundland as a nanny, Patience said helpfully.

'That was in a *play*,' said Ash; pausing then to wonder how a lurcher came to know about *Peter Pan*. Of course, it was entirely possible that she didn't – that none of the things she seemed to say to him were objectively real. That it was a form of confabulation, where he projected onto his dog comments and ideas that were in fact emanating from elsewhere in his disorderly brain.

But that made it even more important that he get some professional help with raising his sons.

If he really was going doolally, they'd need someone who wouldn't wake up one morning unable to operate the toaster.

Till then, it seemed only polite to keep up his end of their conversations. 'It's a kind offer,' he assured the dog, 'but I'm not sure the social workers would be much happier about you raising the boys than they are about me. We need a genuine professional – someone who can produce her credentials like John Wayne pulling a six-shooter.

'They'll have people for me to interview by the beginning of the week. It was funny,' he said, frowning at the memory. 'They were quite shirty with me to start with. I don't know why. The first thing I said was that if the nanny my friend recommended wasn't available, I'd be happy to consider someone else.'

The dog appeared to consider for a moment. Then: Nanny McPhee?

'That's the one. She must work for another agency; none of the ones I spoke to seemed to have her number.'

Patience was apparently still formulating a response when the doorbell rang. She gave what appeared to be a shrug, or as close as someone without collarbones can manage, and voiced the resigned bark of a dog doing her duty.

It was PC Budgen, from Meadowvale. He greeted Ash with cautious affability, as people tended to when they weren't sure if they were dealing with the organ grinder or the monkey.

Instantly, the sight of the uniform drove Ash's thoughts to his sons. 'What's happened?'

'Nothing,' said Budgen quickly. 'Everything's fine. It wasn't actually you I was looking for. It was Hazel. But she isn't at home, and I wasn't sure that kid who lodges with her would pass on the message. I thought she might be here.'

Ash shook his head. His heart was still racing. 'I saw her outside the school this morning. I don't know where she went after that.'

'Well, if you do see her, will you ask her to give me a bell? It's nothing urgent, but she wanted to be kept informed.'

'I will of course. Informed about what?'

'The guy in the hospital. You know, the one who tried to blow up the museum? She asked me to let her know if he woke up. Well, he's woken up.'

Eleven

Gabriel Ash had no idea what to expect of a twenty-first century nanny. In the picture-books of his own childhood, they'd been plump, uniformed persons of severe but kindly mien wheeling sit-up-and-beg perambulators, but he suspected even this most conservative of professions might have moved on a little since then. He was determined to keep an open mind.

The first to present herself at Highfield Road arrived the following day, a tall, angular young woman with spiky hair and a nose stud. Her name was Charity. 'But everyone calls me Chaz. Parents, kids – everyone.'

She was very far from Ash's image of what he needed. She spoke rather loudly in a marked Lancashire accent, and appeared to dress from the rummage-box in an Oxfam shop; and when he asked about her views on discipline she gave a great honking laugh and said, 'Well, I don't believe in beating kids into submission! On the other hand, by the time you're old enough to know the difference between right and wrong, you're old enough to take the consequences of making bad choices. You can tell kids not to play with matches until you're blue in the face, but it doesn't sink in until they burn themselves. It's my job to make sure they don't burn them-selves too badly.'

Ash wasn't confident that a goth nanny would reassure Family Support that all was now well in the boys' lives. In spite of that, he found himself rather warming to Chaz. They parted on good terms, and he promised to let her know.

The second candidate, who arrived two minutes early for her noon appointment, looked much more promising. She was indeed rather stout, and wore a dark suit with a silk scarf in the neckline that almost looked like a uniform, and she introduced herself as Mrs Burns. She might have been a few years older than Ash. He knew immediately that producing Mrs Burns would get Family Support off his back. She was even Scottish, which he vaguely understood was a bonus.

But there was a problem. At first he wasn't

sure what it was, but as they talked it became unavoidably apparent. Mrs Burns preferred little girls. She managed to make Ash feel vaguely inferior for only managing to father sons. She made it clear that, as a matter of professional pride, she was perfectly willing to consider a family with boys, but there simply wasn't the job satisfaction in caring for them that there was with girls. Her whole demeanour switched between doting and disappointment, depending on which she was talking about.

Chaz the Lancastrian goth was looking more appealing by the moment. But could she do what he needed her to do, which was not so much to look after the boys, a task he could in fact manage himself, but *appear* a suitable person to look after them? He remembered the careful, watchful social workers who'd visited him and rather suspected she could not.

'Third time lucky,' he told himself, and waited for Ms Kelly, who was due on Monday morning.

When, answering the doorbell, he found himself looking clean over the top of her head, for a brief but surreal moment he thought the agency had misunderstood and sent him another child to care for. She was tiny. Even standing on the top step, she barely came up to his shoulder. So the first thing he saw was the top of her head, straight black hair pulled back into a simple knot that reminded him a little of Hazel's – or what Hazel used to do with hers when it was long enough – except that Ms Kelly's stayed where it was put, and Hazel's never had for long.

'Mr Ash?' She looked up at him with a small, polite smile. 'I'm Frances Kelly.'

We all make assumptions. About how people will behave based on their appearance, about how they will appear based on their names. Ash had expected Frances Kelly to be a plain but good-hearted Irishwoman, either a redhead with freckles or an olive-skinned, dark-haired west-coaster, displaying the Spanish genes that arrived in Ireland after the wreck of the Armada.

He was right about the hair, wrong about everything else. Ms Kelly had the almond eyes, peach-coloured skin and delicate bone-structure of the Far East, and she spoke English with the precision of someone who had spent years perfecting it. She looked about twenty. Only as he adjusted his filters, and listened to what she had to say, did Ash realise she was a grown woman with children of her own back home in the Philippines.

She must have realised he was doing some internal adjusting because she said, 'I'm not what you expected.'

Sometimes it's less offensive to be honest than polite. 'No,' he confessed. 'I thought you'd be a Dubliner.'

Ms Kelly bubbled a small but genuine laugh. 'My grandfather was from Ireland. The Philippines is a nation of immigrants.'

'So's Britain,' said Ash. 'No island is an island now, but it seems our ancestors got around even when they'd nothing but their own feet and the odd dug-out canoe.'

They talked about the boys. About how Ash came to be caring for his boys alone, and why Social Services doubted his competency. He held nothing back. It was important that she understood the nature of the job, the back-story of the people she'd be working with.

When he'd finished, Ms Kelly reflected for a moment. Then she said, 'Where is your wife now?'

'No one knows,' said Ash. 'On the run from the police. She may still be in England, she may not – I've no way of knowing.'

'Are you afraid she may try to abduct your sons?'

Ash tried to answer honestly. 'Afraid, yes. Do I think it's likely? – probably not. I don't think, wherever she is, she's in any position to complicate her life any further.'

'As a mother, she may not see it like that.'

'That's why I'm afraid.'

He realised he was being more open with Ms Kelly than he had been with either of the previous applicants. They talked about the legacy of the Ash boys' unsettled early years. About their very different personalities – clever, intense Gilbert, easily moved to anger and resentment, and pleasant, easy-going Guy, everybody's friend, the human Labrador.

On which subject: 'How do you feel about dogs? No allergies or anything?'

'I'm very fond of dogs, Mr Ash. Most nannies are. Dogs and small children are not terribly different, you know. Both respect fairness, and return love four-fold.'

Ash asked, as he had asked Mrs Burns, about discipline.

'Computer games,' replied Ms Kelly promptly.

'You give them computer games when they misbehave?'

'No, I take them away. I put them in a big see-through box with a padlock that I keep in the kitchen. Every time they sit down to eat, they see them. They see them, they want them, they remember how they lost them, and they think maybe they should behave better in future. Oh, computer games are a wonderful invention!'

'When do you give them back?'

'When they've earned them. By being good, or helpful, or kind. Everything we do has consequences, Mr Ash. Positive consequences or negative consequences. I don't think children should be burdened with the ills of the world, but we all need to try to make it a little better.'

They talked a while longer, then Ms Kelly left, in the hatchback she'd parked at the front gate. A car very like its owner: diminutive, outwardly modest, quietly classy. Ash had had to restrain himself from offering her the job on the spot. 'I'll be in touch with your agency.' But before that he wanted to talk to Hazel.

Even before that, there was Patience's opinion to consider. Behind the closed door he raised an eyebrow at her. 'Well?'

Dogs are like children! said the lurcher indignantly. If I leave paw-prints on the kitchen floor, is she going to lock Spikey Ball away?

Spikey Ball was Patience's only treasure. She

never visited the park without him. He was pink and squidgy, and gave her the sort of guilty pleasure that a grown man might get from a collection of comic books – knowing her enthusiasm was rather childish did nothing to diminish it. (He was also, by common consent, male. Patience always referred to him as He; and, worryingly, Ash had started to do the same.)

'I'll get you a spare Spikey Ball, just in case.'

It won't be the same, grumbled Patience; but she raised no further objections.

Which left only Hazel. He hadn't seen her since their argument at the school gates on Friday morning. He thought about phoning, decided to go round to her house before collecting the boys from school. He was pretty sure he owed her an apology – another one – and it was hard to do it properly over the phone.

Her car was parked in Railway Street, so Ash expected to find her at home. But Saturday answered the door, and only shrugged when Ash asked for Hazel.

'She isn't here?'

The boy shook his head, slouched back to the sofa.

'Well, I'll wait. She won't be long or she'd have taken the car.'

'She wasn't back last night,' muttered Saturday. 'I don't know when she'll be home.'

That surprised Ash more than it should have done. He was so used to her being there that he often forgot she was a young woman with a life of her own. 'Is she with someone?'

'Oliver Ford.' The acid in Saturday's voice would have stripped varnish.

The years Ford had been a household name were the same ones Ash had spent as a virtual recluse. He had to think longer than almost anyone in England would have had to. 'Oh – yes. The historian. The one she rescued from the fire-bomber.'

'Yeah. Him.'

Puzzlement knitted Ash's brows. The former street-kid was a born cynic, unlikely to be much impressed by celebrity, but this overt hostility was unexpected. 'Saturday – has something happened?'

'No.' The boy leaned over to pick up one of Hazel's magazines, feigning an interest in soft furnishings and cleaning products.

Ash gave an oddly gentle sigh. He checked his watch, but there was time enough, and anything that Saturday was this keen to keep from him he probably needed to know. He took the chair on the other side of the little coffee table and rephrased the question. '*What* has happened?'

'Nothing,' insisted Saturday. He looked up. 'I don't like him, all right? I don't like his fancy car, I don't like his fake tan, I don't like his expensive suits and I don't like *him*. I don't know why Hazel's hanging out with him. She can do better.'

Ash blinked. Surely the boy wasn't thinking . . .? But no. His concern, his indignation were more brotherly than proprietorial. 'You think a famous, highly paid, much-admired television presenter isn't good enough for her?'

'I think that one isn't,' growled Saturday. 'I think he's a two-faced git, and if she doesn't wipe him off her shoes pretty damned fast she's going to find out for herself. I don't want her to get hurt.'

'Me neither. But Saturday, we don't have to like her friends. Maybe she sees something in him that we don't. Maybe she's right, maybe not, but it's her call. Even if it proves to be a mistake, it's hers to make.'

'Mistakes can be costly,' muttered Saturday darkly.

'I think she can look after herself. She's been looking after all three of us for months. If Ford gets uppity, she'll have his arm up his back and frog-march him down to Meadowvale before he knows what hit him.'

The boy managed a rueful grin at that. 'She's nobody's doormat,' he admitted.

'No, she isn't. I don't expect there's anything that the pair of us can do that Hazel can't do better. Still . . .'

'What?'

'Maybe we'll keep an eye out for her all the same. Let me know when she gets home, will you? I need a word with her.'

Saturday promised that he would, and Ash left the boy somewhat happier than he had found him.

Twelve

Hazel Best had never been a silly teenage girl. She'd never screamed at pop-stars, mooned over local heroes or moped over matinee idols. She'd been level-headed to an almost disturbing degree. She'd always been able to see the big picture, always taken the long view, always known there were plenty more fish in the sea. She was the teenage girl that the mothers of other teenage girls pointed out as a shining example.

Privately, she'd suspected she was a deeply boring teenager, but at least avoiding problems saved you the trouble of having to resolve them.

Now, at the age of twenty-seven, she was behaving like a silly teenage girl. She was hanging on the arm of a man older, wealthier and more famous than she was, and enjoying the heads that turned and the eyes that widened. She was flirting. She was charming and provocative. She was going to clubs she'd only ever been to on drugs raids, dancing as if her feet were on fire, and drinking dubiously coloured concoctions with little paper umbrellas in them. And she was enjoying herself immensely. She bought three new outfits, none of which her mother would have approved of.

Ford was excellent company: witty and urbane, socially skilful, a practised summoner of taxis and cajoler of head waiters. He was fluent in the language and all the nuances of social interaction.

When he remarked, self-deprecatingly, that if the television work dried up he might try his chances as a gigolo, Hazel giggled appreciatively and said he'd make another fortune. She meant it. He was as polished, and successful, a seducer as he was at everything else he turned his hand to.

Not the least pleasing of his attributes was the interest he took in her: her history, her activities, her opinions. As far as Hazel could tell, it was genuine: when, afraid of boring him, she gave him only the edited highlights, he demanded more detail and seemed flattered by the most mundane of confidences.

In a rare moment of introspection, Hazel realised that this ability to be interested in anyone and anything was, much more than his qualifications as an historian, what elevated Oliver Ford to the status of celebrity. She was not so dazzled as to think she was the only woman he'd ever shone the searchlight of his personality upon. His outstanding talent was for making everyone he dealt with feel special. He was a flatterer; but a flatterer of supreme artistry, so almost perfectly sincere that even people who knew what he was doing liked him for it.

When the shooting script left Ford at a loose end and he suggested quitting grimy Norbold for an away-day in Devon – 'Nothing improper, nothing you should tell the chief constable about' – Hazel gave no thought at all to whether she should go, only to what she should wear.

As the days passed and he still hadn't heard from Hazel, Ash found himself growing anxious. He knew he'd annoyed her, and he wanted to update her on his search for a nanny. There was also PC Budgen's message. Ash tried her mobile but she didn't answer. He sent her a text, picking out the letters as clumsily as an arm-wrestler doing *petit-point*; but he may have done it wrong, or perhaps she never received it. In any event, she didn't reply.

The day after he interviewed her, Ash telephoned the nanny agency to offer Ms Kelly the job, starting as soon as she could manage it. He was asked if he wanted her to live in or out, and didn't know how to answer.

'Has she any preference?'

Either, he was assured, would be entirely acceptable to her. She had lived in with her last family; she was currently renting a room in Coventry and could commute if that suited him better.

Finally they agreed that, for a trial period of a month, she would come in daily, from eight in the morning until five at night, five days a week, unless he needed her to stay late; after which, if all parties were satisfied, they would review the question of living in.

Discreet enquiries were made as to whether he could afford the financial commitment he was entering into. Ash understood their concern: he made an immediate transfer of funds to cover the initial month, grateful for the money he'd made while he was capable of well-paid work. He'd had a lot of different things to worry about in the last few years, but money had never been one of them.

That settled, and the boys in school for the day, Ash addressed his next dilemma: what, if anything, he should do about the young man in the hospital. He hadn't been able to pass on the information Hazel had asked for. Should he let Budgen know?

Curled up on the sofa, without lifting her head, Patience said, You could go to the hospital yourself.

He expected to be refused access to the prisoner. But as luck would have it, PC Budgen had drawn the short straw again. He was propped disconsolately on a plastic chair that had probably seemed a lot more comfortable two hours earlier, at the shut and shuttered door, and Ash was a welcome distraction from his tedious duty.

'Hi, Gabriel. Is Hazel with you?'

Ash had never, in forty-one years, come to terms with his given name. On the lips of a twenty-five-year-old police constable he hardly knew, it sounded more alien than ever. He took some comfort from recognising that (a) it was an improvement, however slight, on what they used to call him at Meadowvale; and (b) if he was on first-name terms with the local constabulary, it was as a friend of Hazel Best's and marked her own gradual rehabilitation back into their ranks.

He still couldn't bring himself to call PC Budgen 'Wayne'.

'I couldn't get hold of her. I left her a message but she hasn't called back.'

Budgen shrugged. 'I don't suppose it matters. I don't think he's going anywhere.' He gave a sideways nod towards the door.

'How's he doing?'

'On the mend, apparently. He was pretty sick for a while there, between blowing his hand off and burning his face to a crisp, but he's conscious now and seems to be making sense.'

'Has he been able to explain?'

'Why he crossed Europe in order to blow up a little local museum?' Budgen shook his head. 'No. DI Gorman's tried talking to him a couple of times. He wasn't interested in answering any questions.'

'Perhaps he doesn't speak English.'

'I think he does – at least some. "Please" and "thank you" to the doctors and nurses. Seems quite grateful for their attentions. His mother would be proud of him,' he added sourly. 'They're sending a specialist up from Counter Terrorism Command in London. Someone who can talk to him in his own language. Maybe the spooks will make more progress with him.'

Ash kept a diplomatic silence. Budgen had clearly forgotten that, in his years as a security analyst, Ash had worked under the Home Office umbrella in that division which might loosely be described as 'spooks'.

But Budgen had his mind on other matters. He looked furtively up and down the corridor. 'Gabriel, are you rushing off?'

Ash shook his head.

'You wouldn't sit here and look official for ten minutes? I'm bursting for a pee, and I could murder a cup of coffee. I'll bring you one back,' he offered hopefully.

Ash took his place on the plastic chair. 'What do I do if he's knotted his bed sheets together into a sub-machine gun?'

'Do what I'd do,' said Budgen. 'Look for something really solid to hide behind.'

The constable was longer than ten minutes. The plastic chair quickly grew uncomfortable. And Ash found himself doing what he had no business doing, which was opening the door and looking at the frail figure under the white sheet in the only bed in the room.

Rachid Iqbal looked back.

Ash gave a start of momentary fear when he realised he was alone with a terrorist. But Iqbal was tethered to the bed not only by his weakness but by the tubes drip-feeding the life back into him. Illness had replaced the coppery warmth of his skin with a greenish pallor, except where areas of his face and neck were dressed with some glistening unction.

His arms lay on top of the sheet. One of them ended in heavy bandages, midway between wrist and elbow.

'I didn't mean to disturb you,' said Ash quietly. 'Do you need anything? I can call a nurse.'

'No.' The voice was breathy, and accented, but clear enough. The terrorist added politely, 'Thank you.' He eased his slight form fractionally under the sheet. Even that minimal action made him catch his breath and squeeze his eyes shut.

'You're in pain,' said Ash. 'I'll get someone.'

'No. Really.' The young man managed a fragile

95

smile. 'It will soon be time for my medication.'
He pronounced the four syllables carefully, as if
one might otherwise escape. 'I will wait. I must
be a good patient.'

'If you're sure.' Ash went to back out of the
room.

'Please . . .' The likelihood that he would be
left alone again instilled a timid urgency in
Iqbal's voice. 'May I ask you something?'

'You can ask. I may not be able to answer. I'm
not a doctor. I'm not even a policeman.'

Iqbal acknowledged that with a dip of his
eyelids. He had long, fine eyelashes like a girl's.
'Then perhaps you will not know. But . . . there
was a young woman. She tried to stop me. Do
you know, was she hurt?'

Ash fisted his hands deep in his pockets. 'As
a matter of fact, I do know. She's a friend of
mine. And yes, she was hurt. Her face was
burned. But she'll mend.'

'Is she in the hospital here?'

'Not now. They sent her home.'

The young man sighed. 'That is good to hear.
I have been most worried about her. I never
meant for her to be hurt.'

Ash said mildly, 'If you don't want to hurt
people, perhaps you should avoid fire-bombing
crowded places.'

Flat under the white sheet, the boy's chest
attempted to swell. 'It was a matter of honour.'

'Really? You think there's something honour-
able about burning a young woman you'd never
met before? All I can think,' said Ash, 'is that
something's getting lost in the translation. In

96

English we use the word to mean noble, self-sacrificing, putting other people's needs ahead of our own. But you think it means forcing people to see things your way and torturing them until they do.' He pursed his lips reflectively. 'Have you considered the possibility that you might be wrong?'

'You think this was . . . politics?' Even in its frailty, the young man's voice managed to convey surprise.

'I hope so. I'd hate to think it was a passing whim.'

'Not . . . politics.' This was the most talking Rachid Iqbal had done since he woke up and it was beginning to take its toll. He was struggling to keep his eyes open, and the unpractised words were slurring together.

'You're going to tell me that jihad isn't a political imperative, it's a religious one,' guessed Ash. 'So I'm going to do what nobody in polite society ever does, which is tell you what I think of your religion. Of all religions. None of them are worth a damn unless they make their followers better people. And you are not a good advertisement for yours. Anyone who'd do what you've done shames the cause for which he does it. People stopped cutting bits off one another in the name of their gods when the notion of civilisation began to catch on. What you do or don't believe is your own business; but when you maim and kill people for believing something else, you immediately revert to barbarianism.

'And you will lose. Because there's something in human beings, those of many religions and

97

those of none, that aspires to be better. Fairer, kinder, more caring. Kindness is stronger than hatred. It endures longer and it spreads wider. Hatred is ultimately self-defeating. You're going to lose because you have nothing to offer. You think you can frighten people into thinking in old, discredited ways, but you're fooling no one except yourselves. You're an intellectual dead-end. The world will run you down and move on, and all that will be left will be a footnote in history: Hitler, Stalin, Pol Pot, and you. You're an anachronism. You're a freak show, and everyone knows it except you.'

Ash heard himself then and winced. Had the damaged boy before him any idea what he meant by *anachronism*? Had he any idea what Ash was trying to tell him?

Probably not. Because Rachid Iqbal had entirely exhausted his reserves. He could stay awake no longer, not even to be lectured on the error of his ways by this big, quiet, angry Englishman using words he'd never heard before and attributing to him attitudes that he did not recognise. The best he could do was simply repeat, 'No . . .' as clearly as he could before the comforting darkness swept up to claim him.

Gabriel Ash went on looking down at him for some moments after he realised that the young man was unconscious. Then he padded quietly from the room, and waited outside until PC Budgen – finally and apologetically – came to relieve him.

Thirteen

Ash sat down with his sons that evening, with the television off and gadgets put away for the night, and explained about the new nanny.

Predictably, Gilbert was unimpressed. 'Why?'

'Because I'm not doing as good a job of looking after you as I want to,' Ash said honestly. 'It's a long time since I got any practice, and even then I wasn't doing it alone. Ms Kelly knows more about raising children than the three of us put together. She'll make our lives easier, and more fun. Yes, Gilbert, that includes you. Don't decide you don't like her before you've even met her. She's made of sterner stuff than Saturday – you should probably avoid making an enemy of her.'

'*Nobody's* called Saturday,' growled Gilbert rebelliously.

Promptly at eight the following morning the doorbell rang, and the boys hurried to answer it – Guy, who suffered from the same crippling shyness as Billy Graham and Liberace, making no secret of his curiosity, and Gilbert struggling to get there first while still appearing coolly uninterested.

Frances Kelly stood on the doorstep, dressed in a bright yellow smock over dark trousers, wearing a smile as bright as the smock. 'Good morning, Mr Ash. And Guy, and Gilbert. Ready for school, I see. That is a very good start.'

Guy, beaming, grabbed for her hand, shook it manfully and pulled her inside. Gilbert stood back with an expression of shock on his narrow face. 'But she's . . .'

Ash had a pretty good idea what was coming, hurried to change the subject. 'Do come in, Ms Kelly. You'll have to tell me what you need, how we should organise things. And what the boys ought to call you.'

'Most people call me Frankie,' she said. 'That would be fine. And I suggest we talk about routines and such after I've walked the boys to school. I need a word with their head teacher – introduce myself and so on.'

'Yes, fine – excellent,' nodded Ash, keenly. He knew he was behaving like an idiot, but he was anxious to leave no gap for his elder son to fill. Perhaps he should have told them the name was misleading. But that would have given Gilbert all night to formulate a strategy, and this way he could only be as unpleasant as he could manage at a minute's notice.

Gilbert Ash was always ready to rise to a challenge. 'But she's Chinese!' he protested loudly, and Ash cringed.

Ms Kelly appeared entirely untroubled. 'No, I'm from the Philippines. Do you know where the Philippines are, Gilbert?'

His powder may have been drawn by her prompt and cheerful response. But he wasn't ready to back down. 'Near China?' he hazarded, stonily.

'Not *very* far from China,' agreed Frankie. 'I'll show you in the atlas after school. That is where

100

my children live. You do have an atlas? No? Then we must ask your father if we may go shopping . . .'

If she'd asked to buy them both Samurai swords, he'd probably have agreed out of sheer relief. Not until that moment had Gabriel Ash admitted to himself just how difficult getting his lost sons back had proved. Be careful what you wish for . . . Already – she hadn't been in the house for five minutes – he had the sense that Frances Kelly had been one of his better decisions.

The away-day in Devon stretched somewhat, but they were back in time for Oliver Ford to resume filming at the museum on the Saturday. Hazel watched from the sidelines. It was more interesting now that she knew some of the people involved. She was amazed how long it took to get two minutes of programming into the can – there was no longer a can involved, but some of the production team were old enough to remember when there was – and impressed by Ford's ability to keep his narration seamless, even though it was filmed in bite-sized chunks. She warmed to Emerald, who bossed her male colleagues around shamelessly and reminded Hazel of the captain of her school hockey team. She started to appreciate how a shot could be set up so that it was more than just another image of a man pointing at a glass case. Some of the techno-speak she heard started to make sense to her.

A man turned up with a horsebox and a pile

of armour. Hazel puzzled over the shape of some of the armour, until the man decanted his horse and started fitting some of the odder bits of metal to it. It gave her a resigned look that reminded her of Patience.

When horse and man were proof against anything short of an Exocet missile, the one struggled up on top of the other and they cantered across a convenient field while Ford spoke to camera about the crusading classes in the thirteenth century.

Then, unexpectedly – or at least, as unexpected as a storm could be in England in October – the heavens opened. The carefully constructed shots were no longer of a gaily caparisoned horse cantering across medieval England, but of an angry, muddy man on foot pursuing a muddy horse across a muddy field after it had fallen in the mud. Emerald threw up her hands in despair and called an end to the day's shooting.

With the weather forecast promising more of the same for several days at least, Ford cornered Emerald and suggested that they abandon filming for a week.

'But we're already running behind! You buggering off to Devon didn't help.'

Ford remained unchastened. 'You didn't need me until today. I've seen the schedule, I know when I'm going to be needed and when I'm just going to be sitting round drinking coffee. And really, Emerald' – he directed her gaze to the window: it was like peering through a waterfall – 'you can't blame me for this. Look, we've finished the inside work, and we can't do anything

102

outdoors in this, so you might as well give everyone a few days off. It won't cost any more than keeping us here waiting for a break in the weather, and it'll earn you Brownie points with the whole crew. Let's meet back here on Thursday, say. If the weather's better by then, we'll quickly catch up on lost time.'

She did some rough sums in her head, blanched at the financial implications, but had to acknowledge that the probability of doing any useful work outside in the near future was minimal.

Satisfied, Ford linked his arm through Hazel's and steered her back towards his trailer. 'Four days. Where can we get to in four days that they don't have mud?'

He knew – of course he knew – the perfect place. No mud, but a sapphire sea breaking in lace-trimmed waves against a rocky red shore. No rain, but a blue-tiled pool surrounded by potted palms and wicker loungers. No Emerald tapping her clipboard with the end of her pen to demand attention, but a hotel staff in white tunics who knew when they were required before their guests did, and a head chef who knew exactly – *exactly* – how Ford liked his steak.

Morocco was one of the many places Hazel had never been. Foreign holidays had never been on the agenda when she was a child – as a serving soldier her father had got all the travel he'd wanted at work, could never be persuaded to venture beyond Cornwall when he was on leave. After her mother died they never bothered with holidays at all. She'd ventured as far as Brittany with some university friends once, and to the Canary Islands with a group of police probationers while they awaited the results of their exams, but that was about it. Her passport had seen about as much sunshine as Dracula.

And four days in Morocco sounded . . . amazing. Every fibre of her being wanted to jump at the chance. But there was this little chirping cricket on her shoulder, primly pointing out that while a few decadent days in the sun with a celebrity might be the sort of thing that lots of girls would jump at, Hazel Best had always been too sensible for that. Too aware of where such indulgences might lead. Too smart to dive headlong into a blue tiled pool without knowing exactly where the ladder was that would enable her to get out. And fully aware that another word for *decadent* was *dirty*. If someone who wasn't Oliver Ford had offered her a dirty weekend in Brighton . . .

Hazel brushed the cricket off her shoulder and began ransacking her wardrobe for some clothes that hadn't just come back from Devon.

Fourteen

Before Frankie Kelly had been working for him for a week, Ash knew that he and his sons were in safe hands. They'd agreed a plan of campaign which would allow him to spend as much time as he wanted with the boys, to contribute as much to raising them as he was able, but still provide him with daily support and emergency back-up.

Frankie too seemed satisfied with the arrangement. Ash wasn't quite sure why. Much as he loved them, he doubted that his children were outstanding examples of the species, and he knew the house was shabby. He even found himself apologising for Patience, and promised to brush her more often to keep her hairs off the boys' clothes.

Frankie gave him the same warm, generous smile as she gave her charges. 'My goodness, Mr Ash, don't apologise for your fine dog! A dog is a wonderful thing for children. It keeps them active, it teaches them care and kindness, it makes them think of something beside themselves. A little hair on a school blazer is a very small price to pay.'

Patience thumped her tail in agreement.

Frankie laughed in delight. 'Goodness, Mr Ash – I believe she knows exactly what we are saying!'

Ash sidestepped that carefully. 'I feel a little awkward being called *Mr* Ash. People at work used to call me Ash. My friend Hazel, and my therapist, call me Gabriel.'

'Yes? But then *I* would feel awkward. No, I'm afraid you must get used to it, Mr Ash.' And that, he realised immediately, was that.

He couldn't wait for the people from Family Support to come round again and try their disapproving stare on Frankie Kelly.

* * *

105

They went to Casablanca. It wasn't what Hazel expected: much more middle-class and respectable. Less 'Rick's Café' and more 'Lyons Corner House'.

Ford took her shopping. Anything she admired he wanted to buy for her, so she was careful only to admire – at least aloud – the gaily coloured scarves and artisan brasswork created before their eyes in the little open-fronted shops. Some of the jewellery was fairly cheap-and-cheerful too: Ford bought her a silver bracelet and half a dozen charms. 'We can add to them as we go along.'

Hazel bought souvenirs for Saturday – a keffiyeh to knot about his thin throat on winter days when he considered himself too cool to wear a scarf – and Ash. That was harder. Not because he had everything: in fact he had very little in the way of personal possessions. The difficult part was knowing what might give him some pleasure. She finally bought him a finely tooled leather collar for Patience.

She also wanted to buy Ford something. This was as difficult as buying for Ash, if for a different reason. Ash wanted little; Ford already owned everything he wanted. She watched covertly to see what took his fancy among the goods on display; but his tastes ran mostly to luxury, and she didn't want to give out the wrong signals. She enjoyed his company – she was very much enjoying this trip – but she didn't see it as anything other than a pleasant interlude and she didn't want Ford to think differently.

In the end she bought him a shirt. She realised that he probably paid more for his shirts at home, and that hand-made hadn't the same cachet in a country where even skilled labour was cheap, but she liked the fabric which was chambray with a little very delicate embroidery around the yoke.

'If you don't like it,' she said, 'you can always sleep in it.'

Ford held it up, inspecting the workmanship. 'I *do* like it,' he assured her. 'And I don't need anything to sleep in.'

But by then she knew that.

After taking the boys to school on Monday, Frankie made an inventory of their belongings. She was serious about Ash buying them an atlas, and any number of other improving and educational toys. She was a great believer in proper building blocks – not the ones that came already assembled into a specific structure, but those that made you use your imagination. Frankie was a great believer in children using their imagination. It was their one window on the world, she said, that wouldn't crash in a power-cut.

Ash had tea and biscuits ready for when she was finished. She sat down with an audible sigh of gratitude. She was also a great believer in the therapeutic properties of tea and biscuits.

'Do you want me to come shopping with you?' he asked. 'Or would you rather go alone and browse? You can take my credit card.'

Frankie Kelly looked up at him – she had to look up at people much smaller than Ash – with exasperation. 'Mr Ash, you shouldn't be so trusting.'

Ash shrugged. 'I'm trusting you with much more than my credit card, Frankie. I'm trusting you with my children.'

She nodded approval and took another custard cream.

That was when the phone rang. It was Detective Inspector Dave Gorman from Meadowvale Police Station. 'Gabriel – have you been interrogating my suspect?'

'No,' said Ash promptly. Then, because he was a deeply honest man: 'I did talk to him. But that was days ago.'

'*Why?*'

'I was there when he was waking up. He wanted someone to talk to.'

'It didn't occur to you that questioning a terror suspect was probably a job for an expert?'

Ash refrained from pointing out that, when it came to terrorism, he was something of an expert himself. 'I didn't question him. I asked if he wanted me to call the doctor. I asked if he was in pain. He wanted to know if Hazel was all right, and I told him she would be.'

'And you told him he was a poor advertisement for his religion.'

Ash was surprised the injured youth had repeated that to the policeman. 'You want to argue the point?'

'What I want to argue about is you saying that, or anything else, to a man facing charges of attempted murder! Gabriel, you know how the system works. Putting him away won't come down to what he did – dozens of people saw what he did! – but to proving it. The first thing his brief will want to know is, were all the procedures properly followed? You giving him a lecture on religious freedom does not constitute proper procedure!'

'But I'm not a policeman,' Ash pointed out reasonably. 'I'm a private citizen. Nothing I say to him can compromise your case.'

Which was probably true; but Gorman was still annoyed. 'I suppose I can always say you're just the local lunatic who happened to wander by.'

'You've said it before,' murmured Ash.

'But that doesn't help me with the problem you've created.'

'What problem?'

'Now he's refusing to talk to anyone *but* you! He must have recognised you as some kind of a kindred spirit. He thinks he'll get a fairer hearing from you than he will from Counter Terrorism Command.'

That was certainly a problem. 'You did tell him I'm not a policeman? In fact, *I* told him I'm not a policeman.'

'He doesn't care. He won't talk to CTC, he won't even talk to me. He says he *will* talk to you, at least about some things. I think he wants to debate religious dogma with you. Will you come to the hospital and talk with him?'

'I'll come,' said Ash reluctantly. 'I'm not sure how much good it'll do.'

'Me neither,' admitted Gorman. 'But if he starts talking he may end up telling us more than he intends to. It's worth a try. Shall I send a car?'

'Certainly not,' sniffed Ash. 'I've got a car. I've got a perfectly good car.'

'You've got a perfectly good car that's older than some of my officers,' said Gorman. 'I'll see you at the hospital in half an hour. Unless you break down on the way.'

From Casablanca they headed inland to the red city of Marrakech. It was everything Hazel had hoped: vibrant, busy, colourful, full of strange sights and stranger smells, at once deeply exotic and entirely familiar. It was a market town full of people doing business. The fact that their businesses involved dyeing great swags of wool and drying them over the street, or tanning leather in huge vats whose stench travelled two blocks against the prevailing wind, didn't alter the fundamental ethos of the place. Residents, farmers coming in from outlying areas and foreign visitors met and mingled on the cheerful, noisy streets, making way – eventually, under protest – to traffic comprising modern 4x4s, big old sedans that even Ash would have traded in, and the occasional donkey.

The invitations to shop, shouted across the alleys of the impossibly convoluted souk, came in a variety of languages – French, English, and some which Hazel didn't recognise and so were probably Berber or Arabic – but in essence were the same that market traders shouted across the town squares of middle England. 'What're you looking for, missus? Got it here somewhere. You know what you need to go with one of those? – one of these. Bargain of the day, this is. Not fifty quid. Not twenty quid. Not even a tenner. You got eight pounds? There you go. You know it makes sense.'

Dazzled by the colour, drunk on the smells, Hazel wandered from one tiny emporium to the next, admiring the craftsmen busily finishing their wares in front of her, sometimes buying trinkets, sometimes getting lost, enjoying the experience with all five senses. At times she forgot about the man who had brought her here, and spent minutes haggling in schoolgirl French with a man turning little fruitwood boxes on a pole-lathe indistinguishable from the one his great-grandfather had used; only to find, when she'd succeeded in striking a deal that she was pleased with (and the wood-turner probably ecstatic about), that Ford was watching her affectionately.

Hazel wanted to buy camel stew from one of the street kitchens in the Jemaa el-Fnaa, and eat supper at communal tables grouped around the cooking fire. Ford shuddered, muttered something about Delhi belly, and steered her to an altogether more prestigious establishment where they ate, reclining on cushions, at a low table under silvery lanterns. The stew served here was perhaps from a better class of camel, and the kitchens were probably more in line with European expectations, but Hazel regretted the lost opportunity to share in the camaraderie she had glimpsed at those communal tables in the great square.

After they had eaten she dragged Ford back to watch the street-theatre and listen to professional storytellers working the crowd in a language she couldn't fathom.

Ford understood enough to give her a rough translation. The Arabic in use was not identical to that spoken in those areas of Syria and Iraq where he'd worked, but it was close enough to follow. When the storyteller finished, Hazel gave him a small banknote, and a single *dirham* to Ford for the translation.

He didn't put it in his trouser pocket with the rest of his change, but folded it in his handkerchief in the breast pocket of his jacket.

On the Tuesday evening Ford phoned Emerald. The call didn't last long, but the outcome was clearly to Ford's satisfaction. 'It's still raining cats and dogs in the Midlands. No point going back yet.'

'We can stay another couple of days?' Hazel heard the hope in her own voice, knew Ford must have heard it too. She frowned. 'But Oliver, what about . . .?'

He knew what she was going to say, stopped her with a wave of his hand. 'The expense? What about it? I work like a Trojan for eight months of the year so I can enjoy my ill-gotten gains for the rest of it. If you weren't here, I might save a bit on mint tea' – Hazel had developed a taste for the local brew – 'but the only real difference would be that I wouldn't be enjoying myself as much. You're giving me much more than you're taking.'

In truth, she knew that a few more days in Morocco would make little dent in his financial situation. Not paying her share still went against the grain with her; but somehow, less than it had in Norbold. They say that travel broadens the mind. Hazel was still, just, narrow-minded enough to worry that she could get used to being a kept woman.

But before she could propose a more equitable solution, Ford had taken her silence for consent. 'Good, that's settled then.' And when she didn't immediately correct him, they both knew she would not raise the matter again.

Half an hour later Ford's phone rang. He talked for several minutes before ending the call. He came back with an expression Hazel couldn't read. 'Now, that's remarkably good timing. If the sun had been splitting the heavens over Norbold, and Emerald had had her cameras ready to roll, I wouldn't have known what to do about that.'

'What?'

'An old colleague has painted himself into a corner over some artefacts rescued from Palmyra. Wants me to pour oil on troubled waters at the Turkish Ministry of Culture & Tourism. I have some contacts there. I'll take everyone for a good lunch, dole out a bit of flattery, point out that the items would have been lost if they'd been left *in situ*, and that one day Syria will be very glad its good neighbours in Turkey cared enough to keep its artefacts safe. In the meantime they'll look good on display in Istanbul. It won't take twenty-four hours. We'll be on our way home before the rainclouds have cleared over Wittering.'

About the only part of this that Hazel took in

was that 'we'. 'You want me to come with you? To Istanbul?'

Ford laughed. 'Well, I can hardly abandon you in Morocco, can I? If we get a flight tomorrow, we'll be back in England by the weekend.'

Hazel hardly knew what to say. There had been times, she knew, when people she cared about worried that she was becoming impulsive. But even if it was true, underlying that was a solid stratum of common sense that gave foundation to all her judgements, all her actions. If she seemed impulsive, it was only because it didn't take her long to weigh up pros and cons and reach a decision. She thought quickly. But she did always think.

She didn't know what to think about this. All she knew about Istanbul she'd learned from the cinema, and girls who allowed themselves to be taken there by men they hardly knew *always* came to a sticky end. Ford said he'd have her back by the weekend. But there was little to stop him changing their plans again. She'd agreed to a few days in Morocco. Now he was assuming her consent to a few more days, further from home, further into the unknown.

Hazel Best hadn't been a police officer for very long. But she'd been an intelligent, rational, healthily sceptical human being for twenty-seven years now, and the last time she'd been tempted by an invitation to adventure she'd been thirteen years old and her best friend had wanted them to run away to sea together. (Even at thirteen, though the idea appealed, she had known that nothing but trouble would come of it and regretfully declined. In the end Harry Beswick hadn't gone either. Running away to sea meant first reaching a port, and he couldn't work out the train timetables. He'd gone on to become a librarian and an authority on maritime fiction, thus enjoying much of the romance of sea travel without the inconvenience of actually having to go anywhere.)

If a friend had consulted her on a similar offer, Hazel's response would have been uncompromising. It wasn't a good idea. No amount of charm on the part of the person issuing the invitation would make it a good idea. It wasn't wise and it wasn't safe. What, after all, did she really know about her companion? How far could she trust him? And whether or not she knew the answer, wasn't the mere fact that she posed the question enough to tell her what the answer ought to be?

Ford was waiting, looking expectant rather than hopeful, as if there was no doubt in his mind what her response would be. He was wearing the chambray shirt she'd bought him, and a straw trilby tipped at a rakish angle over one eye, and fourteen years after she'd disappointed Harry Beswick she opened her mouth to visit the same disappointment on Oliver Ford. It was, after all, the sensible thing to do.

But, to her astonishment, the words that came out were: 'You organise the flights and I'll pack.'

Fifteen

Constable Budgen – a chastened Constable Budgen, who wouldn't be asking anyone to hold the fort for him again any time soon – let Ash into the side ward.

Rachid Iqbal appeared to have been waiting for him. At least, his narrow, fine-boned face registered satisfaction at Ash's arrival.

Ash nodded a cautious greeting from the door. 'I was told you wanted to see me.'

Iqbal nodded too, politely enthusiastic. 'Yes. Yes, please. Thank you.'

It was a week since they'd last met. Since then, care and rest had worked a magic of healing in Iqbal's body. Not his hand – no amount of time, or surgical skill, would restore that, and the bandaged foreshortened stump lay on top of the covers in mute, devastating testimony. But his colour was better, and there was an animation in his face that suggested the return of a little strength. Even that energetic nodding would have been impossible last time Ash was here. But Iqbal was a young man, he'd been in good health before he blew himself up, and his body was winning its battle to get well.

Soon, thought Ash, his problems would really start. 'Do you want to tell me why?'

Iqbal appeared to give it some thought. Of course, he was doing his thinking in one language before translating his conclusions into another. As someone who had never achieved proficiency in any language other than that he had grown up with, Ash had the utmost respect for people who could make themselves understood in foreign tongues. He'd once had some rudimentary French and German, but he'd never had any understanding of Arabic. He hadn't much regard for the young jihadi, but he could admire his command of English.

'I wish,' said Rachid Iqbal carefully, 'to explain to you why you are wrong.'

Ash had been about to pull out the chair and sit down; now he changed his mind. He didn't intend to stay that long. He sighed. 'Sunshine, if you're looking for converts, you've come to the wrong shop. I thought I made that clear when we talked before. Perhaps you nodded off at the critical moment.'

The young man was frowning, ready to take offence. 'Sun Shine? This is a reference to my . . .?' He went to raise his right hand, remembered he had no fingers on that side, raised his left instead and touched his cheek. 'My skin?'

Ash coloured deeply. Despite the disproportionate scale of their transgressions – he had made an innocent comment that had been misunderstood, the boy in the bed had tried to murder people – Ash was mortified. 'No. It's just something we call people. Sometimes because they're friends, and sometimes because we don't know their name.' As if there was any room for doubt, he added: 'I don't know your name.'

Iqbal considered. 'I do not know *your* name. Sun Shine.'

Ash gave a little grin. It mightn't be offensive, but it was pretty silly. 'My name is Ash. Gabriel Ash.'

'Jibra'il?' The boy brightened. 'Like the angel?'

'I can only think my mother was still feeling the effects of the epidural.' Ash waited.

Finally the boy gave a tiny nod. 'My name is Rachid Iqbal. I am happy to make your acquaintance.'

After a moment longer, Ash pulled out the chair after all and sat down. 'I really wish I could say the same, Rachid.'

'You think I am a bad man. I am not a bad man,' he insisted.

'Perhaps gods can see deeply enough into men's hearts to judge their motives. The rest of us have to judge people by their actions. You did a very bad thing. Speaking as a mere human being, I think that makes you a bad man.'

'I *did* do a bad thing,' agreed Rachid Iqbal. 'I failed.'

Ash shook his head, bewildered by a hatred so comprehensive that all Iqbal regretted was that the people he had burned survived. 'If that's how you feel, I don't think we have anything to talk about. You tried to kill my friend and a bunch of innocent bystanders. I don't care why. It was such a monstrous thing to do that you forfeited any right to have your voice heard. When you're well enough, you'll be put on trial, and no one will care what was in your heart. They'll only care about the spray-can in your right hand and the cigarette lighter in your left, and your decision to bring them together.'

'I did *not*!' said Iqbal indignantly. 'Try to kill your friend. Or the innocent bystanders.'

'Then what *were* you doing? A bit of impromptu hairdressing? Of course you . . .'

Then Gabriel Ash did what, at one time, he'd been better at than almost any man alive. He picked up the tiny pieces of a scattered jigsaw, and looked at the shapes of the pieces that were missing, and made an inspired guess about the picture. 'Ford? You were trying to kill Oliver Ford? *Why?*'

Immediately the boy in the bed was on his guard. Which was all the confirmation Ash needed. If he'd guessed wrong, Iqbal might have been scathing or amused or relieved. He would not have retreated almost physically into his pillows and muttered, guardedly, 'I did not say that.'

This was what Detective Inspector Gorman had been hoping for. Ash knew he should probably leave now, call the policeman and tell him that he'd got two significant pieces of information that Iqbal had refused to give to his interrogators: his own name, and the name of his intended victim. It didn't explain everything. But it would allow Gorman – or CTC, since it was officially their case now – to focus their inquiries. They might still not get the right answers, but at least they'd be asking the right questions.

Ash stayed where he was. 'That's what you meant when you said it wasn't political. Oliver Ford is an historian: nothing you could do to him would affect British overseas policy. What you did wasn't an act of terrorism, it was

119

attempted murder. Not political but personal. Why? How do you know Ford? What has he done to you that you'd travel hundreds of miles to make an attempt on his life?'

But Rachid Iqbal knew he'd said too much already. He had never intended to unburden himself to Ash. These were matters he didn't intend to discuss with anyone. But he'd felt besieged by all the policemen – the big, ugly, perplexed one from Norbold Police Station, who knew nothing about any country where they didn't play rugby but still struck Iqbal as a basically decent man; and the smaller, quiet, dark-eyed one who'd been sent up from London, who spoke Arabic as well as Iqbal did, and was much more to be feared. Someone in London must have thought their shared heritage would give them common ground. But Iqbal had met a lot of small, quiet, determined men in Turkey, and before that in Syria, and he knew how dangerous they could be.

He'd thought he could buy himself a little time by offering to talk again with the big shambling man, almost as ugly as the Norbold detective, who had treated him with some kindness when Iqbal was at his most vulnerable. He hadn't intended to tell him anything useful either; but while there was the possibility that he might, the dark-eyed policeman from London would leave him alone. Iqbal had heard that English policemen relied on guile and persuasion to extract the truth from their suspects. But he didn't believe it. He thought that, sooner or later, when they thought he was sufficiently recovered from his injuries, if he still wouldn't answer their questions they would beat him.

Iqbal was still young, and on the whole older men endured beatings better, but he was moderately confident that he could hold his tongue. Not out of pride, or because a great cause hung on his silence, but because the reputation of someone precious to him depended on it. He would keep it safe as long as he could. He believed he could suffer a few broken bones without betraying his purpose. But Iqbal was mortally afraid that if the London policeman wanted an explanation enough to put the blackjacks back in the toy-box and take out . . . well, he didn't know how long he would be able to hold his tongue then.

So the longer he could keep them guessing, keep them hoping that he might tell them what they wanted to know carelessly, or foolishly, or unsuspectingly, the better. Asking to speak to Ash had been a delaying tactic, no more. But the fewer tools a man has in his kit-box, the more value he will put on each of them. Iqbal had been genuinely pleased to learn that Ash was willing to visit him again.

He was wondering now if that had been a mistake. Gabriel Ash looked like many westerners Iqbal had seen – large, pale, awkward, infinitely less impressive than they believed themselves. But already it was clear to Rachid Iqbal that this westerner thought with more agility than he moved. And he had the disconcerting ability to hear what hadn't been said. Iqbal wondered if he might have been better taking his chances with the policemen after all.

He lay back, mumbled into his chest, 'I am not well. You will go now, please.'

But Ash stayed where he was, his deep-set eyes boring into Iqbal's face. Iqbal thought it entirely possible that, even if he said nothing more, Ash might at any moment drill down into his brain and syphon off the thoughts and memories he had considered safe there.

But perhaps actual mind-reading was beyond the Englishman after all. After a minute Ash straightened in his chair, and looked away briefly, and when he looked back it was with an apologetic little half-smile. 'I'm sorry, I know you must be tired. I'll go in a minute. First though, I need a straight answer to a very simple question. I'll explain why I need to ask, because I think – I hope – when you understand, you'll be willing to answer.

'You remember the girl you asked about? The one who got burned. I told you she's a friend of mine. Well, that's a bit of an understatement. She's been the best friend anyone could ask for. She looked out for me when I was in trouble; she believed in me when I lost belief in myself; she risked her own neck to rescue me from danger. And not because it was her job, but because she has a heart the size of Warwickshire and will do just about anything for just about anyone if it's in her power. You know this. It's how she got burned.'

He waited. After a moment Rachid Iqbal nodded reluctantly. 'Yes.'

'You were concerned about that. You never meant for her to get hurt. Almost the first thing you said, when you regained consciousness, was to ask if she was all right.'

'You said she would be.'

'I did,' agreed Ash. 'I thought it was true. Now I'm not sure. Rachid, I could be wrong about this too, but I think that – despite the evidence – you are basically a decent young man. I don't know why you did what you did, but I think you must have had a reason. You know Oliver Ford, or you know something about him, or someone you care about has known him and had cause to regret it. Am I right?'

Iqbal refused to answer. But his face answered for him.

'She's with him now. My friend Hazel. She went on holiday with him. I don't know where they are, or when they're coming back. I need to know if she's in danger.'

For the longest time it seemed as if Iqbal wasn't going to answer that either. But Ash had read his silences well enough. Finally he nodded. He had no idea if he was making things better or worse for himself, but the big Englishman needed to know.

'Yes,' he said simply.

Sixteen

Fifteen minutes earlier, Detective Inspector Gorman would have been able to refer Ash to his colleague from Scotland Yard. But Detective

123

Inspector Serai was on his way back to London, to discuss his lack of progress and his next move with colleagues whose views he valued more than those of a provincial DI. His train was pulling out as Ash presented himself at the front desk at Meadowvale and asked for an urgent meeting with the senior CID officer.

Gorman had him shown up. He was hoping for some useful information from Ash's visit to the hospital. Ash's obvious agitation startled him. 'Sit down, man. What's happened? What did he tell you?'

Ash did as he was told; and took the tacky plastic cup that Gorman pressed on him. 'It was Oliver Ford he was after. I don't know why – he wouldn't say. He just kept saying it was personal, not political.'

Gorman frowned, the heavy brows gathered over the lopsided nose. 'OK. Well, that's good, isn't it? One man with a grudge rather than a gang of conspirators with a cause? We bang this one up – did you get his name, by the way? – and that's an end to it.'

'His name's Rachid Iqbal,' said Ash. He sipped the scalding coffee – at least, he thought it was coffee; the machine on the landing also dispensed tea and oxtail soup, and occasionally an unholy combination of all three. 'And I wish that *was* the end of it. Hazel's with Ford, and I don't know where they are, and Iqbal says she's in danger. We have to find them, Dave. We have to bring her home.'

At a time when Hazel Best had had very few friends at Meadowvale Police Station, DI Gorman had given her a fair hearing. He still had a lot of time for her, thought she had the makings of a good CID officer – if she could stay out of trouble long enough. By the same token, he couldn't think of anyone better capable of looking after herself. He seriously doubted that a TV historian could give Hazel more problems than she could deal with. 'What sort of danger?'

Ash shook his head. 'I don't know. Iqbal wouldn't say.'

'What *did* he say?'

'Just that. That if Hazel was with Oliver Ford, she was in danger. He was concerned for her. He knew he'd hurt her at the museum, wanted to know if she was all right.'

But Gorman knew that everything Ash said, everything he worried about, had to be passed through the filter of his own history. The man had gone into free-fall after his wife and children disappeared – naturally that affected how he viewed the world. Gorman knew he wasn't lying about this. He also knew he could be over-reacting.

'She went away with him,' he said. 'What, for a holiday?' That was fairly non-committal. 'You've no reason to think Ford kidnapped her?'

'No, none,' said Ash quickly. 'The weather put his filming on hold, he invited her away with him for a few days and she went. But I don't know where they went to.'

'Is there any reason you should?'

Ash blinked. 'No, of course not. She does what she wants, with whoever she wants to. I thought nothing of it' – that wasn't strictly true – 'until

125

Iqbal said he was trying to kill the man. That Ford had made an enemy who was willing to cross Europe to try and kill him.'

'Why?'

'He wouldn't say.'

'Then why assume it's Ford that's dangerous? It's Iqbal who's dangerous. But he's not going to be anywhere near Hazel again.'

Ash was finding it hard to explain. He knew what Iqbal had done. In spite of that, and despite his account being more holes than fabric, he believed what Iqbal had told him. He tried again.

'Rachid Iqbal went to a lot of trouble to get at Ford. It's not easy to travel here from Turkey when you've no passport. God knows how he got together the money for his air fare, let alone the false papers. Without the clout of an organisation behind him, it must have taken him months. So he didn't do it on impulse. He didn't take a swing at someone who'd offended him – he followed Ford from the far side of Europe to a little museum in a village he could never have heard of, and he tried to burn his face off.

'Even without knowing why, we have to assume it was a matter of importance. I don't expect Iqbal knew it would cost him his hand, but he must have known it would cost him his freedom. And he still thought it worthwhile. That says Iqbal is a hot-headed, bloody-minded young man with little regard for the rule of law. But it says something about Ford as well. That he did something to provoke that kind of hatred.'

Almost against his better judgement, Gorman was intrigued. 'What do you think he did?'

126

'I don't know. I tried to press him, but Iqbal wouldn't say any more. I think he regretted saying as much as he had. But he's an intelligent, rational young man, and he doesn't strike me as a fanatic. I don't think this is because of anything Ford wrote in an academic paper.'

Gorman didn't think so either. He still didn't see why a feud between the young Arab and the historian meant that Hazel was in trouble. 'As far as I understand it, Ford's people haven't finished filming at Wittering. He'll be back as soon as the weather improves. Talk to Hazel then. Maybe she'll know why Iqbal came after Ford with a flame-thrower.'

It wasn't the response Ash had hoped for, but it was a reasonable suggestion. Perhaps because he no longer had a job, he tended to forget that most people had schedules to meet, places they had to be. He cast Gorman a rueful little smile. 'You're right. They're probably on their way back now.' He stood up. 'I'm sorry I couldn't get anything useful out of Iqbal.'

'At least we know now who the target was. And that Iqbal was probably working alone. I'll sleep sounder in my bed tonight just for knowing that.'

'Thank you for the coffee.'

Gorman scowled. 'There's no need to be sarcastic.'

The next morning Ash walked Patience across town to Railway Street. The curtains in the front room of the little terraced house were drawn back, but there were no other signs of life, and no answer to his knock. He rapped the door again, louder, and waited. After a couple of minutes Saturday appeared, tousled, in shorts and a ragged T-shirt bearing the legend 'Eventers do it three different ways'. It must have been a cast-off of Hazel's: equestrian jokes were outside Saturday's remit.

'Did I get you up?' asked Ash, pointedly.

But that was unfair. Saturday had a job now, he worked the evening shift from eight until midnight in a petrol station; over and above being a teenager, he had every excuse for sleeping late. The youth didn't complain. He yawned, and scratched the bird's nest of his hair, then waved a hand vaguely in the direction of the kettle and wandered off upstairs. He reappeared a minute later, still unwashed but at least wearing a T-shirt that hadn't been slept in.

'Hazel's not back yet?' It was a rhetorical question: by now Ash had seen the state of the kitchen.

Saturday gave an ambiguous grunt, bent to pat the dog.

Ash tried again. 'Have you heard from her? A postcard, phone call? Do you know where she is?'

The boy shook his head.

'Or when she's due back?'

'No idea.'

'It's not like her to drop off the radar.'

But actually, he didn't know that. All he knew was that for the past six months Hazel had been where he needed her when he needed her; and that had more to do with the state of Ash's mind than Hazel's. For all he knew, except when she was nurse-maiding the village idiot, she might have jetted off to foreign parts every available weekend. She might only have been waiting for Ash to get his act together, to gather up the remains of his family and start creating a normal life, so she could quit feeling sorry for him and get on with the things that free-spirited young women liked to do.

Saturday muttered something into his coffee. Hunched over his mug, straw-coloured hair falling unkempt in his face, he looked like someone conducting a conversation from behind a haystack.

Ash sighed. As the father of two sons who would in due course become teenagers, he considered dealing with Saturday as a kind of dry run. 'Hello? I'm over here.'

Saturday looked up, half exasperated, half amused. He enunciated clearly, as if speaking to someone very old who had mislaid his ear trumpet. 'I said, it's not like her to take up with a thug like that, either.'

Ash shrugged. 'She must see something in him that we're missing. She's not the only one: the man clearly has a following. Perhaps it's a woman thing.'

'Perhaps it's a *Too much oestrogen swilling round your system screws your head up and makes you think you're kissing Prince Charming when actually it's just another frog* thing,' said Saturday. Then he saw Ash's expression. 'What?'

Ash recovered himself enough to shut his mouth and shake his head. 'Nothing. It's just, you never cease to amaze me.'

129

'Why? Because I know some words with three syllables in them?'

'No. Because somewhere in that seventeen-year-old body dwell the heart and soul of a fifty-year-old cynic.'

'Yeah?' Saturday finished his coffee and headed back upstairs. 'Well, it's his turn to do the washing up.'

Ash had one more avenue to explore. If it too proved a dead-end, he saw no alternative but to wait for Hazel to return, when and indeed if she did. He drove out to Wittering, expecting to find the film crew still camped out in the museum car park. But the big vehicles, including Ford's trailer, were gone.

For a moment Ash was nonplussed. Gorman had said that filming was not yet finished, that the crew were merely waiting for the weather to improve. And then it struck him that the rain had stopped. If Ford had taken Hazel away because the weather had made it impossible to film, shouldn't they have returned when the sun came out again? But if Ford was expected back, why had the film crew packed up?

Deeply uneasy, Ash went inside to ask if the museum director knew when and where the film crew had gone.

Herbert Jennings was a man to whom routine mattered. (He was also possibly the last child in England to have been christened Herbert.) He liked to sit at his desk on a Monday morning, before the public were admitted, and plan his week meticulously. Though he had initially welcomed the publicity that would accrue from the new museum being televised, he soon discovered that routine was the first casualty when there was a film crew in attendance.

They wanted to film during the time he'd set aside for staff training. They wanted to move the exhibits around. They wanted – saints preserve us! – to *take them out of their cabinets.* Herbert Jennings passed a cotton handkerchief across his brow at the very thought. When the tall woman with ginger hair had said they were taking a weather break, he had felt his heart soar like a lark. And when, this morning . . .

'She telephoned to say that they wouldn't be back,' he told Ash, relief purring in his voice. 'At least, she didn't know *when* they would be back. She couldn't get hold of the presenter, and two cameramen and a sound recordist had other jobs to go to, so she was *pulling the plug*' – he said it as if it was some strange foreign expression he'd memorised by heart – 'until she could put together a new schedule.'

Ash felt cold fingers stroke his spine. 'She couldn't get hold of the presenter?'

'Apparently he's gone abroad and isn't answering his phone,' said the director, unaware of the pike he was driving into Ash's vitals. 'Celebrities. Hah!'

'The woman with ginger hair,' said Ash. 'Did she leave a number where you could call her?'

'I'm afraid not. You could try the hotel where they stayed, though. They might have a contact number for her.'

Seventeen

The receptionist at The Crown – which is to say, The Crown in Wittering, not to be confused with any number of other hostelries of the same name in the cavalier counties of Warwickshire and Worcestershire – knew exactly how to get hold of Emerald. She showed Ash to the residents' lounge, where Emerald was drowning her sorrows with a large balloon of brandy.

She brightened momentarily at the sight of Ash. 'Are you my taxi?'

'I'm afraid not. I'm a friend of Hazel Best's.'

'Who?'

'Constable Best.' Ash was irritated at having to remind her. 'The police officer who was burned in the bombing.'

Emerald had her mouth open to say 'Who?' again, when memory stirred. Her eyes narrowed and her broad mouth pinched. 'Oh. Her.'

Ash felt a rising indignation. 'Surely you haven't forgotten, Miss . . .?'

'Emerald,' said Emerald.

'That Hazel Best risked her life protecting your headline act from someone he'd failed to charm?'

Emerald looked surprised, the gingery eyebrows elevating. 'Really? Ford was the target? I thought it was an attack on the museum.'

Ash winced, kicking himself mentally to save Detective Inspector Gorman the trouble of doing it physically. But in truth, did it matter if Emerald knew? 'It seems to have been personal, something between Ford and the boy. We don't yet know what it was about.'

'Isn't he an Arab?' Emerald seemed to think this said it all.

'Possibly. He flew here from Turkey, but he probably isn't Turkish.'

'They're pretty unpredictable,' suggested Emerald. 'Arabs.'

Ash hung onto his patience. 'So are television personalities. We don't know which of them started the feud. But we do know which one thought it was worth crossing a continent and sacrificing his own liberty to end it.'

Emerald sniffed. 'Like I said – unpredictable.' She checked her watch, a large man's affair strapped to her big-boned wrist. 'I don't know how you think I can help.'

'Mr Ford may be able to shed light on what happened. I'd like to talk to him. Do you know when he'll be back?'

'Hah!' The brandy was beginning to take effect. 'I know when he *should* have been back. I know he called me yesterday to say he'd be delayed. I told him the weather was brightening up, but he wasn't interested. When I tried to phone him back he didn't answer, and when I checked with his hotel in Marrakech he'd gone. Nobody knew where to.'

Anxiety stirred the contents of Ash's stomach. 'Was Hazel still with him?'

Emerald shrugged. 'I presume so. The receptionist kept saying "they". To be honest, I blamed your friend. I thought she'd spirited him off somewhere.'

Ash's heavy eyebrows rocketed. 'You thought Hazel Best had kidnapped Oliver Ford?'

'Don't be silly. I thought she'd led him astray. Turned his head. Given him something more enjoyable to do than coming back here to finish my film.' Emerald checked her watch. 'Where *is* that damned taxi? Look, darling, I don't know what they're up to. I don't even *care* what they're up to. I just wish he was here, working, instead of playing at Lawrence of Arabia!'

'And you've no idea where they could have gone?'

'After Morocco? Could be anywhere. Oliver knows the whole of the Middle East like the back of his hand. It's where he made his name – Turkey, Iraq, Syria. I wouldn't know where to look for him, even if I felt the inclination.'

'What will you do about your film?'

'Put it on hold, darling. Hope it all comes together later.' She sighed. 'You'd be amazed how often things like this happen in our industry. Too many damned prima donnas. All stars and no chorus.'

Defeated, Ash went home. If he couldn't find Hazel, he could at least feed his family. But Frankie had put something in the oven before she went to collect the boys from school. Feeling oddly disappointed that even this small achieve-ment had been denied him, he retreated to his study. When he'd had the big house to himself, he'd lived mostly in the kitchen. Now he shared it, he appreciated the private space Frankie had created for him. The rule – also established by Frankie – was that, when he was in the study, nobody too young to vote was allowed to disturb him unless the house was on fire.

Patience regarded rules the way she regarded her car harness: a splendid idea in principle, but not something to get in the way of what she wanted to do. She was lying on the conker-coloured leather sofa, curled round like a croissant.

Ash frowned. 'How did you get in here?' He was sure – almost sure – the door had been shut.

The lurcher thumped her tail in friendly greeting.

'Well – at least move up.'

She did as she was bid, leaving him a perfectly circular dip in the sofa cushion lined with fine white hairs. Ash sat down, and the dog put her long head on his knee. He stroked her ear. The speckled one: the other was tan.

'I can't find her,' Ash said simply. 'She's with Ford, but nobody knows where they are. Nobody knows when they'll be back. Or even, with any certainty, if.'

Dogs are good at sensing distress in their owners. Patience pressed herself along Ash's thigh, holding his troubled face in her steady golden gaze.

'Dave Gorman thinks she can look after herself. And of course she can – we both know that. But it's a big world out there, and I think Oliver Ford may be more at home in it than Hazel is. I'd hate to think she was in some kind of difficulty and I didn't know.'

What would you do if you did know? asked Patience.

'I'd be on the next plane. Frankie would look after the boys. I'd pull whatever strings were necessary to find her, and I wouldn't come back without her.'

How would you find her?

'I still have friends in Whitehall. This used to be my field, remember? We'd pull passenger lists from every flight departing Morocco in the last forty-eight hours. If she was on one, we'd know where she'd gone. If she wasn't, then we'd know she was probably still in Morocco, and that's where I'd start looking.'

You could do that now.

Ash frowned. 'And tell her what? I can't charge in to rescue her from someone she doesn't want rescuing from! No, I'm over-reacting. I'm sure everything's fine. She's just headed off for a romantic interlude with someone glamorous. She'll come to her senses soon enough, and then she'll come home. The best thing we can do is pretend we weren't worried about her.'

Patience appeared to give that some thought. Then: I wonder what Saturday meant.

'About what?'

When he called Hazel's friend a thug. Wasn't that odd? I've heard him call you all sorts – a prat, a moron, Grandad – but never a thug. Why would he call Oliver Ford a thug?

* * *

Saturday wasn't surprised to see Ash back again so soon. It took a lot to surprise him. Being on the streets from the age of fourteen will do that.

'You called Oliver Ford a thug. Why?'

The youth shrugged, pushed down the knob on the toaster. Left to his own devices, he survived exclusively on things you could spread on toast. He never tired of the exercise: bread in, knob down, knob up, toast out. Of course, an electric toaster is a novelty to someone who has only recently had access to electricity.

'Saturday. Look at me. I want to know what you meant.'

'I don't like the guy. What can I tell you? Some people you like, some people you don't. I don't like Oliver Ford. Hazel does. Maybe you do. Lots of people do, but I don't. OK?' He applied himself to the toast, spreading marmalade until it dripped off the sides.

Ash breathed heavily at him. 'What is it that you're not telling me?'

Saturday rolled his eyes. 'Can you narrow it down a bit? I mean, are we talking nuclear physics here? Street dance? The history of the northern Semites, or how long it takes to boil an egg?'

Gabriel Ash was a big man, and because he was also a decent man, he very seldom got physical with anyone. He had noticed – they'd thought he hadn't, but he had – the alarm in people's eyes as he used to shuffle past on the weekly torture that had been his trip to the shops, and he'd always taken care never to justify their concerns. He might have been the local idiot,

137

but he'd been scrupulous about being a harmless idiot. Rambles With Dogs. He might have mumbled to himself, but he never raised his voice. He never swore. And he never, ever laid his hands on anyone.

He gathered the front of Saturday's T-shirt in one hand and lifted him off the kitchen chair. The boy's eyes flared whitely at him – but old habits die hard: he never let go of his toast.

Nose to nose Ash said, very quietly, 'I know when you're lying, Saturday – your lips move. Now, I asked you why you called Oliver Ford a thug. Not a bastard, or a prat, or a pompous twat or a blithering idiot, but a thug. That wasn't casual abuse: it came from somewhere in particular. If I find out that Oliver Ford has laid a finger on Hazel, and you knew . . .'

Saturday shook his head vigorously, the straw-coloured hair flying. 'I don't! I didn't . . . I've never seen him touch her, and she's never said anything like that. Gabriel, I would have told you. Honest I would.'

Ash lowered him slowly back onto his chair. 'Then what . . .?' And then he had it. 'He hit *you*?'

The boy got up to feed the toaster again. Perhaps he wanted more toast; perhaps he just wanted to turn his back. 'Yeah,' he said negligently. 'It's no biggie. I mean, maybe to *you* it is, maybe people who live in Highfield Road and work for the government don't expect to walk into a door once a week, but some of us aren't so precious about our personal space.'

But there was something infinitely sad about his

dismissiveness. He was claiming not to care about being struck only because he'd been helpless to prevent it. As a street kid Saturday had had no rights, no influence, no protection, and he'd had to accept whatever came his way, good or – much more often – bad. Ash had believed that had come to an end when Hazel took him in. It turned a knife in his gut that the boy had been hurt once again, by someone he would never – left in his own world – have met, and hadn't even thought it worth mentioning.

Ash swallowed. He reviewed all the things he'd been about to say and put them away. Finally he said simply, 'What happened?'

For some seconds it seemed that Saturday wasn't going to answer. Ash suspected he was trying to come up with a plausible lie, something that might cast him in a better light than he deserved. Then he realised the boy was embarrassed. Embarrassed by his own helplessness, because someone could hit him and there was nothing he could do about it.

'Start at the beginning,' Ash said softly. 'What day was it?'

'The day after . . .' And there Saturday stopped. That was something he hadn't wanted to share, least of all with Ash.

Ash considered for a moment and then filled in the blanks. 'The day after the boys gave you the slip. That's it, isn't it? My boys ran away; you called Hazel, and Hazel left Ford on his own at the museum. He blamed you for spoiling his big day. So – what? He came round here to bawl you out and ended up thumping you?'

'Pretty much.' Moved by some impulse of honesty Saturday added, 'He didn't really thump me.'

'Were you hurt?'

'He's not exactly Arnold Schwarzenegger! No, I wasn't hurt. I got a back-hander across the mouth. It wasn't the first time, I don't expect it'll be the last.'

'Did you hit him back?'

''Course not. He may not be Arnold Schwarzenegger,' said Saturday, amusement in his sideways glance, 'but he's still bigger than me. I high-tailed it out the back door.'

Ash reviewed the conversation thus far. 'You haven't told me why he hit you.'

'Yes I have.'

'Not yet,' said Ash judiciously. 'But you're going to.'

The boy sniffed. 'I may have called him . . . something.'

Ash's knowledge of teenage terms of abuse was limited; he genuinely wanted to know. 'What?'

'A gigolo.' He pronounced it Giggle-O.

Ash laughed out loud. There was something unexpectedly old-fashioned about this Nobody's Child; it was one of the things that made people warm to him. Well – some people. 'He must have loved that!'

'He's a professional charmer. And he's old enough to be Hazel's father.' Saturday sounded quite indignant. 'It's pathetic.'

'He is *not* old enough to be her father. He's younger than me.'

'Yeah, but you're not . . . you don't . . .' Embarrassment overtook him and the sentence died.

Ash sighed. 'Saturday, who Hazel chooses to have relationships with – even if they're nearly as ancient as me – is none of your business. You are her lodger, and her friend. You are not her father, her husband or her priest. Any more than I am. It's not for us to tell her who she should spend her time with.'

'You're happy to see her with a guy who lashes out when he's angry?'

And that was exactly the right question. When Rachid Iqbal said Hazel wasn't safe with Oliver Ford, Ash had been worried enough to go to the police. Now Saturday was telling him the same thing. Oliver Ford may well have wanted to hit the cheeky brat his new girlfriend had unaccountably taken in. Almost everyone who knew him had wanted to hit Saturday at one time or another, including Ash. But most people stopped short of actually doing it. Ford hadn't. And he hadn't stopped short of whatever he'd done to earn Iqbal's enmity either. Without knowing what that was, it was hard to know how it fitted in, but there was at least the suggestion of a pattern emerging.

'No, I'm not,' he told Saturday. 'If I knew where she was I'd go and talk to her. She'd tell me to mind my own damn business, but after she'd sent me away with a flea in my ear she'd think about it. She's a police officer – she knows that domestic violence isn't only about labourers drinking their wages on a Friday night and taking out their frustrations on their wives. She knows almost anyone can be a perpetrator, and almost anyone can be a victim. Even if she didn't believe it, at least at some level she'd be ready for him.

'But I don't know where she is. No one seems to know where she and Ford are now. The last address the film crew had for them was in Morocco, but they moved on from there. I know almost nothing about film-making, but the one thing everyone knows is that it's expensive. If Ford has left his team in the lurch, that undermines his professional reputation. I can't believe he'd do it on a whim. Which raises the possibility . . .' He didn't even want to put it into words.

Saturday needed him to. His pale, pinched young face – still pale because he worked at night and slept much of the day, still pinched because it would take time to undo the damage of two years living on the streets – was anxious. He needed Ash to make the fear go away. That's what grown-ups did. They took care of things. Ash, though he might have baggage of his own, was not only a grown-up but an intelligent, influential grown-up, and he could make things happen that someone like Saturday could only dream of. His eyes begged Ash to make things right. 'What possibility?'

Ash was too wrapped up in his own anxieties to soften the blow. He was thinking aloud. In truth, he was using Saturday as a sounding board in the way he used Hazel when she was here. 'That he's already done something that means he can't come home.'

Eighteen

Frankie agreed without hesitation to move into the house in Highfield Road and assume responsibility for Ash's sons. She arrived for work on the Friday morning with a suitcase.

'I think we'd better make this permanent, don't you?' said Ash through the open bedroom door as he threw a few necessities into a bag.

'That would be entirely acceptable, Mr Ash,' said Frankie, simultaneously unpacking in the guest room across the landing.

The boys had raised tearful objections to Ash leaving, at twenty-four hours' notice and unable to say when he'd be back. Predictably, Gilbert came up with the most hurtful thing he could say in the circumstances. 'If you didn't want to be with us, why didn't you leave us with Mum?'

Ash had immediately gone down on his knees and gathered the angry child to his breast. 'Of course I want to be with you. You mean everything to me. *Everything*,' he repeated fiercely. 'But Hazel is my friend, and I think she's in danger, and if I didn't try to help her I wouldn't be a good enough man to be your father. Please try to understand, Gilbert. It's not that I want to do this – I have to do it. Frankie will look after you until I get back. It might only be a couple of days, but I'm not going to promise that because I don't know.'

Before flying to Marrakech he spent half a day in Whitehall, talking to people he knew and people *they* knew, putting together a support package he could call on when – if – he found Hazel, or Ford, and needed the kind of help that British consuls don't routinely offer.

Although he had spent five years as a government security analyst, he had never been the guy who gets on the plane. He'd worked at a desk, sometimes in a library, occasionally in a nice coffee-house where he could talk to people who wouldn't be seen dead entering the Home Office, even by a back door. He had never been licensed to kill; he'd never been licensed to shout at people, or poke them with a stick. He was essentially an academic.

Except this time. This time there was no alternative but to blow the cobwebs off his passport and do the job himself.

Heathrow is one of the busiest airports in the world. It handles seventy-five million passengers and almost half a million aircraft movements every year. Aircraft queue up on the ground to take off, and in the air to land.

It was years since Ash had flown anywhere. He didn't allow enough time to check in before his flight closed. Afterwards it was hard to believe this wasn't a higher power at work, but while he was trying desperately to pay off his taxi with one hand, shoulder his bag with the other and figure out the shortest route to the check-in desk, it just seemed another example of the world getting too damn fast for a man who'd spent four years in purdah. Every time he checked his watch another three minutes had unaccountably disappeared. Before he could shut the door on the taxi he'd just climbed out of, someone else was climbing in. Behind them, another party was ready to hail the next one. And behind them . . .

'Gabriel? Whatever are you doing here?'

For a moment – only a moment – he really thought he'd imagined it. That his troubled mind, so preoccupied with her safety, so anxious to hear her voice, had conjured it out of the babbling mayhem of the taxi rank. Some other woman hailing a friend – some other Gabriel? – maybe he'd misheard . . .

Almost nothing else in the English language sounds like Gabriel. And when he looked around – eagerly, anxiously, unable to bear the disappointment he was sure must follow – there she was: Hazel Best, golden-tanned, spiky fair hair sun-bleached, in a cotton shirt nowhere near warm enough for Britain in October, and high-heeled sandals. Hazel Best, safe and well. Not murdered; not, so far as he could see, molested; just sun-kissed and happy, and back a few days late from a holiday she'd clearly enjoyed. If she ever guessed the things that had been going through his mind, and what he'd planned to do about them . . .

She pushed through the taxi queue to reach his side. Several heads away, standing guard over the luggage, Ford nodded a greeting but didn't move.

'I said, what are you doing here?' There was something indefinably different about her. She looked . . . more sophisticated, somehow. Older. More prosperous. She pulled a pashmina out of the straw bucket she'd used as carry-on and threw it round her shoulders, and Ash knew immediately that it was cashmere.

There were many things Gabriel Ash was good at. Some he was better at than almost anyone else. Lying wasn't one of them. 'Er . . .'

She put it another way, as if talking to a small child. 'Where are you going? Which terminal? Which airline? Show me your ticket . . .'

Ash threw up his hands in surrender. 'I'm not going anywhere. Look, I've got a taxi . . . Oh. It's gone.'

Hazel regarded him fondly, head on one side. 'You came to meet us? How did you know when we were getting in?'

'I got lucky,' mumbled Ash; and though he knew it was a rubbish explanation, he hoped she'd be tired after the flight and let it go for now.

'Did you drive down? Where's your car?'

'I left it in Whitehall.'

By now Oliver Ford had flashed his profile and secured another taxi. Their bags were disappearing into the capacious boot. 'We'll drop you off there,' he offered, coolly. He'd been as surprised to see Ash as Hazel had been, but not as pleased.

Ash blinked. 'Won't you let me drive you home?'

'We're not going back to Norbold, not yet. Oliver has some people to see in town.' That was part of what had changed: she had never described London in that way before, as if it was her natural milieu. 'Town' had meant Norbold; even 'going into the city' had only meant Birmingham. 'We'll stay over a couple of nights. I'll call you when I get back.'

'I tried to call you,' said Ash. He heard the whine of complaint in his own voice. 'Your phone was switched off.'

'Bloody roaming charges,' she explained airily, 'they cost a fortune. What were you calling me about?'

'Oh – nothing. Just . . .' Inspiration struck. 'I've taken on a nanny for the boys. I wanted you to tell me it was a good idea.'

'Excellent,' said Hazel enthusiastically. 'Gabriel, we'll have a catch-up when I get home. You can tell me about your nanny, and I'll tell you about our trip. Is Saturday all right? He hasn't burned the house down?'

Ash glanced at Ford just quickly enough to see Ford think about glancing at him and change his mind. 'Saturday's fine. The house is fine. But he's been worried about you. You might at least have sent a postcard.'

'I *did* send postcards,' Hazel protested. 'They'll probably turn up next week. Where I posted them, they probably come part of the way by camel.'

It's a tedious drive from Heathrow into central London. Ford pretended – Ash was sure it was a pretence – to fall asleep. Hazel too dozed, her head against Ash's shoulder. Not for worlds would he have moved it.

He didn't want to get out of the taxi at Whitehall. But there seemed to be no alternative.

'You'll call me as soon as you're home? You promise?'

Hazel stared at him, her fair brows gathering. 'Are you all right, Gabriel? You seem . . . distracted.'

He forced a smile. 'I'm fine. Why wouldn't I be? But call me.'

She waved as they drove away.

Before collecting his car, Ash returned to the anonymous office behind Whitehall to update Philip Welbeck. To thank him for the assistance he'd offered, and explain why he wouldn't need it. Something rather disturbing happened. No one shouted at him. Neither Welbeck nor any of the others who'd been roped in to help called him an idiot, or laughed at him, or told him he was getting too old for chasing young blondes halfway round the world.

Men and women who, recently, had been treating him almost as they had before his breakdown were being careful around him again. Not saying anything unkind. Not saying anything that might upset him. Just quietly sliding the paper-knives off their desks and putting them away in drawers.

Ash wanted to tell them that it wasn't necessary. That he'd made a mistake but he wasn't irrational, they didn't have to worry about him losing his marbles again. But instinct warned him that would only make things worse – that protesting his sanity would only draw attention to the question marks surrounding it. Ash felt something inside him curl up and die. He

148

apologised again, and left, and did not expect to set foot in the building again; and he supposed that no one there would share his regrets. In that at least he was mistaken.

He drove the long road home. Only when he turned into his drive in Highfield Road and caught a glimpse of the boys at the window of their playroom, and felt the surge of love and relief that still had the power to overwhelm him, was he able to put events into some kind of perspective. Perhaps there were things he had lost: the respect that came from doing an important job well, the regard of people he himself respected. But nothing could take away from the value of what he had gained. From the knowledge that everyone he cared about was safe.

Nineteen

Oliver Ford made his peace with Emerald and a new schedule was agreed for completing the shoot. The earliest everyone could be brought together again was five weeks hence, by which time the winter would be looming and the settled weather so vital for filming could not be counted on. Not that it ever could in England, even in summer, but the latter part of the year was always the least predictable.

Ford proposed waiting until spring, so he could spend the winter indoors, on his book, but Emerald was having none of it. She knew from bitter experience that TV personalities were even less reliable than the weather: if Ford began work on another project, there was no knowing when or even if she'd get him to come back.

She would dearly have loved to replace him, with someone less well-known but more dependable, but that would have meant reshooting everything she already had in the can, and trying to persuade broadcasters that viewing figures would hold up without Ford's name supporting them. On the whole she thought it better to finish the project at the earliest opportunity, and make a note in her diary never to employ Oliver Ford again. Or if she really had no choice, to take him to the vet first.

With no certainty as to when shooting would resume, Ford decided to take a house in the area. The glorified camper-van he had occupied back in September was barely adequate, he insisted, for a single man in warm weather. Hazel refrained from pointing out that whole families had been born and raised in houses no bigger, her own included. If he wanted to rent a house, no doubt he could afford to.

She did not immediately realise that she was a part of his plans. She had imagined that when they returned to Norbold he would find himself a smart service flat and she would return to Railway Street and the faint but pervasive smell of Saturday's trainers. On their last night in London, Ford watched her carefully sorting her clothes from his and packing them in separate bags. For weeks now their clothes had shared a proximity as intimate as that of their owners.

He frowned. 'Aren't you coming with me?'

'Coming where?' asked Hazel. 'You haven't even looked at flats yet, let alone taken one. Why don't you stay with me until you find something?'

He could hardly have been more horrified if she'd proposed erecting a tent for him in her back garden. 'Your house? Hazel, I don't want to be rude, but . . .'

People never said that, she had noticed, unless they were about to be very rude indeed. So it proved.

'. . . But if I had a flunky, and the flunky had a wastrel brother, and the wastrel brother had a drug dealer, the drug dealer would live in your house. In fact, I suspect he already does.'

Hazel froze, even more astonished than she was offended. Only when her eyes burned did she remember to blink; only the dry, centrally heated air on her tonsils reminded her to shut her mouth. She swallowed. 'How *dare* you . . .?'

At which Ford flashed the big, handsome, TV personality grin. 'Come on, Hazel, I'm only teasing. It's a perfectly nice little house. But that's the point – it's a little house. And we wouldn't even have it to ourselves, unless you gave that feckless boy his marching orders, and you're not going to do that, are you? It makes much more sense to rent somewhere we can be alone. And not in Norbold – somewhere nice and quiet. There's some really pretty country around Norbold,' he added seriously. 'Who'd have guessed?'

'Er – everyone who lives in Norbold,' said

151

Hazel tersely. She was still mentally reeling from the force of his insult. 'Oliver – I can't rent a house with you. It's all I can do to find the rent for the one I've got. I'm sorry it isn't smart enough for you, and I'm sorry you don't like my friends, but I'm not about to change either of them any time soon. If you need somewhere better suited to your image, take a look at the property ads in *Country Life*. Let me know if you find something. I promise I won't visit without fumigating myself first.'

Only then did Ford seem to realise how much he'd upset her. The big, handsome grin disappeared, to be replaced by something slightly apologetic but also critical. 'Don't be like that, Hazel. It was just a joke. Don't they have jokes where you come from?'

'We do have jokes,' said Hazel, zipping the last case and straightening up. 'You can tell that they're jokes because they make people laugh. We also have snobs. They're pretty laughable too.'

Ford threw up his hands in exasperation. 'Well, of *course* I'm a snob, dearie! I believe that people who've worked hard to achieve something are better than people who haven't. I'm also an elitist, because I believe that taking the trouble to learn how to do something makes you better than someone who's spent their time playing video games. I believe that knowledge is power, and that power is better exercised by people with some acumen than by people who couldn't organise a piss-up in a brewery.

'I believe that all men *are* created equal,' he

went on, warming to his subject. 'But for the next sixty-odd years, what they become is largely down to themselves. Not everyone is cut out to be a mover and shaker. Not everyone wants to be one. But if *nobody* wanted to be one, the world would stagnate. It may be politically correct to think that some hippy making daisy-lace in a log cabin in the Forest of Dean is as important as the managing director of a big multi-national company, but it simply isn't true. No one dies from the lack of daisy-lace. People do die if there's no power to heat their homes, or nobody keeping the drinking water clean, or no one to keep the garbage from festering. All life is precious. But some lives are only precious to their owners, and some lives are important to thousands of other people as well.

'That's what I believe. Call me a snob if you like. I think of myself as a realist. I suspect most people actually feel the same way, but haven't the guts to say so.'

Hazel wanted to tell him that he was wrong. That most people believed in the intrinsic worth of all human beings, and recognised that who they were was not defined by what they were. That it was not normal to value people according to their dollar-earning capacity.

But Oliver Ford was a professional communicator, skilled at marshalling arguments and presenting them both forcefully and persuasively, and Hazel recognised – and it gave her an odd little thrill of satisfaction, as if his talent reflected credit on her – that anyone who went up against him in a debating contest was going to lose on points. He was clever and articulate. Perhaps he believed what he said, perhaps he just enjoyed playing devil's advocate. Hazel could disagree with every word Ford said, and still admire his skill as a presenter.

'OK,' she decided, trying not to smile. 'Ground rules. My friends are my friends. You don't have to like them, you don't have to spend time with them, but you don't insult them, at least not in front of me. For the record, Saturday isn't a drug dealer. To the very best of my knowledge – and this is something I do know something about – he isn't a drug user. He's a decent kid who had some bad luck, and I'm helping him get back on his feet.

'Also, my house may not be in the smartest part of Norbold, and even the smartest part of Norbold may not be smart enough for you, but it's clean and it's warm and it's mine, and you may think you're being funny but if you disrespect my home it feels as if you're disrespecting me.'

She took a deep breath. 'I've enjoyed the time we've spent together, Oliver. But you have to understand that I don't belong to you. You don't get to say what happens in my life – where I live, who I live with, what I do with my time.'

Half contrite, half offended himself, he murmured, 'I wouldn't dream of it.'

'Good,' said Hazel. 'Then let's try again. Where are you going to stay while you look for this palace suitable to your image? There's still time to change your mind and say you'll come home with me, as long as you'll at least pretend to be grateful.'

154

Ford looked at her, head slightly on one side, as if he'd never come across anyone quite like her before. As kind, yet as forthright. As feminine, yet as strong. Who clearly enjoyed his company, but wasn't prepared to tolerate the excesses of his personality.

Being with her was a bit like being with his mother. But when she wasn't telling him to mind his manners, checking that he'd got a clean handkerchief and reminding him to visit the little boys' room before going out, she made him feel more alive than he had in years. He wasn't sure why. She wasn't a particularly inventive lover, and he didn't feel other men's gaze turning his way in envy when he walked with her. Apart from the haircut, she was an essentially conventional young woman, and Oliver Ford tended to look for something exceptional in a companion.

Perhaps it was the very fact that Hazel Best remained steadfastly unimpressed by his celebrity status. Many of the women he'd known had claimed to be unmoved by the doors it opened, the envy it provoked, the way crowds tended to gather around him and then part as if he were Moses dipping his toe in the Red Sea. But in Ford's experience, all of them were seduced eventually. Perhaps Hazel would be too. Certainly it would be interesting to find out.

Aloud he said, 'I've already got somewhere.'

Hazel stared at him in rank disbelief. 'How? We've not left London since we got back.'

'My agent,' Ford said smugly. 'Miriam's been looking for me. She e-mailed me some details. I'm going to look at a couple of houses this afternoon, and I shall take one of them. Will you come?'

Hazel demurred. 'I have to get back. It's time I got back to work. And I promised I'd meet this nanny of Gabriel's.'

'Please will you come?' said Ford.

Still she hesitated. Ford waited. Everyone said yes to him in the end.

'Oh, all right,' said Hazel.

Twenty

Purley Grange occupied a wooded dell eight miles from Norbold. The name was inscribed on a slate plaque almost completely obscured by ivy: they drove past it three times before realising the gap in the hedge was actually a driveway. From the road there was no sign of the house. But there were new tracks in the mud showing someone had been here recently, so they followed them, the crowding trees closing darkly behind them as the drive veered.

'The place has been abandoned,' ventured Hazel. 'It'll need months of work before it's fit to live in.'

'Miriam knows what I want,' said Ford confidently. 'She wouldn't have sent me here if it was a wreck. She knows I don't do DIY.'

Up ahead the sky broadened as the trees drew aside, and a final flourish of the drive – track, rather, its gravel long since compacted into the

156

mud – revealed the house. Ford took his foot off the gas and let the car cruise to a halt while they studied it.

It wasn't what either of them was expecting. Hazel had been wrong: the place hadn't been abandoned, or even neglected to any extent that showed from here. The roof was good, the wood-work recently painted, and someone had polished the windows until they sparkled in the October sunshine.

Ford had been expecting something grander. It wasn't a mansion but a two-storey brick building with gables in unexpected places and dormer windows like eyebrows in the roof. There was a little wooden porch round the front door, and a long wooden bench against it looking out over the garden. The plants were dying back now, but someone had devoted skill to their care, and the lawn had been recently mown. It made a charming picture.

'Shall we go inside?' asked Ford, head tilted impishly.

'Oh yes.' Hazel was already out of the car.

The key had been left under a flowerpot; which outraged Hazel's instincts for crime prevention, until she remembered that they'd had trouble finding Purley Grange even though they were looking for it. It would probably have been safe to leave the front door wide open, and a bottle of whisky and a stack of unmarked banknotes on the hall table.

'It's Arts & Crafts, isn't it? Nineteen hundred, nineteen ten – something like that.' Hazel had only recently developed an interest in property.

She had been born an army brat, living in married quarters that changed every couple of years but all looked the same. Then her father retired to become handy-man on a small country estate in Cambridgeshire, settling his family in the gate-lodge that came with the job. After that, Hazel had a succession of rented rooms convenient for university, her teaching job, the police studies course and her Norbold posting, until circumstances nudged her into renting the little house in Railway Street. A few weeks of buying curtains and slapping on emulsion had her talking like the editor of *Ideal Home*.

Ford was right: the house was ready to move into. The rooms were furnished, mostly with antiques, the cupboards stocked with pots, pans and cutlery, the linen-press with linens. There was even warm water in the taps. It was as if the owners had nipped to the shops shortly before their visitors arrived.

'Are you sure this isn't somebody's home?' asked Hazel, feeling like an interloper.

'It *is* somebody's home,' said Ford, 'but he's abroad for two years. Something to do with the EU. He's arranged for a local woman to come in twice a week to keep the chill off, but ideally he'd like someone living here.'

'You?'

Ford smiled. 'Perhaps. Do you like it?'

Hazel tried to be sensible. 'It's pretty remote. You'd be stranded if anything happened to your car.'

Ford looked surprised. 'If anything happened to my car, I'd buy another one. And actually, it feels more remote than it is. Wittering is only four miles in that direction.' He pointed. 'And Norbold only about as far again. Fifteen minutes – twenty if you get behind a tractor. It isn't that much of a commute.'

Now Hazel was staring. 'Commute? You mean me? I'm not going to be living here.'

Ford smiled. 'Can I persuade you to think about that for a little longer?'

She had been effectively living with him for a fortnight. But that was abroad and then in London – and London was another country for someone from Norbold. She had imagined that when the holiday was over, she would return to her house and Ford to whatever he decided to rent, and they would meet up after work. She hadn't realised he hoped to move her into Purley Grange along with his books, his computer and his suitcases.

She did as he asked and considered it now. 'You don't even know how long you're going to be here. If Emerald can reschedule the filming, you could be finished by the end of the month. What will you do then – throw me out on my ear? Send me back to Railway Street and Saturday?'

Ford gave an expansive shrug. 'Nothing's forever. Well, not many things. What will *I* do when you find someone as smart, handsome and rich as me, but ten years younger? I'll remember you fondly and get on with my life.

'I don't know how long it'll take to finish filming, or even when we'll be able to get started. I don't know what I'll do next. But the house is to let for two years, and if you want me to, I'll take it for two years. You can live here and work in Norbold, if you insist on working; I'll shoot off when I'm needed elsewhere, come back when I'm not. If we're still a good thing after two years it might be time to buy something anyway.'

Once again he'd managed to surprise her. It wasn't exactly a proposal, but it was rather more than a proposition. While Hazel had been thinking of Ford as an extended holiday, he'd been thinking of her as at least a medium-term commitment.

She found a window-seat and lowered herself carefully. She picked her words even more carefully. 'Oliver, I think you know – I hope you know – how much I enjoy being with you. The whole Arabian Nights thing was a riot, the sort of thing I never do, never even *think* of doing. I'll never forget it.

'But now you're talking of us setting up home together, and that's a whole different ball-game. A holiday is a break from reality, and it comes with a natural time limit. What you're suggesting now is that we create a new reality, with the intention that it should be a lasting change. And I'm not ready for that. I like my life – my ordinary life, where I go into work and dodge terrorists and come home to Saturday's laundry dripping in the bath. I'm not sure I'm ready to give it up in order to be half of a couple. It's too . . . grown up for me. I'm not ready to be somebody's significant other.

'I've never been much of a party girl. I like to let my hair down – well,' she amended ruefully,

'I *used* to like to let my hair down – as much as the next person, but at heart I've always been pretty conventional. At heart, I still think of a family as being a man, a woman, two-point-four children and a cocker spaniel. If I was to set up home with you, or anyone, that's what I'd be looking for. I never have gone in for quick-change, flavour-of-the-month relationships. If I want to be with someone at all, I want to try and make a go of it.

'This sounds as if I'm asking you to marry me,' she said, looking up with a quick grin. 'Relax: that's not what I'm saying. We aren't a good enough match to be talking about forever. We've had a lot of fun – at least, I've had a lot of fun, and I hope you have too – but it would be a mistake to read too much into that. It was a great holiday. I never for a moment thought it was the beginning of the rest of our lives.'

'Is it the age difference that bothers you?' Ford made it sound like an accusation. All the proprietorial pleasure with which he'd shown her round the house had gone from his manner, leaving him frowning.

Hazel shook her head. 'The age difference doesn't trouble me. Nor does the fact that you're rich and famous and I'm not. We're just very different people, Oliver. And that's fine for ten days in the sun, and a few more in a smart hotel. But if we tried to base a committed relationship on nothing more than a fortnight's fun, I think we'd break each other's hearts. We'd each be expecting things that the other couldn't possibly deliver.'

'I don't expect anything of you,' insisted Ford.

'Of course you do! You expect that I'll keep you company when it's more fun than being alone, and keep out of your way when you need your own space. You don't expect me to go to work with no clear idea of when, or in what state, I'll come home. You expect that I'll cook us a nice meal on a Sunday night. You *don't* expect that, if the phone goes just as we light the candles, I'll dash off and leave you to eat your beef Wellington on your own. That's not what you need in a partner. You'll come to resent it. You'll want me to give up my job and let you provide for us.

'And that isn't going to happen, Oliver. The life I have is too valuable to me. Let's stay friends. Let's enjoy a nice meal out from time to time, and a dirty weekend if the fancy takes us, but don't let's make promises we're not going to be able to keep. I don't want to disappoint you. I don't want us to end up angry at one another.'

If he'd snapped back with what was in his mind right then, that would have been the end of them. She'd have made him drive her back to Norbold and never seen him again. Ford had the sense to swallow the surge of recrimination before even a word of it was spoken, and say nothing for the minute and a half it took him to consider what she'd said and formulate a response.

Then he said, quietly, 'Hazel, I've had a great time too. It *has* been fun – that's exactly what it's been. I don't remember the last time I enjoyed myself so much, and with so little obvious reason. We didn't do anything very special. We

162

didn't spend a fortune going places and doing things neither of us had ever felt the need to do before. We didn't do anything very much. So what I was enjoying was you.

'You say you're ordinary, but actually you're anything but. There aren't many people as completely without artifice as you. With you, what you see is what you get – and that's incredibly rare in my business. Being with you is like opening the windows to my soul and letting the fresh air blow through.'

She smiled at that, and he smiled back.

'You say you're not ready for commitment. Hazel, that's fine. I can wait until you are. I may be older than you, but I'm not in my dotage! I can afford to be patient. One advantage of getting older – there aren't many, but there are some – is that you know your own mind. You know what you want, and how to get it, and whether it's likely to be worth the trouble. I want us to stay together. As friends, yes, but more than that. I want you to be the last thing I see when I fall asleep at night. I want to wake up with your curlers poking me in the eye—'

'I do *not* wear curlers!' Hazel interjected indignantly.

'I don't want anything from you. I just want you to be there. I want a home – a proper home, not just a succession of places to live – and I want you to be the warm heart of it. And if I have to wait until you realise it's what you want too, that's what I'll do.'

'But Oliver . . .' Her voice had sunk to little more than a whisper. 'What if it isn't what I

163

want? What if you wait, and I never come to feel the same way?'

'Well . . .' He reflected. 'I suppose I'll just bill you for my time and expenses.' He grinned in delight as he saw her think, just for a moment, that he meant it. 'You don't get many guarantees in this life. You do what you think is for the best, and most of the time you don't even know if you were right or not. If things work out, you think you were clever. If they don't, you think you were unlucky; but you never know what would have happened if you'd chosen differently.

'Of course I can't *know* that a time will come when you feel the same way about me as I feel about you. It's an act of faith. I *believe* I can make you feel that way. I may be wrong. If so, we'll go our separate ways. And it'll be awful. But I'd rather risk losing you than be too scared to give us a chance.'

There was a long pause. Then he said it again. 'Give us a chance.'

All her life Hazel Best had been the sensible one. The sensible girl at school; the one who could be trusted with the pencil sharpener and the milk money. The dependable teenager, who made sure everyone got home before the parents organised a search party. The reliable probationary constable, who could be counted on to defuse difficult situations rather than exacerbate them.

And common sense said, *This isn't what you wanted.* Common sense said, *If someone had asked you three months ago, you would never have said it was your ambition to shack up with a celebrity!* Common sense said, *You could be getting in over your head here. And there's no need to. You don't need what he's offering. You were content before you ever met him.*

Common sense, Hazel thought in a flash of understanding that was almost an epiphany, would wait at a bus stop in the rain rather than accept a lift in a Ferrari. Sometimes you have to take a chance. If it all goes pear-shaped, you sort it out. But it would be sad to go to your grave regretting all the chances that came along and you were too sensible to grasp.

'Yes, all right,' she said.

Ford wanted to be sure he hadn't misunderstood. 'I should take the house?'

Hazel looked around. The leaded lights of the many windows were winking like diamonds in the sun. She nodded. 'You should take the house.'

Twenty-One

In twenty-seven years, Hazel remembered feeling like this only once before. That too had meant following her heart rather than her head: becoming a police officer instead of a teacher. She hadn't been able to rationalise that either. She'd enjoyed teaching, had a certain talent for it, was beginning to enjoy the rewards that came with success. Friends had thought her mad to throw away the years of work that had brought her to that point in order to start afresh as a police trainee.

Yet at some level she had known that it was right for her – that this was what she wanted to do. It was the same with Ford. She couldn't have explained to anyone – she couldn't explain it to herself – why she wanted what he was offering so much that she was willing to smother the sensible Hazel Best who had made a reasonable job of being her so far and become someone else entirely: less cautious, quicker to take risks, ready to act without even assessing the risks involved. It was a little like demonic possession, only in this case the imp taking control of her was herself. Herself as she had so often, if only fleetingly, wanted to be: braver, more spontaneous, free-spirited.

And that, she realised, her eyes widening at the recognition, was precisely what Oliver Ford did for her. It wasn't the trappings of wealth or celebrity that she was so enjoying. It was being that other Hazel whom he had somehow liberated. As if being cautious and sensible and rational was a guise that only now, with him, she was able to cast off. If he left her next week for someone prettier and with more hair, she would always be grateful to him for introducing her to that daring alter ego whose existence she had never before suspected. With or without Ford, she thought the two of them were going to have a whale of a time.

She needed to collect her car, and she needed to collect her clothes. Her first thought was to go back to Railway Street that evening, when Saturday would be working, and leave him a note. But that was cheap and cowardly. She

166

didn't have to explain herself – not to Saturday, not to anyone – but nor did she have to avoid old friends as if she had something to be ashamed of. The least she owed them was to take a proper farewell, and promise to keep in touch, and promise always to be there for them if they needed her. She told herself that she really meant that, and ignored the knowing chuckle of the gleeful imp in the background.

So she went back to Norbold the next morning, late enough to find Saturday awake, early enough that he would not yet have left the house.

He was in the kitchen, yawning over his breakfast. The evidence of his supper, and quite a few meals before that, was stacked beside the sink. Hazel forbore to comment. He'd wash up when he ran out of plates. She didn't think now, when she was effectively moving out, was the time to criticise his housekeeping.

Saturday must have known who it was when he heard the front door open. No one else had a key. He had a few moments to swallow his surprise, or alarm, or whatever was his immediate reaction to the return of his landlady, so that the face that met her was – as well as slightly sticky with jam and in need of one of his still infrequent appointments with a razor – entirely without expression.

'You're back, then.'

'Not really,' said Hazel. 'Just collecting some stuff.'

The youth twitched one eyebrow in the least possible gesture of enquiry. 'Another trip?'

'No.' She threw herself down on a kitchen

chair. He was entitled to ask; he was owed an answer; but Hazel was damned if she was going to stand in front of him like an errant schoolgirl before the headmaster. 'We've taken a house out past Wittering. Well, Oliver has. I'm moving in there.'

Under the T-shirt, Saturday's thin chest swelled with a deep breath. Hazel wasn't sure whether to expect congratulations or a tirade. But it was simpler, more to the point than either. 'You're letting this place go.' He said it as if he'd been expecting it, had got used to the idea of being homeless again.

Remorse made Hazel hurry out an answer. 'No, Saturday, of course I'm not. At least, not in the foreseeable future. I have no idea, right now, how long I'll be with Oliver, and I'm certainly not giving up my bolt-hole on the strength of a holiday romance! If it turns into something else, maybe. But I won't leave you in the lurch, whatever happens. You can stay on here if you can find the rent. If not, we'll find you a bed-sit somewhere. I'll make sure you're all right before I give the keys back. You're my friend, Saturday. Nothing that happens between me and Oliver Ford will alter that.'

He looked slightly mollified, and slightly relieved. Hazel knew him well enough by now to know that much the greater part of his feelings remained, like an iceberg, hidden from sight. 'All right.'

He'd made his tea in the mug, the little string from the tea-bag still hanging over the rim like the tail of a drowned mouse. If he'd made a pot she'd have helped herself, but she didn't want to boil the kettle again. She'd hoped to be in and out of here in no more time than it took to pack a couple of bags.

But she couldn't rush away now, leaving Saturday to wonder how much of what she'd said was sincere and how much mere lip-service, designed to placate. She caught his eye and held it. 'Is that what you thought? That I was going to chuck you back on the street because it suited me to sow some wild oats with Oliver Ford?'

Saturday shrugged negligently. 'You're a free agent. I'm not your responsibility. I'm nothing to you. I've always known you might want me out at some point, and if I got a week's notice I'd have nothing to complain about.' A tiny spark of annoyance sounded in his voice. 'I'm not helpless, Hazel. I got by before I knew you, and after I leave here I'll get by again. Don't worry about me. You learn a lot living on the streets. The first thing you learn is, if you can survive there, you can survive anywhere. When you can't fall any lower, the only way is up.'

'"We are all in the gutter,"' Hazel quoted softly, '"but some of us are looking at the stars".' The boy frowned, uncertainly. 'You're wrong about one thing. You are not nothing to me. You are my friend, and I care what happens to you. I will never, ever not worry about you.'

He blinked and looked away quickly, which is what he did if he was afraid he was about to show some weakness. 'You'd better leave a forwarding address. For your post.'

Hazel didn't actually know the address of the

169

house she was about to move into. 'I'll have to call you. Just hold onto the post. I'm going back to work as soon as I can organise it, so I'll call in every few days. Leave it on the hall table.'

He was looking at her again. 'Have you seen Gabriel?'

She hesitated for a moment. 'Not since I saw him in London.'

'Are you going to see him?'

Hazel didn't understand the reluctance she felt. She and Ash were good friends, but not *that* kind of friends – there was no reason for her to feel embarrassed about her relationship with Ford. A part of Gabriel Ash was still in love with the wife who'd betrayed him. If Hazel had found someone to love too, Ash would be happy for her. And yet . . . and yet . . . Only the fact that she'd promised stopped her from leaving Norbold without seeing him.

'Yes,' she said finally. 'Of course.'

In the mornings, after she'd walked the boys to school, Frankie took a few hours for herself. Sometimes she sat in her room, reading, sewing, or writing letters to her family in the far Philippines, but often she stayed in town and Ash never asked what she did there. He didn't want to give the impression that he resented her absence, and they hadn't known one another long enough that he could ask out of mere curiosity.

Perhaps his reticence was due in part to the fact that he did rather miss her when she was out. The big house in Highfield Road seemed to slip back into the dusty quiet that had enveloped it since he returned there after his illness. The first chink of light had appeared when Patience arrived; a great wave of activity had swept through the slumbering rooms when the boys came, shouting and laughing and arguing and losing things and throwing things; but the advent of Frankie Kelly had been the catalyst that turned the man, the boys, the dog and the big old house into more than they had been. She'd taken them all in her small, capable hands and fashioned a family out of them.

Now the whole house was in use, not just the kitchen and the small back bedroom. After organising the boys' rooms and his study, Frankie had moved Ash from the room where he'd slept as a child into the master bedroom. She'd arranged for a decorator to scrape off his mother's faded roses, and consulted him as to what should replace them. The back bedroom she meant to occupy herself, to free up the guest room. Knowing Ash as she was coming to, she accepted that it could be a while before he needed it for visitors; still, in her opinion every household of consequence required a guest room, and guests could not be expected to share with the help.

For years Ash had asked nothing more of a house than that it keep the rain off him. He was amazed how much satisfaction the new arrangements afforded him, and in particular the comfortable study, a sanctuary where no one would disturb him unless in a real emergency. Admittedly, opinions varied as to what constituted an emergency. Frankie set the bar fairly high: fire, flood or imminent structural failure. The boys were more liberal in their definition, and included wanting ice-cream when Frankie was only offering fruit, and disagreeing over the relative merits of competing channels on the playroom television.

Patience, of course, came and went as the mood and her own purposes took her, just as she always had. She liked the new study, but she liked the new bedroom more. The double bed gave her space to stretch out.

In all, Frankie Kelly had been an unmitigated success, and Ash couldn't imagine how he'd managed without her. He was unreservedly glad that the nanny recommended by Hazel had been unavailable. If Frankie had demanded an Aston Martin as a perk of the job, he'd have bought her one, if it had meant selling a kidney to fund it.

And yes, when she was out he missed her. He missed her quiet, cheerful efficiency. He missed hearing her hum the little songs of her home as she tidied the playroom and loaded the dishwasher. (She was taking on more and more of the housework as the days passed. So, when she went into town, Ash would wander round for half an hour looking for something to do, defeated in the end by the fact that she'd left him nothing.)

He found himself considering again the alarming, but at the same time seductive, possibility of getting back to work. Caring for the boys was no longer an issue. The obstacle that remained was the one that had stood in his way for the last four years: what possible work was he fit for? Not his old job as a security analyst. The government liked its advisers to be more or less sane. Before that he'd worked as an insurance investigator. But that was a long time ago: the skills he'd honed were now a decade out of date.

There must be other jobs, he thought. Lots of people, even those without many skills, had a job. There ought to be something he could do. He didn't actually need the money, but there are other reasons for working. Self-respect is one, feeling useful another. Perhaps he could start by volunteering somewhere. A charity, a good cause of some kind. It was a pity he wasn't better with people . . .

He heard the back door and thought, with a sudden lift of the heart, that Frankie had returned early. He'd make her sit down – tie her to a chair if necessary – while he made her some lunch for a change. He left the book he'd been reading open on the arm of his chair and headed through to the kitchen.

It wasn't Frankie. It was Hazel.

It was only for a fleeting moment, but she saw disappointment flicker across Ash's expression. Something deep inside her curled up and moaned. Then he smiled warmly and ushered her inside. 'You're back, then. Come in, sit down. Tell me where you got to, what you saw.' For the first time ever in this house, she didn't have to tidy something away before she could take a seat.

She made herself return his smile. 'I can't stay long. I've just been to Railway Street to gather up some belongings. Oliver and I have taken a house out beyond Wittering.' She'd put it that way, she realised, because – although it wasn't strictly accurate – it sounded better than saying she was moving in with Ford.

'Ah.'

She couldn't tell if she'd surprised him. No one she knew, not even Saturday, could hide his feelings like Ash. It was as if a gauze curtain dropped between them, filtering the information that normally passes between people engaged in a conversation. Hazel understood where it came from. For years, revealing what was going on in his head would have put him at the mercy of men in white coats. Though both his life and his mind were more stable now, protecting himself from scrutiny had become a habit.

'Well?' The lightness of her tone might have fooled someone else; she doubted if it would deceive Ash. 'Aren't you going to give me a lecture?'

'What about?'

Hazel felt the stirrings of exasperation. He could still do this to her: provoke her to anger by refusing to argue. 'Behaving like a groupie.'

'Is that what you're doing?'

'Of course not!' She heard her voice rising and reined it back. 'I thought – you give the impression – you think I'm behaving badly. Well, I'm not prepared to feel guilty about this. Oliver and I are both adults, we're neither of us cheating on anyone else, and I'm sorry if I've shocked you but right now this is what I want to do with my life. I don't need your permission, or your blessing. I would like to think you'd wish me well.'

For a split second Ash wanted to throw his arms around her. He managed to stop himself, but the thought went all the way. Hazel felt it as a wave of warmth sweeping over her, and her skin flushed in response.

Ash too had more colour to his cheek than usual. 'Of course I wish you well! Hazel, I want everything for you that you want for yourself. I want you to be happy, and I want you to be safe. If this is what you want to do, I hope it'll work out for you.

'Why would I be shocked? You're not a child. You're the most grown-up person I know. You've been a rock for me. It's thanks to you that I have a life worth living. Nothing would please me more than to see you settled with someone who deserves you.'

Through the glow of pleasure, Hazel sensed a *but*. 'But?'

His broad, heavy-browed face flinched as if with a momentary pain. 'I worry about you. I don't want anything bad to happen to you. When you left the country with him, and no one could tell me where you were, I was scared to death that . . .' The sentence faltered.

Hazel tipped her blonde cropped head to one side. 'What?'

'That something had happened to you,' Ash finished lamely.

Hazel blinked. 'You mean, you thought Oliver had sold me to white slavers? Cut my throat and buried me under a convenient sand-dune?'

Here, in dull predictable *safe* Norbold, the very idea seemed absurd. But that was only because she'd come home unharmed. It hadn't seemed absurd at the time. 'You could have let us know you were all right . . .'

'What are you, my mother?' Then memory threw up the image of him outside the airport, paying off the taxi, looking lost amid the noise and bustle of a world he hadn't ventured into for years. 'Gabriel – when we bumped into one another at Heathrow – were you coming to look for me?'

He could have lied. He didn't think he could have lied convincingly. 'Yes,' he said simply.

All the irritation she felt for him – not just now but at regular intervals – vanished as if someone had pulled a plug. Circumstances had thrown them together, mutual regard had made them friends. But that was something else. You'd only do that for someone you really cared about. Someone you loved. And there are different kinds of love – Hazel didn't suppose for a minute that he felt about her the way he had once felt about Cathy – but all kinds of love have this in common: they change the world. Knowing that Gabriel Ash valued their friendship that highly changed the world for Hazel.

She blew out her cheeks in a quiet pant of amazement. 'But whatever made you think I was in trouble? So much trouble that I needed someone to come and bring me home?'

It was decision time. Now he had either to tell her the truth or to lie to her. And he wasn't going to lie to her.

'The boy at the museum,' he said quietly. 'Rachid Iqbal. He wasn't a terrorist. He had a grudge against Oliver Ford. I don't know why, but he hated Ford enough to travel fifteen hundred miles to try to kill him. And I wondered if you were safe with a man who could inspire that kind of hatred.'

Men, Hazel thought in amazement: men and their sudden furies and their festering grievances and their willingness to wage war over a line in the sand. And their great hearts, and their generosity, and the way they wouldn't let cold facts ruin a good emotion. Women were supposed to be the emotional ones, but that hadn't been her experience.

She marshalled some words to reassure him. 'Oliver's done a lot of work in the Middle East – he must have caused some offence to someone. Perhaps someone was angry because what Oliver called treasure turned out only to be old bones and old stones. Maybe he took the wrong side in a local dispute. He's not the most tactful man in the world: he may well have ruffled feathers.

'I don't believe he did anything you and I would consider dishonourable. He can be thoughtless sometimes, he can be pompous, but that's the television thing – it goes to people's heads. I think it's turned Oliver's head a little. He needs someone to remind him not to take himself so seriously. But I can't imagine he's ever done anything that would earn a justifiable hatred. That isn't who he is.'

Ash's voice was low. 'Are you sure you *know* who he is?'

Hazel bridled. 'Of course I am. At least, I know the important things. I wouldn't be with him if

I thought he'd done something to be ashamed of.' She made herself remember what Ash had done and overlook why he'd done it. 'Look, Gabriel, when things have settled down a bit, let's all get together for a meal or something. I think if you got to know Oliver you wouldn't have these silly concerns.'

Almost before the word was out she wished it unsaid. No concern is silly until it's been disproven, and then all of them are. Ash didn't object, but she knew he'd noticed and felt it as a criticism.

But all he said was, 'Yes, I'd like that. Will you call me?'

'Yes.'

'Soon?'

'As soon as I've figured out how the Aga works.'

Twenty-Two

The weather turned problematic again. There was no word from Emerald about the resumption of filming. Ford spent much of his time at Purley Grange. In the mornings he worked in his study, and preferred not to be interrupted except by a mug of strong black coffee around ten-thirty. He was writing a textbook on Richard the Lionheart. He would finish by half past twelve, and often they would go out for lunch.

Hazel had advised Meadowvale that she

considered herself fit for work and was waiting for an interview with the medical board. Her invitation to attend failed to arrive. At first she thought Superintendent Maybourne didn't want her back on the beat until she could see small children across busy roads without the sight of her burns making them cry. But as the days passed and there was still no summons, she began to suspect that she was being subtly punished. She wasn't quite sure for what. She and Ford had been thrown together by a police Press Office eager for positive coverage: was she to be ostracised because their match-making had succeeded?

In the meantime, it was pleasant to spend time making herself at home and getting to know the surrounding area. Wittering, with its new museum, was the nearest village, a robust hour's walk away, or eight minutes in the car. There were no other houses close by. Woodlands, currently turning from green to flame, surrounded the house entirely, reducing its vistas to no more than fifty yards in any direction. Hazel wondered if, in winter, the proximity of all those dark trees, dripping moisture into the dark ground, would feel claustrophobic – and whether she'd still be here to find out. She felt that the uncertainty ought to distress her more than it did. In fact she was content to let events unfold as they would. For the moment, the woodland setting with its carpet of gold and red and rich brown was both calming and charming.

She thought, I must get Gabriel over for lunch soon. Patience would run off a week's worth of energy chasing rabbits. Hazel ran the idea past Ford, who said she must of course ask her friends round if she wanted to; but his lack of enthusiasm made her reconsider. Perhaps, she thought with a secret grin, he wanted to keep her to himself a little longer. There was no rush. The woods weren't going anywhere, and she couldn't imagine that Ash was either.

Ford watched her getting ready for bed. She let him, enjoying his admiration. This was the first thoroughly grown-up relationship she'd had, and it was quite different to the fun she'd had with teenage boyfriends, with fellow students or even with her contemporaries on the police studies course. It wasn't just that Ford was older. She was too, and the rhythm of their life together was naturally slower. But it was also more focused, more deliberate, arguably more intense. And that, she realised, was because this was the first time that she'd been with someone and been open to the possibility that it was for good. That Oliver Ford might be her last lover.

As she brushed her cropped hair, growing a little shaggy now as well as asymmetric, Ford said thoughtfully, 'You'd look terrific as a redhead.'

Hazel was momentarily taken aback. 'You mean, I don't look terrific as a slightly singed blonde?'

He was immediately contrite. His arms went round her, folding her against his chest. 'You'd look terrific bald and covered in tattoos. With your teeth filed to points and a bone through your nose. But one of the privileges of being a woman is that you're allowed to have fun with your appearance. If I dyed my hair red, my colleagues would point and snigger and my bosses would tell me to stay off work until I looked like a serious historian again. If you dye yours red – or purple, or green – people will applaud your daring.' He shrugged. 'It'd soon grow out if you didn't like it.'

She was staring at him in the mirror. 'You're serious? You think I should dye my hair?'

'No,' he said judiciously, 'I think you should let a hairdresser do it for you. Some things a professional is always going to do better.'

Hazel didn't know what to say. It wasn't an outrageous suggestion, it was just that she'd never considered it before. 'Let me sleep on it.'

'Of course.' And as he turned back towards the bed, he ruffled her hair and grinned. 'Whatever you want, sweetheart.'

Ruffled her hair.

In fact, though, he'd piqued her curiosity. Hazel had never dyed her hair before, partly because she liked its natural colour and partly because she couldn't be bothered. Now she found herself wondering how she'd look as a redhead. Ford made an appointment with a stylist in Birmingham, drove her to the salon and helped her pick the precise shade, or blend of shades, from an album. As well as colouring it, the stylist reshaped her angular cut. A little less punky this time, now she had more hair to work with. Hazel sat through the whole procedure – it took most of a morning – like someone waiting her turn at the guillotine, but afterwards she had to admit to liking the result.

'Told you so,' Ford said smugly.

As if she'd done something for him, he wanted to reward her with a new outfit. Hazel frowned. 'I've got plenty of clothes.' In fact, she'd never owned so many clothes in her life.

He explained as if to a child. 'You don't buy new clothes to have more clothes. You buy new clothes to have *new* clothes.'

It was like describing heat-stroke to an Eskimo. In the end it was easier just to agree. He picked her out a floaty dress in waterfall shades that she thought would clash with the red hair. In that she was wrong. She still couldn't see herself wearing it. 'I never wear dresses.'

'You've done a lot in these last few weeks that you never did before,' Ford pointed out. 'Look, I know I'm never going to wean you off your jeans and boys' shirts. I know you're a country girl at heart. But not for every minute of every day! It's nice to dress up sometimes. To have somewhere nice to go to, and something nice to wear. Isn't it?'

Hazel remembered a similar conversation between herself and Saturday. 'It's nice to have a good soak in a hot bath sometimes . . .' She grinned at the recollection, and nodded.

Ford didn't understand the grin. He frowned. 'Are you making fun of me?'

'No,' said Hazel truthfully. But then, impishly, she added: 'Would it matter if I was?'

He had to give that some thought. Clearly he would have liked to say Yes, but suspected that she'd accuse him of being precious. And she might be right. Oliver Ford wasn't a man much given to introspection; it was a measure of the value he vested in this relationship that he was, if grudgingly, open to the possibility. In the end he said, 'Not if you do it in a loving, empathetic and generally supportive manner.'

She chuckled and hugged his arm.

Ford bought her turquoise high heels to go with the dress.

Ford had business in the bank. While Hazel was waiting outside, watching the people hurrying along the pavement for no better reason than that they weren't trees, Dave Gorman almost passed her by. He started visibly. 'You look different.'

She couldn't resist preening. 'It's the hair.'

'Yes,' he agreed after a moment, 'that too. When are you coming back to work? We're missing you.'

'Really? I always think I hear a collective sigh of relief when I leave Meadowvale.'

'Not always,' said Gorman defensively. 'And you do . . . liven the place up a bit.'

That was unarguable. 'I've sent in my request. I'm just waiting to hear.'

'These things take time,' he agreed. 'How's the face now?'

'Fine,' said Hazel. 'I can barely feel it. It's a bit shiny under the concealer, but as long as I can avoid punch-ups for another week or two, it'll be fine.'

'Maybe that's the delay,' hazarded Gorman. 'In this job, you can't always avoid punch-ups.'

Hazel heard a note of – possibly unintended – criticism in that. 'Dave, no one can accuse me of hiding behind the furniture when the shit hits the fan!'

'I didn't mean that.' He seemed genuinely concerned that she'd misunderstood. 'I just mean, the powers-that-be are wary of approving anyone for duty if they aren't fit for every kind of duty. They don't want to be responsible for exposing you to unnecessary risk.'

'I can man the radio,' said Hazel. 'I can run the computers. There are lots of things I can do if they want to keep me off the streets a little longer.' She heard the echo of that and realised it could have been put better. 'If you'll pardon the expression.'

Gorman grinned. 'I'll have a word with Maybourne if you like – say I've seen you and you look fine to me.'

For a moment she was about to give him her new address, in case they wrote to her at Railway Street and Saturday lost the letter. Something – discretion, a desire to protect her privacy, even a touch of embarrassment – stopped her. 'You've got my mobile number?'

Gorman nodded, and they parted.

Twenty-Three

Hazel's car refused to start. Though she knew very little about the workings of the internal combustion engine, she lifted the bonnet and poked things for a minute or two, in a spirit of showing willing. If she'd found something that was plainly a plug and something else that was plainly a socket, and the two had become disconnected, she would have reintroduced them and hoped for the best. But nothing so obvious presented itself, so she admitted defeat and went back inside.

'My car won't start.'

Ford looked up briefly from his papers. He was on something of a roll with the book and hadn't left the house for days. 'Bummer.'

'Will you have a look at it for me?'

He seemed astonished by the suggestion. 'I don't know anything about engines.'

Hazel had always rather assumed that a certain level of mechanical knowledge came, like deep voices and hair loss, with the testicles. 'Can't you jump-start it or something?'

'How? With what?'

They stared at each other in mutual incomprehension. Finally, irritably, Hazel shrugged. 'All right, I'll call the garage.'

But she couldn't get a signal on her phone. All the trees, she supposed. She asked Ford to try his network.

With an exaggerated sigh, Ford put his work aside and took out his phone. 'No, nothing. What's the number of your garage? I'll keep trying till I get a signal.'

She called it out to him, and Ford made a note of it. Then he looked up. 'Where were you going? Was it anything urgent?'

It wasn't urgent. She'd thought she might look in on Ash; she'd considered reminding Detective

Inspector Gorman of his promise; mainly she felt the need to get out of the house and go where there were more people than trees. 'Just into Norbold. Can I take your car? I'll call at the garage while I'm there.'

But like many men who could afford to buy another if anything happened to it, Oliver Ford was protective of his car. Not very knowledgeable, it seemed, but protective. He hummed and ha'ed, and thought he might have business in town as well, and suggested they have a nice lunch at The Crown on the way home.

By then, though, Hazel was going off the whole idea. What she had really wanted was a little time to herself – away from the house, away from Ford, checking that the threads of her old life were still where she could pick them up when she wanted to. If he had been a different sort of man, she would have said briskly, 'Love you dearly, Ollie, but I don't actually want your company twenty-four hours of every day.' And held her hand out until he dropped his keys into it.

But Ford lacked much insight into his own failings, or what Hazel perceived as his failings, and she knew that if she told him she wanted some personal space he would ask her why, what he'd done to displease her, and keep coming back to it like a sore tooth. Instead she gave a slightly forced smile and said, 'Never mind. Maybe I'll go for a walk instead.'

'All right. How long will you be?'

His attentiveness could be wearing. 'An hour or so. I need the exercise. Don't wait lunch for me.'

Ford nodded. 'OK. Take care. I'll keep trying the garage.'

He was as good as his word. Two hours later, muddy and breathless but lighter in spirit for her tramp through the woods, she returned to find only Ford's car in front of the house. Her own had gone.

'Diego took it away?' She was surprised and a little alarmed.

'I'm afraid so. It was the . . . distributor? Or was that what he said it *wasn't*?' Ford gave a sheepish grin. 'Sorry, but I did warn you about me and engines. Bottom line was, he needed to work on it at the garage. He'll bring it back when it's fixed.'

'How long did he reckon it'd be?'

'Two or three days,' said Ford. 'Tell you what: if it isn't back by the weekend, we'll drive into town and rent you something.'

'Yes, all right,' said Hazel, and Ford returned to working on his book.

Since Hazel had left the little house in Railway Street, Ash had made a habit of dropping round a couple of times a week to make sure Saturday was all right. That he had enough money to buy food, and that food was what he was spending his money on. He didn't want the boy to feel he was being spied on, though, so he started walking Patience the long way home from the park. By the time he got to Railway Street it was no longer a lie to claim he needed a cup of coffee and a sit-down before walking the last mile home. Gabriel Ash had never been a terribly active man. For much of his life, the only part of him that got regular exercise was his brain.

He thought he was being quite subtle. But by the third visit, Saturday knew exactly what he was doing and also when to expect him. Ash would arrive to find the front door ajar and the kettle already on.

Saturday was managing fine, but he too felt Hazel's absence like a small bereavement. He'd been alone, and he'd lived with someone who cared enough about him to ask how his day had been and remind him to eat vegetables, and he knew which he preferred.

And Ash, though he now had his sons to think about, found that they did not fill the precise spot in his mind that Hazel had occupied. He missed her: the inconsequential warmth of her chatter, her well-meaning interference in his life, the way she involved him in the affairs of the world from which he had for so long withdrawn. She had coaxed him back to life; and to a life richer and more fulfilled than he had ever expected to enjoy again. Perhaps that was only partly her doing, but it was certainly true that it would not have happened without her input. He owed her so much. Now she wasn't around, he felt guilty that he hadn't done a better job of thanking her.

In thinking about her, he missed what Saturday had said. 'Sorry – what?'

'I said, have you heard from Hazel at all?' So they'd been thinking along the same lines.

'Not for a couple of weeks. I suppose' – Ash

shrugged, lamely – 'she has other things on her mind.'

'Have you called her?'

Ash blinked. He hadn't thought of that. 'No, I haven't. And I must. I have her number at home . . .'

Saturday gave him a long-suffering look. It was the one he'd learned from Hazel, the one with Ash's name on it. 'I think you'll find your phone knows the number.'

Ash patted his pockets until he found it, keyed up the phonebook. Looked at her name and wondered if she'd welcome the sound of his voice or think he was intruding.

'Call her,' urged Saturday. 'Call her now.'

So Ash did.

A voice he didn't recognise told him the number was currently unavailable, and suggested he try again later. Ash rang off. 'No reply.'

Saturday was doing the Hazel look again. 'Did it go to voice mail?' Ash shook his head. 'Then she must have switched it off.'

Ash frowned. 'Why would she do that? She's never done it before. I've never not been able to get hold of her when I needed to. Do you suppose there's a problem?'

Saturday gave him that special grin that young people reserve for their elders when the subject of modern technology comes up. 'Everything's fine, Gabriel. Either she's turned it off so it won't disturb her, or there's a gap in the coverage where she is. A dead zone. The further you get from centres of population, the more of them there are. Try her again later – sometimes it's a question of where the satellites are at a given time.'

Ash was a little reassured, and also a little rueful. 'When it comes to mobile phones, there's a bit of a dead zone in my head. You grew up knowing this stuff. I had to learn about it – and then they changed it around while I was out of circulation and I'm having to learn it all *again*. I struggle to remember what half the expressions actually mean. 3G, 4G – that used to be something pilots had to worry about. A mobile communications device was a carrier pigeon, and when you talk about instant messaging I think of semaphore. When you talk about social media, I think of *The Tatler*.'

He was making a joke of it, but in fact he was hardly exaggerating. It wasn't even the four years he'd been a hermit. His wife had accused him of being born middle-aged, and Ash suspected she was right. It didn't justify what she had done, but perhaps it helped explain it.

'You need a refresher course,' said Saturday. 'Things move fast in the world of consumer electronics. Today, people do on a phone what you probably used a mainframe computer to do when you were working.'

Ash elevated an indignant eyebrow. 'Mainframe? How old do you think I am?'

Saturday regarded him kindly. 'Well – pretty old, Gabriel. You can't expect to pick it up the way people my age do, just by hanging around together and trading tricks. And it's not like you'll ever want to do the really cool stuff.'

Ash stiffened. 'Really cool stuff?'

'You know – hacking. You don't need any of that. You just need to update the basics. Work out what you need it for, and learn how to do that. Er – what *do* you want to do with it?'

Ash took a deep breath. It was a now-or-never moment: he had the powerful feeling that if he didn't put it into words now, the whole idea would shrivel and drift away on the wind. 'I want to go back to work. If I can find a job I can do, that someone's willing to pay me for.' There: it was said.

To his credit, Saturday didn't immediately hoot with laughter. He had never known Ash as a working man. But he did know that he was an intelligent man, and that he had once held impor-tant, well-paid positions – so well paid that, even after four years of economic inactivity, he was still financially secure. 'Why?' he asked, puzzled. 'You don't need the money.'

'Why not?' countered Ash. 'Twelve months ago I didn't work because I wasn't capable of working. Two months ago I didn't work because looking after my boys took all my time. Now I have the time, and I have the capacity, and I'm starting to feel I'd like to put them to some use again. Less for the money than the self-respect. It's what you do if you're an adult, particularly if you have children. You find work and that's how you raise them. So they can tell their friends, "My dad's a butcher. My dad drives a taxi. My dad"' – he flicked Saturday a little grin – '"works in a service station." Anything that's both legal and respectable. I owe it to them.'

'But you're not a butcher,' Saturday pointed

191

out, reasonably. 'And taxi drivers have to drive faster than you do. And the job in the service station is mine, so keep your paws off it. Besides which, those aren't the sorts of job you want. They're the sorts of jobs you could do with half your brain, while using the other half to solve quadratic equations.'

Ash stared at him in astonishment. 'Saturday, what the *hell* do you know about quadratic equations?'

'I went to school. Don't change the subject. You shouldn't be doing little fill-a-bit-of-time, pay-for-the-piano-lessons jobs. You should be doing proper, important stuff again. You'll never be satisfied with a nine-to-fiver. There's only one good reason to take a boring job, and that's in order to eat. That isn't a problem for you. If you get a job painting the stripes on humbugs, you'll be climbing the walls within a week. You might think you'll be satisfied with just working. But it won't last. It won't be enough for long.'

Ash might have argued, but the youth knew him too well. That came as a bit of a shock too. But he'd started this conversation: he couldn't pull the plug just because he didn't like Saturday's answers. Honesty – total honesty – seemed the only way forward.

'I couldn't get an important job now,' he said quietly. 'Nobody would trust me with anything that mattered. You need to be reliable for those kinds of jobs. People need to feel they can count on you, that you'll still be up to the task on a bad day. And nobody is going to look at my track-record and feel that.

'I have a history of mental illness. That's a bit like being a murderer: potential employers are always going to feel that, just because you haven't done it for a while, you're still more likely to do it again than someone who never murdered anyone. And there are lots of people available for work who've never seen the inside of a straitjacket.'

Saturday said nothing. He let Ash talk, and he listened and didn't interrupt.

'I might find someone willing to trust me with an assistant-under-manager sort of job, where I won't scare off the customers if I go into melt-down someday. I will never find anyone willing to give me a position of real responsibility. Why would they? Why would someone who owes me nothing risk me ruining his business? I'm not even an unknown quantity – I'm someone who's already proved himself unreliable.

'So I need to start small. Get a foot on the ladder, and try to persuade an employer that I just might be promotable. That's the only way I'm ever going to earn an honest wage again.'

Saturday regarded him with compassion. It was a bit like seeing a great boxer reduced to serving as a bouncer in a backstreet nightclub. 'There *are* people who'll take a chance on you. The manager at the service station knew I'd boosted that laptop from his washroom when he took me on.'

'The age of miracles is not yet over. Well, maybe your manager has a brother who'll take a chance on me. Anyway, I'm going to find out.' Ash thought for a moment, frowning. 'Do they really pay people to do that? Paint the stripes on humbugs?'

Saturday nodded innocently. 'Oh yeah. And toothpaste. It's a fiddly job, not everyone can do it. Also, hollowing out chocolate bars to insert biscuits, and squeezing the walnut into the centre of a Walnut Whip.'

Ash gave a superior smile. 'I'm unreliable, not an idiot. Everyone knows the walnut goes *on top* of a Walnut Whip.'

'Oh yes,' murmured Saturday. 'Silly me.'

Twenty-Four

Now the idea of finding work had occurred to him, Ash was troubled by his lack of marketable skills. Everything that he once knew was out of date.

He was good with figures – but he had no accountancy qualifications. Perhaps he could work in a shop – a small shop, with not too many customers – where his ability to do the books would be a bonus. Books . . . A tiny light-bulb flickered in his head. A bookshop, perhaps. Crowds don't gather twelve deep around the till of a bookshop, and customers who were them-selves not wholly persuaded by the twenty-first century might not notice, or care if they did, that he was an analogue man adrift in a digital world.

The idea had some appeal. He saw himself dusting rows of leather spines, and heading unerringly for a top-shelf treasure with the aid of sliding library steps. (How Frankie would have laughed at this! He showed no talent for dusting at home.) People who worked in bookshops were allowed to be a little out of touch, he was sure, as long as they knew their shelves inside out and could match their customers to their stock. ('A little light holiday reading, madam? May I recommend Miss Austen? Such a subversive wit . . . And perhaps Mrs Gaskell to follow.')

How would the boys react? He suspected there was more cachet to having a father who was a fireman, a stand-up comedian or a professional footballer, but presumably a father who worked in a bookshop was better than one who did no work at all.

There were only two obstacles that Ash could see. One was the perennial one, of persuading any business that he would be an asset rather than a liability. The other was that there was no bookshop in Norbold. He pondered the problem as he walked home, Patience trotting quietly at his side.

The shortest route from Railway Street to Highfield Road was through the park, but Ash had to call at the garage behind Arkwright Street first. The old grey Volvo that had been his mother's had started making a strange noise, somewhere between a rumble and a rattle, particularly noticeable on corners, and after listening with mounting unease for a week he'd taken it in for a check-up.

The young man who ran the garage spoke with

a powerful Brummie accent, wore – even in November – T-shirts designed to show off his muscles, and decorated his workshop with calendars that in any other context would be deemed pornographic. But he was a very good, very reliable mechanic, and even if he laughed because someone was still driving a car that was old enough to vote, he still made sure the Volvo would get Ash and his family everywhere they wanted to go.

'Did you have any luck tracking down my rattle?' asked Ash.

Diego the mechanic nodded solemnly. 'I did.'

Ash didn't blame him for not going into detail. They hadn't known one another long, but still long enough for Diego to realise that if he started talking about the arcane world under the bonnet, Ash would go glassy-eyed and start shuffling out of the garage backwards. 'Big job?' he hazarded.

Diego rocked an oily hand. 'Not particularly. But it did take a fair bit of technical expertise to pin it down. Still, this is what us top-flight mechanics are trained for. Once I knew what was causing the problem, resolving it was easy enough.' He waited.

Ash steeled himself. 'What was causing the problem?'

Diego took something off the bench behind him, dropped it into Ash's hand. 'A boiled sweet in the glove compartment.'

Ash insisted on paying him for his time, although Diego would have been more than satisfied with the look on Ash's face. He opened the passenger door for Patience before climbing in behind the wheel.

He was about to leave when Diego ducked down to the open window. 'Do you know when Hazel's coming back?' It was Hazel who had introduced them.

'She's back now,' said Ash. 'She's staying with a friend. Why?'

'Her car's ready, but she isn't answering her phone. I thought she must still be away.'

Ash was puzzled. 'You've been working on it since she went to Morocco?'

Diego shrugged. 'I don't know where she is. I just know the car came in three days ago, for a service and a valet. Some bloke brought it in. I told him, "Are you sure she wants it valeting?" After they've been upside down in a ditch, valeting is a bit like polishing the silverware on the *Titanic*. But he insisted. Said she wanted it looking like new. I said, "If she wants a car that looks like new she'll have to buy a new car." He just said to do the best I could and got into a taxi.'

Some bloke. 'A man about my age? Couple of inches shorter? Good looking, and not unaware of the fact?'

Diego grinned and nodded. 'That's him. Who is he?'

Maybe the mechanic kept his television tuned to Formula One. But Ash was obscurely pleased to know the man was less universally recognisable than he imagined. 'His name's Oliver Ford. He works in television.'

Diego nodded wisely. 'That explains the spray tan.'

Ash laughed out loud. 'I think the tan is probably genuine.'

'And I'm a blond, blue-eyed Scandinavian,' said Diego cynically.

Ash drove slowly home. In fact he drove slowly most places – he'd been off the road for four years, and anyway the Volvo was built for endurance not speed – but today he was driving slowly because he was thinking.

He had that uneasy feeling again. Last time he'd got it he'd made a fool of himself, and he'd sworn he was going to stop jumping to conclusions. Hazel hadn't been kidnapped by white slavers, she'd been on holiday, and she'd returned safe and well. Nothing untoward would have happened to her this time either. Her partner – Ash still tripped over saying it, even inside his own head – had brought her car in for a service. Wasn't that exactly the sort of things partners did for one another?

Why wasn't she answering her phone? Could be any number of reasons. The simplest was the most likely: that Diego had called at a bad time. Ash pulled over to the side of the road to test this theory; but again he got a female voice – not Hazel's – informing him that the person he was calling was unavailable and asking him to call back later.

Perhaps the house Ford had taken was in a mobile black-spot. Or perhaps she'd lost her phone and hadn't got round to giving him the number of the new one. It was even possible that she'd simply switched it off and forgotten to switch it on again, and any time now would be sufficiently puzzled by the way the world had gone quiet to take it out and call someone herself.

Ash really hoped it would be him.

'I know I'm being neurotic,' he said apologetically as he parked the car in his drive. 'It's just . . . I don't like it when I don't hear from her.'

No, said Patience quietly. You're not being neurotic.

'I'm sure I'm imagining problems where no problems exist. Blowing things out of proportion.'

I know what neurotic means, said Patience. It's not neurotic to worry about someone when you have reason to think they might be in trouble.

They went inside. They had the house to themselves, so the dialogue continued.

'What reason? What makes you think Hazel might be in trouble?'

The lurcher looked surprised. How a dog whose face is little more than bone and teeth with skin stretched over them can convey expressions is something of a mystery, but they can. Even the ones who don't talk.

She said, Have you forgotten what Rachid Iqbal said?

'Rachid Iqbal said almost nothing. Only that Oliver Ford wasn't to be trusted. He wouldn't say why not, or how he knew.'

He said enough to worry you.

'Yes, he did. If I hadn't bumped into Hazel at the airport, I'd probably still be traipsing round the Middle East looking for her. And she was fine. I was worrying for nothing. I'm pretty sure I'm still worrying for nothing.'

No, insisted Patience, you're not. If you were

sure we wouldn't be having this conversation. You're worrying because she's your friend and she could be in trouble.

Ash breathed heavily at the dog. 'And you think this because Ford took Hazel's car in for a service?'

No. Because she doesn't seem to want it back.

Ash had almost persuaded himself there was nothing to be anxious about. Now Patience – or that alter ego he personified as Patience – had all but persuaded him the very opposite. 'Even if I thought you were right, what could I do about it? She isn't answering her phone, and I don't know where she's living now.'

You don't need to know where Hazel's living. You need to find out where Oliver Ford is living.

Ash nodded slowly. Of course: it seemed so obvious, when the dog pointed it out. Obvious, but problematic. 'Who's going to tell me that? Anyone who knows will see it as their duty to protect his privacy.'

Patience had the answer to that too. Who? – his agent. And how? – lie.

Twenty-Five

Hazel was struggling with the shoes Ford had picked out for her. They were beautiful, but they felt . . . wrong. It was years since she'd worn heels – they weren't practical for police work – and even then she hadn't worn them often.

Now she was wearing them around the house to try to learn the knack again. At first she found herself tottering from chair-back to door handle like an old lady with a new hip. But as her balance returned, she felt that indefinable presence, that stature, that a three-inch stiletto confers.

She smiled condescendingly down at Ford as he came into the kitchen in search of coffee. 'My goodness, is that the beginnings of a bald spot?'

If she'd thought for one moment that he would be offended, she would never have said it. But then, if she'd thought for one moment that he would be offended by a casual little joke, a friendly insult of the kind she traded daily with Saturday and Ash and her other friends, she probably wouldn't have been here.

But he was offended. His eyes flickered hotly at her and his lips compressed to a thin line. His fingers twitched as if he'd been about to check but refused to give her the satisfaction. 'I doubt it,' he said shortly. 'My father had a full head of hair on the day he died.'

Hazel blinked. 'Hey – humour alert? I know the male ego is a delicate thing, but don't take yourself so seriously. I don't love you for your hair. I wouldn't love you any less if you lost it.'

'I am not losing my hair!'

'Well, thanks for making me feel so good about losing mine!'

They stared at one another for a moment in anger and mutual incomprehension. As if neither could understand how this sudden argument had blown up when their own sensitivities should have been obvious to the other. Every second Hazel expected Ford to pass a weary hand in front of his face, shake his head bemusedly, apologise and say he'd been over-working. But he went on looking at her, hard-eyed, as if he was waiting for the apology.

Hazel was frankly shaken. She'd been living with this man now for over a month. She knew that he was touchy. She knew that his sense of humour, which could be delightfully impish and droll, never quite extended to his own shortcomings. But she made allowances for this – was happy to – because of how he made her feel. Intensely alive and stimulated. She enjoyed his quick wit and undoubted intelligence, and also his easy mastery of a social milieu in which she had never moved before. He was internationally recognised for his academic work, and enjoyed wide acclaim for his television presenting; he accepted both as his due and juggled their competing demands with a cool aplomb that still impressed her.

But she had not seen this side of him before. This petty, self-regarding pomposity that could take deep offence at a joke and cling to it like a startled bather hanging onto her towel. It was so . . . *childish*! They shared a bed. Their intimacy was absolute. How could he get this so wrong? Either he'd misjudged her so completely as to think she meant to hurt him, or it was a grotesque over-reaction. It hardly mattered which, because each was as inappropriate as the other.

One of them had to break the leaden silence,

and Ford seemed willing to stand there with his jaw clenched bitterly until he starved to death. Hazel took a deep, steadying breath. 'All right. You're not a stupid man, so this cannot possibly be about a bald spot, real or imaginary. What is it really about?'

He cranked his jaw open just wide enough to hammer out one word. 'Gratitude.'

It was a sort of counter-explanation. She understood less after he'd said it than before. Her face, from which the redness had finally faded, twisted in a puzzled frown. 'Oliver, I don't expect you to go on being grateful to me. I certainly don't expect you to go on *saying* you're grateful. We've moved beyond that. What happened in Wittering is how we met, but it isn't why we're together. We're together because, Lord knows why, we found so much pleasure in one another's company that going our separate ways wasn't an option. I'm here, in your house, because there's nowhere else I'd rather be. I think you'd have to call that love.'

She waited. It would have been nice if he'd picked that up and run with it; but perhaps she'd surprised him. She forged ahead. 'We've talked about the future. About a future together – about sharing our lives for as far ahead as we can see. But if we're going to talk about it some more, there are things we need to straighten out. I need to be sure that gratitude isn't all that's motivating you – because that's no foundation for a lasting relationship. And you need to understand that, while I will never deliberately hurt you, nor am I going to tiptoe round you for fear you might take umbrage at some innocent remark.

'I think it's time you had a proper family, Oliver. Me, or someone like me. You're too used to people saying "Yes, Mr Ford" and "No, Mr Ford" and "Would you like me to tie your shoe-laces, Mr Ford?" You get that from people you employ, and maybe from people who employ you and don't want to risk losing you. You don't get it in a personal relationship between equals. You shouldn't even *want* it in that kind of relationship.'

She took a deep breath. 'Well, the time has come to decide what you *do* want. If you don't want me here, if my jokes offend you and being teased, however affectionately, hurts your feelings, then I can be packed and out of here in half an hour. No blame, no shame – we can just say it didn't work out because in the end we were too different. But if I stay, I need you to do a bit of growing up. You're twelve years older than me – that's too old to be behaving like a spoilt child.'

Ford heard her out in silence. Hazel thought that was a good sign, that she wasn't having to bat aside his denials in order to make her point. Now she was finished, she quietly indicated that it was his turn, tottering on her towering heels to the nearest sofa where she sat and waited for his response. At that moment she could not have guessed which way it would go. Whether he would accept her terms or call her a taxi.

He didn't call her a taxi.

Slowly Ford's stiff expression softened into a

smile. It was an odd kind of smile, though, neither amused nor generous nor even tolerant. It was a superior smile. By the time he spoke, Hazel knew it wasn't going to be an apology. Even so, she wasn't ready for what came.

He reached out and stroked her cheek gently with the backs of his fingers. He said, almost tenderly, 'You're right, of course – you're very young. I forget sometimes. You have a woman's body, but you still think like a child. You think that being pretty is enough to get you what you want. You think that being pretty makes you the equal of people who are older than you, better educated than you, more successful than you and richer than you. And oh, my dear, you have such a lot to learn!

'You think – you really do think, don't you? – that when I talked about gratitude, I meant *I* was grateful to *you*! And of course I am. You did me a service, even though you had to put yourself in danger to do it. But as you keep pointing out, that is your job. That is what you're paid for. I *was* grateful, and I rewarded you – and now it's time you stopped trading on it.'

He took in Hazel's stunned expression. 'I see I have to spell it out. I am disappointed that you seem to feel so little gratitude for what I have done for you. I've shown you a world you didn't even know existed – ancient places the tourists never visit, top hotels, first-class travel. I've bought you clothes from shops you couldn't afford to go in; where the sales assistants make more money than you do. If you'd gone in on your own, they'd have assumed you'd made a mistake and directed you to the nearest Marks & Spencer.

'And now you have the gall to set conditions on me? The day we met, you were nobody. Mere random chance put you in a position to do something valuable, to get your name in the papers, and now you think you're something special. I'll tell you how special you are. You're as special as I make you. The clothes will wear out and you can't afford to replace them; the smart hotels and the first-class air travel are entirely beyond your means; and the places I took you to will be shut if you go alone, and no one will remember you.

'Now stop being such a silly bitch and go back to doing what you're good at: adding a bit of fluff to my life. That's the reason you're here – the only reason you've been anywhere in the last month. I enjoy having you around, being young and pretty and a bit silly – it's a change from the serious stuff I spend the rest of my time doing. So I'll go on paying the bills, and you'll go back to keeping me happy – all right? Because it would be a mistake to make me unhappy.'

Ice had taken a clutch of Hazel's heart. Ice had stiffened her spine and frozen her limbs, and iced water was trickling over the surface of her brain. It wasn't the crude threat that was responsible. Hazel had been threatened before, and by people both better motivated and better equipped to carry out their threats. What made Ford's nastiness so chilling was the context. This wasn't a dark alley round the back of The Flying Horse, popular with drug pushers and their clients, and prostitutes and *their* clients. This was the house she shared with someone she trusted. The confrontation had come out of nowhere, out of an amiable little joke, and she felt she'd been side-swiped by a train. That was how he thought of her? This man she'd contemplated spending her life with? He considered her a *decoration*? Like his Rolex watch and the gold chain which, against her advice, he persisted in wearing around his neck? He thought that, the way he'd bought them – seen them and liked them and bought them – *he'd bought her too*?

She needed to say something, and to say it soon. She couldn't find the breath. It was as if he'd kicked all the air out of her lungs.

Finally she managed, 'I think I should leave now. There isn't much here that's actually mine – what there is, I'll come back for in a day or two. Will you drive me back to town, or shall I walk?'

She had literally no idea how he would respond. Ford was a cultured man: perhaps he would murmur a civilised, 'That might be best,' and carry her bag to his car. But he was also a quick-tempered man: she readied herself for a rough hand to grasp her arm, manhandle her out onto the drive and slam the door behind her. Her mobile was in her bag: she must try to grab it as he hustled her out, though the surrounding forest meant she might have to walk for an hour before she would pick up a signal.

Or might he back-pedal briskly, try to persuade her that she'd misunderstood? That there was still a future for them? She couldn't see him

207

begging her to stay. She couldn't see him dissolving in tears of despair. She could, just, imagine him hitting her.

Ford's hands stayed by his sides. He said nothing. But by degrees his expression changed, the anger and the hardness in his eyes softening until she suddenly realised that, incredibly, he was smiling at her. A genuine smile. That impish, boyish smile she found so hard to resist.

'What?' he said finally, his head tipping on one side like an impudent bird's. 'You're allowed to poke fun at my bald spot, but I'm not allowed to tease you?'

'That . . .' Hazel had to swallow and try again. 'That was a joke? A *joke*?'

He was frankly grinning by now. 'You should see your face! You really thought I meant it, didn't you? Admit it. You really thought I was going bunny-boiler on you.'

'Oliver,' she gasped, 'I had no idea what was going on! You . . . you thought that was *funny*?'

He bit his lip. 'It was from where I'm standing. It still is.'

'I thought you *hated* me!'

'Hate you? My darling, how could anyone hate you? You're utterly adorable when you're confused!'

He put his arms around her, confident of his welcome; and Hazel was too stunned to stop him. All she could do was mumble into his shirt-front, '*Why*?'

Ford laughed richly into the top of her head. 'You started it! Bald spot indeed. If it was true, it would be no joking matter. You think I'm vain? I'm a performer. It matters that I look the part. People expect it. I'd love to be able to say, To hell with it – I'm a man of nearly forty, who cares if I go bald? But the sad fact is, people would care. They expect you always to look as you looked when they first saw you on television. Ridiculous, isn't it? – that the more successful you are, the longer that success lasts, the more you have to lie about who you are.

'But I don't make the rules. For anyone working in television, appearance matters. We spend time and money that could be better used elsewhere on making sure we don't disappoint our audience. It isn't enough to be an authority on the Crusades; it isn't even enough to be able to persuade people who don't know the difference between Saladin and Aladdin that it might be fun to find out. If you want to be successful on television, it's necessary to be eye-candy as well.'

Her heartbeat was returning to something like normal. Hazel levered herself out of his embrace. Ford made no effort to hold onto her. 'It matters that much to you? Being a celebrity?'

He laughed again, a confident throwaway laugh. 'Some are born celebrities, some achieve celebrity, and some have celebrity thrust upon them. Me, I kicked, bit and scratched to get where I am today. Damn right I want it to last.'

Hazel nodded slowly. 'So – no more jokes about baldness?'

'If you wouldn't mind.'

'And no more jokes about' – she couldn't

encapsulate his tirade in a single phrase, settled rather lamely for: 'You know.'

Ford kissed the top of her head. Into her short, springy hair he murmured, 'Did I frighten you?'

'Of course not,' she snorted. But that was the police officer speaking, who could be scared half to death but knew better than to show it. Ford wasn't a gang of lager-louts: he was the man she lived with, the man who had talked about marriage, and she owed him honesty. 'Well – yes, in a way. I thought – suddenly I thought I didn't know you any more. Or maybe that I'd never known you. That I'd misjudged you, and therefore what we have together, so badly there was nowhere left to go.

'I thought it was over, and for the worst of reasons: that it wasn't real in the first place. That I'd talked myself into believing in us because I wanted it so much. That I'd blinded myself to the reality that we're just too different. That the things that matter to us are too different. You can patch over the cracks, and then patch over the patches, but sooner or later the rain's going to come through. I thought that was what was happening. That the rain was coming through.'

Ford reached out for her again. He wasn't a big man like Ash, but the strength of his arms was both assertive and reassuring. 'I'm sorry. I went too far. I was . . . getting my own back . . . and I went too far. I didn't mean to frighten you. You have nothing to be frightened of. You're safe here. You're safe with me.'

'I know,' she murmured into his shoulder.

Twenty-Six

Gabriel Ash was no good at lying. He was very good at seeing through the lies of others, a facility on which he had built not one but two careers; but he never got away with lying himself. As if he was wearing a cap-badge with the word 'Fibber' emblazoned on it, people knew as soon as he contemplated telling a falsehood.

There was, he thought ruefully, only one lie he'd been able to carry off successfully, and that wasn't exactly a lie, more a reluctance to volunteer a truth that no one would believe. No one knew that when he talked to his dog, she talked back. His reputation as the local idiot had afforded the secret some protection. Once when he had let the truth slip out, Hazel had dismissed it as a kind of foolish joke, which wasn't much better.

On the bright side, though he himself might be one of the world's worst liars, Ash knew someone who was among its best. When he'd dropped the boys off for Saturday morning soccer practice, he returned to Railway Street.

Saturday heard him out in mounting disbelief. 'Gabriel – you used to work for MI5!'

'No, I didn't,' Ash said shortly.

Saturday raised one deeply unconvinced eyebrow. 'No, of course you didn't. People have heard of MI5, and the guys you worked for

211

probably keep their number secret. Point is, you have contacts who could find Oliver Ford in two minutes, and have him sweating under an energy-saving low-emission eco-friendly twenty-watt bulb inside half an hour. What do you need me for?'

'I don't want to go through channels,' admitted Ash. 'I've already reminded my old boss that I'm back among the living; if I keep doing it, sooner or later he's going to ask me to repay all these favours, and I really don't want to get drawn into that line of business again.

'And I particularly don't want Hazel's name to start coming up on Home Office computers. If she's got herself in a fix, I'd rather sort it out myself. If I can find her, I'll go and talk to her, see if she's all right, and bring her home if she's not. If I ask Philip Welbeck to find her, I know he'll do it, but it may not end there. I don't want him trying to recruit her. She'd be a good acquisition for him, with her ex-army father, her background in IT and her police training. But it's not the kind of work I'd like to see her doing.'

'I think she'd be good at the cloak-and-dagger stuff,' said Saturday stoutly.

'I think she'd be good at it too. And I think she'd jump at the chance. And I think that, sooner or later, she'd pay too high a price for it.'

'The way you did,' murmured Saturday.

'The way I did,' agreed Ash. 'Well, Hazel's made of stronger stuff than me. But being tough isn't always enough. Even being lucky isn't always enough. I don't want to be the reason

212

she gets involved in something that's more likely to cause her grief than Oliver Ford is.'

Saturday nodded his understanding. The fondness he had developed for both these people – the strong young woman and the broken man – was a firm anchor in the storm-tossed sea that had been his life. He had prided himself on having no friends, had believed that emotional attachments were a weakness, and a luxury no one in his position could afford. Well, weakness or not, he had friends now. Friends he was willing to do much more than lie for.

'Tell me what you need.'

A quick trawl of the Internet on the computer he'd bought with his second month's wages gave Saturday the name and phone number of Oliver Ford's agent. Then things got technical. He asked for Ash's phone, and Ash watched in astonishment as the youth opened it up and ran a wire from it to the computer.

'Whatever are you doing?'

Saturday smirked. 'Watch, my friend, and learn.' He dialled the agent's number.

People employ agents partly as a filter between themselves and the general public. Perhaps Miriam Seward believed Saturday's claim to be a journalist in search of an interview, perhaps she didn't; either way, she was never going to give him Ford's address or phone number. She offered to set up an interview within the next couple of weeks.

'That would be great,' said Saturday enthusiastically, 'only there's a bit of time pressure. I have a slot in a magazine, but I need to get the copy in next week. Which means getting together in the next few days.'

'I doubt that will be possible,' said Ms Seward. 'Mr Ford is out of town – he's working on his book.'

'I know it's asking a lot. But will you call him up and ask him? I'll go anywhere he wants to meet. Can't you at least ask him?' He let a plaintive note catch his voice.

It had the desired effect. 'I'll call and ask. But you shouldn't get your hopes up. Mr Ford values his private time. What's your number? I'll get back to you.'

'Right away? Will you call him right away?'

'I'll call him right away, young man,' she promised. 'But I don't think he'll say yes.'

She rang off. Saturday grinned at Ash. 'Neither do I. But then, it doesn't actually matter what he says.'

Ms Seward was as good as her word. She spoke to Ford, then called Saturday back. 'I'm sorry. He's busy with his book and doesn't want to be disturbed.'

Saturday thanked her for her time and rang off. By then the hack had connected and schematics were already appearing on the screen of his computer. He leaned back with a grunt of satisfaction. 'That's where he is.' There was a red dot superimposed on a road map.

Ash shook his head in wonder. 'Saturday – how do you *know* this stuff? You're not telling me they taught you how to trace phone calls in your school IT class?'

The boy gave a smug chuckle. 'What you learn in IT classes is mostly how to find other guys who know more than you do. Who know more than your teachers do. Everything is out there. Everything. All you need is to know how to find it.'

Even now, Ash was appalled at how much the world had moved on in the time he'd been out to lunch. Though it was a fact that no one of his generation was ever as thoroughly at home with the digital revolution as people who'd grown up with it. The new technology had proved infinitely valuable in the field of national security, but it wasn't people like Ash and Philip Welbeck doing the actual computing. For that, they employed people like Saturday. Computer jockeys tend to be under thirty. The people running the security services tend to be over forty.

On the other hand, Ash was old enough to know how to read a map, an ability that the sat-nav generation don't always share. He fetched an Ordnance Survey of the West Midlands from the Volvo and quickly located the roads around the red dot. There weren't many of them in quite a large area of woodland. 'His agent wasn't lying. Ford really doesn't like being disturbed.'

Saturday was peering over his shoulder. 'How long will it take us to get there?'

Ash stared at him. 'It'll take *me* about half an hour.' He looked critically around the little sitting room. 'You'd better do some housework, in case I can persuade Hazel to come back with me.'

But Saturday had no intention of being left behind. He didn't even argue: he just said,

215

'I'm coming,' in a tone which left no room for doubt.

'All right,' growled Ash. 'But you'll have to stay in the car. I don't want you and Ford coming to blows again. There's no reason for this to turn nasty. I just want to talk to Hazel, and bring her home if I can. I want to get her away from him for long enough to have a proper talk, make sure she isn't being coerced into doing anything she doesn't want to. She's a grown woman; if she wants to go back to him, there's nothing we can do to stop her. But I want to be sure it *is* what she wants, not just what he wants.'

'I'll stay in the car,' Saturday agreed readily. But he winked at Patience when Ash's back was turned.

Hazel tried to call Diego to see if her car was ready. But her phone was still on strike, and now it seemed Ford's was too. She saw no alternative to going into Norbold and seeing the mechanic in person.

Ford said he would drive her, later. He was busy in his study. She drifted round the garden dead-heading the last of the flowers. Then she put together the makings of lunch, and then she went to see how long he was going to be.

'Can we go tomorrow?' he said. 'I'm in the middle of this.'

Hazel frowned. 'Tomorrow's Sunday – he won't be there. We'll be back in an hour. I feel stranded without my car. It must be ready by now.'

Ford shrugged, almost without looking up. 'We'll run into Norbold on Monday, then – collect the car, get some lunch, maybe do a bit of shopping. All right?'

Hazel breathed heavily at him. 'Oliver, I've hardly been out of this house for days. It's a beautiful house, but I don't want to spend all my time in it. I need my car back. Whatever it is you're doing, it can wait for an hour. Take me into Norbold and come straight back. If Diego's still working on the car, someone will give me a lift. In fact, I want to see my superintendent about getting back to work, and Saturday morning's a good time to catch her. So I can beg a lift out with the area car afterwards.'

That made Ford turn round. He looked surprised and a little annoyed. 'You want to go back to work? Why?'

She scowled at him. 'Because it's my job, and I'm fit to do it! I have been for weeks. The longer I put it off, the harder it's going to feel.'

'Then don't go back.' Ford seemed to think it was the obvious answer. 'It's not as if we need the money.'

'Money isn't the only reason to work! I like my job. I like feeling useful.'

'And you don't feel useful here?'

'Since you ask,' she retorted, 'no. You're preoccupied with your work – which is fine, that's how it should be. But what am I supposed to do? I haven't the patience for cross-stitch samplers! I'm a police officer. I should be breaking up fights outside pubs. I should be seeing old ladies across busy roads, and stopping the Mugford twins from

217

riding home on any bicycle they find that's not actually nailed down. I should be getting on with my life!'

Ford looked slowly round the room. 'You don't consider this part of your life?'

'A part, yes! I enjoy being with you, Oliver, you know that. I like this house – I don't even mind living in the middle of the last Wild Wood in England! But it's not a whole life. I have a job. I have friends. I should check that Saturday hasn't burnt down Railway Street trying to dry his socks on the toaster. I need to go into town, and I want to do it this morning. I want you to put your work aside for as long as it takes to drive me into Norbold. Is that so very much to ask?'

Ford turned his gaze from Hazel to the screen of his computer. Then with a sigh he turned back, swivelling his chair to look her full in the face. He held his hands out, palms up, to either side of him – as if, Hazel thought inconsequentially, he was carrying a baguette. He rocked them slightly.

'It's like this. You want to go to town, I want to work on my book. Town, book.' The baguette rocked some more. 'You want to pick up your little run-about, and check on your grubby little lodger, and find out why your services aren't considered indispensable by Norbold police, and I want to complete a book which my publishers are waiting for, which will hopefully form the basis of a new TV series, and which should over the next couple of years bring in several cheques with lots of zeros on them. So I put it to you,

Hazel – which do you think is the most important? Running you into town, or working on my book? Honestly?'

'Honestly?' She set her jaw. 'Right now, Oliver, I would honestly say that the most important thing you could be working on is our relationship. Another hour is neither here nor there to your publishers. If you've got behind with your work, you need to catch up – but you need to do it at another time. Burn the midnight oil tonight. Get up with the larks tomorrow. But right now, I need you to show me some consideration. If you want this relationship to work, you have to make time for me as well. And I need some of that time right now.'

His frown turned imperious, as if she were a minion who had spoken back to him or a cheeky child. 'Don't give me ultimatums.'

She wasn't prepared to back down. 'I shouldn't have to, Oliver. It should be obvious to you that people who think enough of one another to set up home together will have certain expectations of each other. I shouldn't have to ask for your help – you should know when it's needed and offer it.'

Ford gave a cold laugh. 'Not that old chestnut! "If you *really* loved me I wouldn't have to tell you how I feel." You disappoint me, Hazel. Whatever happened to the feminist revolution? You really ought to decide which side you're on. It's ridiculous to insist that you're as strong, as capable and as worth your salt as any man, but play the china doll whenever you don't get your own way.'

Hazel felt herself flushing with anger. She was angry, and upset, and offended, and on top of that she was astonished. She doubted there was a woman in England who was less like a china doll than she was. At thirteen her mother had called her an outrageous tomboy. She probably wouldn't have modified that opinion much if she'd lived to see her daughter at twenty-seven.

It was already too late for a snappy retort. Hazel bridled her anger long enough to formulate exactly what she wanted to say – to get her ducks in line – with the firm intention that something had to change right now. Either Ford's attitude or Hazel's home address, and at this precise moment she didn't care which. She was exhausted by the emotional buffeting that came with loving Oliver Ford. He professed his fondness for her, then set about changing everything about her. How she looked, how she dressed, how she lived. He'd claimed to feel as strongly about her as she felt about him – had he ever *used* the word love? – had she? – but this wasn't the first time he'd turned a perfectly ordinary domestic situation into an unpleasant confrontation.

Not the first time . . .

Hazel let the ducks wander off about their business while she regarded Ford with narrowed eyes. 'Oliver – is this one of your jokes?'

He appeared to give that some thought. Then he drew a world-weary hand across his eyes. 'Do you know, I suppose it is. A joke that got out of hand. All of it. It's a very middle-aged-man thing to do, isn't it? – take up with a young girl and set about turning her into something that she's not. Elegant, sophisticated. Because those are things that you can produce, that you can create, and she already has the one thing that you can't – youth. I suppose it's a last gesture of defiance before the sands of time start sucking at your feet.'

He scowled. 'It's a little pathetic, when you think about it. Trying to avoid growing older by changing someone else. Into – and this is genuinely ironic – the sort of woman there's no shortage of in his own age-group. And for what? To make people envy him? As if being successful isn't cause enough for envy.

'I don't need this, Hazel. I don't need your histrionics. I have important things to think about. I need you to be able to amuse yourself for a few hours while I work. Is that so very much to ask? In return for what I've given you? Now, be a good girl and go and – I don't know – paint your fingernails for a while, and I'll take you into Norbold when I can spare the time. All right? Oh – you could bring me a coffee first.'

Hazel was not someone who responded to provocation with violence. She never had been, even before she joined the police – and as a teacher, there had been ample opportunities if the inclination had been there. All the same, if Oliver Ford had been standing up instead of sitting down, she might very well have slapped him.

She still wasn't entirely sure that he wasn't teasing her. In a way it didn't matter. Whether he was saying these things because he genuinely thought so little of her, or because he considered it funny to make her think so, the inescapable

221

bottom line was that the man she lived with had no compunction about hurting her. The man she slept beside had so little respect for her that he either didn't notice or didn't care about the damage he was doing.

She said nothing. There was nothing she could usefully say. There was no point, and no dignity, in railing at him. She knew now that she'd wasted six weeks of her life – but that wasn't actually Ford's fault. He was who he'd been all along: the error was hers in not recognising who that was. She'd been seduced by his manner, his sophistication, his urbanity – all right, perhaps even by his wealth and his fame – and she'd seen only what she wanted to see. She'd made excuses for his selfishness – he was busy, he was tired, he was better at professional rela-tionships than personal ones. She had made allowances for him because she thought she was or at least might be in love; and he had responded by treating her like – like – like a toy. Something to be taken out and played with when he was in the mood, and put back in the box when he had more important things to do.

She had undoubtedly been foolish, thinking this could be something real, something lasting, when it was clearly nothing more than a passing amusement to Ford. And now it was over. The only question in her mind – a-jangle as it was with how the world had turned widdershins in the space of a few painful minutes – was how best to draw a line under it. Not with a bang; but perhaps not with a whimper either.

So, silently, she retreated to the kitchen and

did as he asked. While the kettle was boiling she went upstairs and put together the few things – her things – she meant to take with her. She left her bag in the hall and finished making his coffee. Thick and strong, the way he liked it, with two spoonfuls of brown sugar, well stirred.

Then, still without a word, she carried it into the study. He saw her, and smiled, and reached for it.

She poured it, with slow deliberation, all over the keyboard of his computer.

Twenty-Seven

Even with a map, it wasn't easy to find the house. Roads entered the ancient woodland and seemed to get lost in there, as if it were the Amazon rain forest. Roads seemed to travel through the woods in an approximately straight line but emerge facing the direction they'd come from. One road Ash tried ended in a sink-hole. Someone had helpfully drawn a stop line across it just short of where the worn tarmac broke up and disappeared.

Finally Saturday spotted a sign tacked to a tree – 'Purley Grange', in poker-work almost obliterated by moss – and though the trail it indicated was unmetalled and barely maintained, after a minute the red tile roofs and glittering windows of a substantial house started to peep through breaks in the trees. There was a wrought-iron gate, overswarmed by ivy, and a driveway refreshed by a recent load of gravel, and then they were there.

It was the sort of house where tradesmen went to the back door. Ash parked the Volvo in front of the main portico, and got out, stretched unhurriedly, and looked around him.

Then he looked back at the car in astonishment. Patience was snarling.

Saturday, who was sitting beside her on the back seat, began edging towards the door. 'What's wrong with her?' She wasn't a big dog. Even Saturday could have lifted her without risking a hernia. But though slender, she was muscular and sinewy, and when she lifted the curtain of her lips the teeth went all the way back to her ears.

Ash shook his head. 'I don't know.' And he didn't know why she was behaving like a dog instead of telling him what was wrong. But he couldn't explain that to Saturday. 'Let her out.'

Saturday's eyebrows expressed misgivings. 'Are you sure?'

'Let her out. Something's upset her. I want to know what.'

The youth opened the rear passenger door. Patience didn't wait but bounded over him, her slim body arching with greyhound grace, and in a scant three seconds had disappeared round the side of the house. Ash followed at a sharp walk. After a moment he began to run.

Sight-hounds do not on the whole give tongue as they hunt. But Ash wasn't a dog expert – Patience was the only one he'd ever owned – and he was alarmed at how quickly she had disappeared both from view and from earshot. He knew the speed she was capable of. By the time he reached the corner she could be anywhere: in the house, in the garden or three fields away. He trusted her not to chase sheep or bite children. He wasn't sure what she would do when she caught up with whatever had angered her.

So it came as a relief when he turned the corner of Purley Grange and saw her immediately, sitting on the gravel, her long scimitar tail making patterns like a Japanese gardener's rake as it wagged, her long pink tongue lolling. Hazel was on one knee beside her, an arm around the dog's neck.

'We came to the right place, then,' said Ash.

That first instinct of relief disappeared the instant Hazel straightened up and turned towards him. She looked dazed and bewildered, and she was bleeding from a two-inch cut under her left eye.

'Gabriel? What are you doing here?'

It wasn't just that she was surprised to see him. It wasn't even the cut, although it was both nasty and fresh. He thought she looked lost. Whatever had just happened, whatever he'd almost stumbled upon, had knocked her sideways, metaphorically as well as literally.

Though the winter was only one frost away, it wasn't a cold day. And Hazel wasn't out here on the gravel in her pyjamas. Still, moved by some instinct of caring, Ash shrugged off his jacket and put it round her; and felt Hazel pull it close about her as if for comfort.

He wanted to go inside, find Ford and take

225

him apart like jointing a chicken. He wanted to bellow his fury, and heave bricks through the pretty sixteen-pane windows, and gather the girl to his breast where she'd be safe.

He could keep himself on a tight rein when he had to. He'd had a lot of practice. Instead he took out his handkerchief, checked it was clean and, folding it into a tight pad, put it into her hand. Even then he had to guide it to her face. 'Hazel – what are *you* doing here?'

She looked up at the house. She looked past Ash to where Saturday had finally extricated himself from his seat-belt and lurched round the corner. She lowered the handkerchief from under her eye and looked at the blood on it, as if she wasn't sure whose it was.

Finally she sucked in a steadying breath. 'I'm getting ready to leave.'

'Yes,' said Ash quietly. 'That sounds like a good idea.'

Patience led the way back to the car. But as Ash went to put Hazel inside she hesitated, looked up the steps to the front door. 'My bag's in the hall. I won't be a minute . . .'

'Damn right you won't.' For a moment the anger in his soul vibrated in Ash's voice. 'I'll get it. Is the door locked?'

'No. Gabriel . . .'

He turned at the foot of the steps. 'What?'

'This.' She gestured at her face. 'It was an accident.'

If he started shouting now, he might never be able to stop. 'Of course it was.' He went up the steps and opened the front door.

The bag was where she'd said, at the foot of the staircase. Ash passed it with barely a look and continued down the hall, opening doors as he went.

He found Ford in the kitchen, dabbing at his laptop with a paper towel. He didn't look round. He must have thought Hazel had come back inside. 'I have six months' work on this thing. Six months! You'd better hope I can get it out again.'

'Frankly, Mr Ford,' Ash said judiciously, 'it's immaterial to me whether you can salvage your work or not. Put the laptop down.'

Startled – he wasn't expecting a man's voice – and irritated, Ford spared him a look that turned into a double-take. 'You? How . . .?' But then he abandoned the query as if it wasn't worth pursuing. 'If you're looking for Hazel, she's in the garden somewhere.'

'Yes. But you're in here.'

On television, Oliver Ford looked bigger than he actually was. People who met him for the first time were always a little surprised. He had the presence, the mannerisms of a more substantial man. By contrast, Gabriel Ash tried not to intimidate people with his bear-like frame, made a habit of stooping slightly to minimise the impact he had on those around him. But not today. Pumped up with quiet rage, he loomed over the smaller man.

'You hit her.'

Ford appeared oblivious of the danger he was in. 'I didn't hit her,' he snarled. 'The silly bitch spilled coffee on my laptop! I tried to shake it out and she got in the way.'

227

Ash was nodding carefully. 'That's what she said. That it was an accident.'

For an instant, no sooner seen than gone, Ford looked puzzled. But he rallied quickly. 'So what are you doing here?'

'Taking her home.'

Ford shrugged, turned his attention back to the computer he was holding inverted over the sink. 'She's not a prisoner. She can leave any time she wants. But tell her to take her things with her. If she comes back in a few days I may not be here.'

'I'll tell her.' Ash was amazed at how calm he sounded. 'As soon as I've done this.'

'Done what?'

If Ash had punched him, angry as he was, he could have broken Ford's jaw. He could have broken Ford's teeth and his own knuckles. He could conceivably have missed altogether – he had no experience of street-fighting, or any other kind of fighting – and put his fist through the kitchen window.

Instead he slapped his face.

Ford didn't go down, or even sprawl across the sink; but both cheeks flooded with colour. Not only from the blow, but because it wasn't the kind of blow that a man delivers to another man. The contempt in Ash's eyes stung more than the slap. Oliver Ford was not much given to self-analysis: what he saw reflected in the pitiless mirror of Ash's gaze startled and wounded him.

Ash's voice never rose from that low intensity which made every word totally believable. 'If you go near her again, I will put you in your grave.'

Ford found himself clutching his cheek like an affronted maiden aunt and dropped his hand quickly, as if hoping no one had noticed. There was nothing he could do about the fact that he was visibly shaking. Not with fear, though Ash in this mood was something to be feared, but with towering, incredulous fury.

'Who the hell do you think you are, threatening me? Coming into my house and assaulting me? You're nothing. You're a charity case. You think Hazel cares about you? That she *ever* cared about you? The kindest thing that can be said is that you're one of her good causes. Lame dogs, lost children and you. What else could it have been? You *surely* didn't think you had anything to offer her?'

Ash looked the trembling man up and down, noting the palm-print picked out in deeper red against the angry flush of Ford's face. 'You're probably right. She was always generous to a fault. Although there are in fact two things I can offer her. Respect, and somewhere she will always be safe. You need to believe me, Mr Ford. If you touch her again, I will put an end to you.'

There was nothing more he needed to say, and nothing he wanted to hear. He turned and left Ford standing shaking beside his kitchen sink, and picked up Hazel's bag as he passed and went down to his car.

There was no conversation as they drove back to Norbold. Ash didn't ask what had passed

229

between Hazel and Ford; Hazel didn't ask what had passed between Ford and Ash. She sat slumped in the front passenger seat, Ash's jacket still tugged around her, occasionally dabbing at her cheek with his handkerchief. It seemed Saturday had nothing to say either, except once when Ash took a wrong turning in the wood. Even Patience was keeping her thoughts to herself.

Ash drove first to Railway Street, but only to let Saturday out. 'I want to take Hazel down to A&E, see if that cut requires stitches.'

'I don't need any stitches,' growled Hazel.

'You don't need any more scars, either. Let someone who knows what they're talking about take a look at it.'

She grumbled some more, but she made no attempt to get out of the car, so he drove on to Norbold General Infirmary out on the ring road.

Then, and only then, did he remember that he should have collected his sons from soccer practice twenty minutes earlier. In a muck sweat of panic and abject guilt, he phoned Frankie, only to learn that their coach had brought them home when the only alternative would have been to lock up the changing rooms and leave them sitting disconsolately on the school-yard wall.

'They're fine,' she assured their horrified parent. 'It's not just you – there's always someone who forgets where he left his children.'

'*Anything* could have happened,' moaned Ash.

'No, it couldn't,' said Frankie calmly. 'They were never alone for a moment. And if they hadn't

230

got a lift home, Gilbert has my number – he'd have had someone call me.'

But Ash still couldn't believe he'd forgotten about his sons.

It turned out that Hazel was right: she didn't need stitches. The nurse in the treatment room zipped the edges of the cut together with tiny strips of elastic plaster. As she worked she said, 'What happened to you this time, dear?'

Hazel rolled her eyes. She didn't even know the treatment room nurse. It seemed all Norbold was familiar with her propensity for getting into scrapes. 'I head-butted a laptop.'

'Ah.' The nurse finished and packed her kit away. 'You probably shouldn't do that again.'

Walking back to the car Ash said, 'Don't go home tonight. Stay at Highfield Road. You've had a shock. You shouldn't be alone.'

'I won't be alone at Railway Street either.' But there was a note in Hazel's voice that suggested she wouldn't take much persuading.

'Saturday is a fine young man in many ways,' agreed Ash stoutly. 'Well – some ways. But when it comes to being looked after, I'll see your Saturday and raise you my Frankie. You've got your bag with you – come and stay with us for a few days. Just till you get your breath back. I'll let Saturday know.'

If it had been his decision, Ash would have tucked her up in bed in the newly decorated guest room with an extra quilt, and brought her soft-boiled eggs and jelly, and hot sweet tea, and kept everyone away from her; and Hazel would have gone quietly mad. Happily, Frankie took

231

control. She tutted sympathetically over Hazel's cut, stretched lunch to serve five, and shoo'ed Guy away when he bombarded her with questions that Gilbert wanted the answers to.

After they'd eaten, she had the boys help her load the dishwasher. 'You eat the food, you deal with the dishes,' she explained briskly, and Hazel and Ash were left alone.

'She's a treasure!' whispered Hazel. 'Where did you find her?'

He was glad she approved; although in truth, it was hard to imagine who wouldn't. Even the notoriously picky Gilbert had decided Frankie was his new best friend. 'An agency sent her. I can't think, now, how I managed without her.

'It wasn't that I didn't like the nanny you recommended,' he added earnestly. 'I couldn't seem to track her down. Lots of people seemed to have heard of her, but nobody knew where she was working or when she'd be available.'

Hazel's frown was puzzled. 'I didn't recommend . . .' But then an echo of the conversation drifted back to her, and a slow smile spread over her battered face. 'Ah yes. Nanny McPhee. So you called round some agencies asking for her?'

'I did,' nodded Ash. 'No one was able to help. But then one of them sent me Frankie, and she's exactly what I need. I just didn't want you to think I hadn't liked your friend.'

'That's fine, Gabriel,' said Hazel generously, 'I'm sure she's fully employed. She's a resourceful woman. Maybe you'll come across her some day.'

There was a hiatus then when neither of them

232

spoke. It wasn't strained, exactly, because they were good enough friends that they didn't need to fill every moment with chatter. At the same time, both were aware that, sooner or later, they'd have to talk about what had happened.

Hazel began. 'How did you know I needed you?'

'I didn't. It was just getting to be a long time since I'd seen you, I couldn't get you on the phone and I wanted to be sure you were all right.'

'Your timing was spot on.' Hazel frowned. 'When did I give you the address?'

'You didn't. Saturday found it. Some time when we're both feeling stronger, I'll tell you how.'

She flickered a smile, but it didn't last. 'I'm not sure what happened. Where it went wrong. We were talking about – at least, I *think* we were talking about – marriage.'

'Well, let's thank every god in the pantheon that talking is all you did. It's a lot easier to pack a bag than to unpick a marriage.'

Hazel didn't argue. Ash was speaking from experience.

He looked at her carefully. '*Did* he hit you?'

She looked away. 'I told you, it was an accident.'

Ash went on as if she hadn't spoken. 'Because, if he did, it isn't too late to go to the police. You might have to take a bit of rough-housing in the course of your job, but nobody has to take it in the place where they live. If he hit you, you should report it.'

Hazel cast him a furtive look. 'And be the

groupie who brought Oliver Ford up before the magistrates? I'd rather have the black eye. Besides, who'd believe me? He's a famous man – a celebrity. Millions watch his programmes. Who's going to believe that, at home, he behaves like a spoilt child?'

'Hazel – everyone who knows you will believe everything you tell them. DI Gorman will, Superintendent Maybourne will. And being a celebrity doesn't give Ford the right to knock people about. The size of his fan club is irrelevant. If that's how he reacts when things don't go his way, he needs to be put on notice. Not for your sake – he's not going to bother you again. But for the sake of the next woman he takes a fancy to. You got a cut on your cheek, and that'll heal. What if he'd damaged your eye? What if he'd done worse than that? If he gets away with it this time, maybe next time he will.'

Hazel didn't want to take the matter any further – she didn't want to have to admit publicly that she'd made a fool of herself with the man – but she might have accepted the necessity but for one thing. 'I couldn't say, hand on heart, that it wasn't an accident. We were arguing, but it was only verbal, and I was making my point pretty forcefully too. We were never going to agree – whatever we'd once had, it had come to an end. I'd packed my bag and I was on my way out.'

She chewed her lip reflectively. There was something like a smile in her eyes at the memory. 'Then I poured coffee all over his laptop, and he snatched it away and flailed round with it,

234

trying to get the coffee out before all his files dissolved. The corner of it hit me under the eye. Gabriel, it's possible he meant to do it. But it's equally possible that he didn't. And it certainly wouldn't have happened if I'd just taken my bag and left. I couldn't swear that it was assault. Even if it was, I think maybe I had it coming.'

There was no question about it: she was definitely smiling now. 'Do you know something? It was worth it for the look on his face.'

Ash smiled too, happy to see her on the way back. The dyed hair and the high heels and the sophisticated clothes had hidden his friend for a while. But that grin and the ripening eye were quintessential Hazel, and he was more glad than he could have said to have her back. He let the subject drop. If the victim of an assault wasn't sure it was an assault, there was no point pursuing it.

But he asked himself, then and again later, what would have happened if he and Saturday hadn't arrived at Purley Grange at the critical moment. If Hazel had gone back into the house alone.

It was one in the morning when the phone went. Still mostly asleep, Ash fumbled for it in the dark before it should wake the house. 'Wadayawant? It's late – or early.'

The very first words he heard snapped him awake. 'Gabriel, I need your help. I need you to come down here, now, and I need you not to ask why.'

'Saturday?' He'd found the bedside light by

now, but looking at the phone didn't tell him anything extra. 'Has something happened?'

'Please. Come now.'

There was never any question of him refusing. 'I'll be there in ten minutes.'

He pulled on his clothes, and he and Patience sneaked out of the house without a sound. He drove away as quietly as he could. But once he was out onto Highfield Road, he hit the gas.

Saturday must have been watching for him, because Ash had hardly pulled into the kerb in Railway Street before the boy had the door open and was waiting on the step, shifting edgily from one bare foot to the other. The light was on in the hall behind him: only as they met in the doorway did Ash get a proper look at him. What he saw shocked him to the core. The T-shirt Saturday slept in was torn and spattered with blood, and his hands were bloody to the wrists. There was blood on his face, too, though the delicate trickle from his left nostril seemed unlikely to have produced the volume evident about his person. There was a graze on his cheek and his knuckles were torn.

'God in heaven, Saturday – what have you been up to?'

Saturday swallowed. 'You should see the other guy.'

Ash gave a gruff chuckle. 'Yeah, right.'

'No, really. You need to come inside and see the other guy.'

Ash followed him down the narrow hall. The other guy was at the foot of the stairs, sprawled motionless on the threadbare carpet, his head resting just inside the kitchen door, one foot on the bottom step, one gloved hand twisted behind him. Blood – much more blood than there was on Saturday – pooled under his face, and there was a cricket bat on the floor beside him.

It was Oliver Ford, and Ash thought he was dead.

Twenty-Eight

'Where is he?'

Detective Inspector Gorman didn't mean to be difficult: he genuinely didn't know who Hazel wanted to know about first. 'Ford is in Norbold General, although they're transferring him to the head injuries unit in Birmingham. Desmond is being processed downstairs.'

Hazel blinked. She heard Saturday's proper name so seldom it didn't sound like someone she knew. 'You know he's a juvenile?'

Gorman nodded. 'Don't worry, I'll organise an appropriate adult before I interview him.'

'He has no family,' said Hazel. 'At least, none he's seen for years. He lodges with me, so I'm probably the next best thing.'

The DI raised one shaggy eyebrow until it merged with his hairline. 'You're too involved, Hazel. It wouldn't be – well, appropriate.'

'How about me?' asked Ash.

'You're a witness.'

237

'I wasn't there when . . . whatever happened, happened.'

Now the shaggy eyebrow dropped censoriously. 'Don't get coy with me, Gabriel, we all know what happened. Ford didn't beat himself unconscious with a cricket bat.'

'And Saturday didn't walk out to Purley Woods and break into Oliver's house in the middle of the night,' said Hazel sharply. 'Until we know who did what, we really don't know who's to blame.'

'Ford didn't break into your house either. He had a key.' He could tell from her expression that it was news to Hazel. 'You didn't give him a key?'

'No. There was no occasion to. When I offered to put him up while he was house-hunting, he thought I was joking.'

'Do you have your keys?'

She couldn't find them. 'I went home with Gabriel so I didn't need them.'

Gorman put a set on his desk. Hazel went to reach for them, but stopped herself in time. Anyway, she didn't need to handle them to be sure. The fob was a small pewter dragon she'd bought in a craft shop in Llangollen: there would be others, elsewhere in the country, but it was stretching credulity to think this might be one of them. 'Those are mine.'

'Did you give them to Ford?'

'I didn't give them to him.' She screwed up her eyes in the effort to remember. 'I suppose, in the . . . excitement . . . of leaving, I may have left them behind.'

Gorman sucked at his front teeth. 'So if Ford says he found them, he thought he ought to return them, but it was late so rather than wake you he let himself in to leave them on the kitchen table, that's entirely plausible?'

Hazel couldn't deny it. '*Is* that what he's saying?'

'Right now he isn't saying anything. He's in a drug-induced coma while the doctors assess his injuries. But I imagine that's how he'd explain his presence at Railway Street.' Gorman changed tack. 'Where did the cricket bat come from?'

'It's mine,' admitted Hazel.

'You play cricket?'

'A boyfriend left it behind, years ago. I held onto it because it's useful to keep something hefty by the front door when you're living alone and you're not always sure of the neighbours.'

Gorman raised an eyebrow. 'You've had trouble with the neighbours?'

'Not at Railway Street. Some of the police station houses I've stayed in, I've been glad of it.'

'And you keep it by the front door.'

She frowned, trying to remember. 'I used to. I haven't seen it recently.'

'So if Desmond says it was under his bed when he was woken by the sound of an intruder, that could be true?'

'Certainly it could. I don't go into Saturday's room if I can avoid it. If it was under his bed, I wouldn't have seen it.'

The DI was nodding slowly. 'Have you ever heard Desmond threaten Mr Ford?'

'*Saturday?*' Hazel was astonished. 'Don't be ridiculous! Why would Saturday threaten Oliver?'

Gorman swivelled his chair in Ash's direction. 'Can you think of a reason?'

Ash would have done a lot to keep Saturday out of trouble, but he wouldn't lie to the police for him. 'I know that they argued, and Ford hit him. But Saturday was in no position to retaliate, and he shrugged it off. The only person that I know threatened Ford was me.'

Hazel couldn't believe what she was hearing. She didn't know which part of that to query first. 'Oliver hit Saturday? When? And *why?* And why did *you* threaten him?'

'Ford hit Saturday because he blamed him for spoiling his big day at the museum. The second time, the time you were there as his . . . companion.' The hesitation was fractional. But Hazel noticed it, and felt herself reddening. 'And I threatened him yesterday morning, because he hit you. I told him that if he came near you again, I would plant him. And I meant,' Ash added seriously, 'every word of it.'

Gorman sucked his lip reflectively. 'And Ford went to Hazel's house, and ended up in Intensive Care. Gabriel – should I be asking where you were last night?'

'I was in my bed until Saturday called. But I can't prove it. If you want to treat me as a suspect, feel free.'

Hazel hadn't finished with Ash. 'I told you that was an accident.'

'I know what you told me.'

It was tempting, but in fact Gorman had no doubt who had put Oliver Ford in the hospital. The issue was not who but why. If the boy, alone in the house late at night, had been disturbed by the sound of an intruder and snatched up the cricket bat to protect himself, even if the force used was excessive, that was a valid defence. But if Saturday, stinging after an earlier encounter, saw an opportunity for revenge, and if instead of asking him to leave he'd waited for Ford to turn his back before setting about him with a blunt implement, that was attempted murder.

'I'll ask the Youth Offending Team to provide an appropriate adult and I'll interview the boy,' said the DI. 'See what he says.'

Hazel nodded sombrely, but Ash wasn't satisfied. 'Not until my solicitor gets here.'

The house in Railway Street was a crime scene. They returned to Highfield Road. Neither of them spoke. Hazel was still in shock, torn three different ways by her fondness for Saturday, her desperately confused feelings about Ford, and her obligations to the police service which employed her.

Ash didn't want to talk either. He was making a mental list of the things he needed to do to help Saturday deal with what was coming. Legal representation was the priority. Whether or not the boy had attacked Ford, he would need good advice and someone to speak for him. Ash didn't think Gorman wanted to nail him for something he hadn't done, or ascribe to him motives he hadn't been acting on. But a public figure had come to harm – possibly a great deal of harm – in Norbold, and there would be pressure to bring a culprit to justice.

Even if Saturday managed to convince the police that he'd acted in self-defence, that might not be the end of it. Ford's public would never believe in his innocence, would clamour for retribution. Nor would the boy be safe in custody. There wasn't a lot of Saturday. His quick wits, grubby charm and cat-like reactions could get him out of only so much trouble. In a Young Offenders' Institution, sooner or later someone slower, less charming, and possessed of a set of home-made knuckle-dusters, would get hold of him and break him in a million pieces. Gabriel Ash had failed, not long ago, to prevent the death in custody of one young man. He would do everything in his power to prevent the same thing happening again.

He spent fifteen minutes on the phone to his solicitor. Afterwards, in the hall, he found Frankie leaving for church. She had the boys with her. 'I've been promising to show them where I go on Sunday mornings. This seems as good a chance as any.'

Ash cast her a grateful smile. Right now he wasn't particularly concerned with his sons' religious education, but he appreciated her getting them off-side while he attempted to deal with this latest crisis.

After the front door had closed, Hazel fixed Ash with an armour-piercing bodkin of a look. 'Oliver hit Saturday?'

Ash nodded. Suddenly he felt very weary.

'How do you know?'

'Saturday told me.'

Hazel picked her words carefully. 'Saturday has been known to lie.'

'I don't think he was lying about this.'

'Oliver blamed him because . . .?' And there she stopped.

Ash finished the sentence for her. 'Because my boys gave him the slip, and you left Ford at Wittering in order to help round them up. It seems Ford came looking for you the next morning. You weren't at Railway Street but Saturday was. Ford was angry, Saturday was cheeky, and Ford slapped him.'

Hazel was remembering that morning. It had begun in Superintendent Maybourne's office, proceeded by means of an argument with Ash, and finished with the encounter – slightly puzzling at the time – with Ford in Railway Street. 'He was waiting in his car when I got home. Saturday had gone out. I thought it was a bit odd at the time. Saturday isn't usually up and about much before lunch.'

'No. Well, Ford came looking for you and got Saturday. They argued, Ford hit him, and Saturday did a runner.' He always used slang as if he'd only just heard it and wasn't sure he was using it right.

'Oliver didn't tell me any of this.'

'Well, he wouldn't, would he?'

'Saturday should have told me.'

'Probably he should. But I understand why he didn't.'

Hazel thought a little longer. 'And' – still

selecting her words with tweezers – 'you slapped Oliver.'

'Yes.'

'And threatened him.'

'Yes, I did.'

'Because of me?'

Ash gave a snort of exasperation. 'No, because I didn't agree with his stance on the Knights of Malta! Of course because of you. He hit you, Hazel. You can make all the excuses for him that you like, but that's what he did. He hit you in the face with his laptop. If I'd been there, *I'd* have taken a cricket bat to his head!'

Hazel considered that in silence. Finally she said, 'Do you think that's what Saturday did? Saw an opportunity for pay-back and took it?'

'I don't know,' Ash said honestly. 'I hope not. I hope he woke up in the middle of the night, heard someone creeping around downstairs, and lashed out with the first thing that came to hand because he thought he was in danger. If it wasn't like that – if he knew it was Ford and decided to take his revenge – I'm not sure what any of us will be able to do for him.'

'I could try talking to Oliver . . .' She didn't finish the sentence. Ash knew as well as she there was no guarantee that, even if Ford woke from his coma, he would be able to conduct an intelligent conversation or reach a rational decision based on it.

Ash hunched his shoulders like a bear emerging from hibernation. 'You can't be seen interfering with a witness, and anyway it wouldn't do any good. This was a serious assault: it's not down to Ford to press charges. The police will bring the case unless Saturday can persuade them he was acting in self-defence. Even if Gorman believes him, he may feel he has to put it before a jury. Because of who Ford is, and the severity of his injuries.'

'We have to do *something*! *I* have to do something. None of this would have happened except for me.' Hazel's gaze was hot on his face. 'If I hadn't taken up with Oliver in the first place. If I'd kept a professional distance.'

'You did nothing wrong,' insisted Ash. 'No one can look into the future and guess what the ultimate results of their actions might be. We'll do everything we can for Saturday, but in the end he may have to pay for what he did. We'll know more after Dick Gervais has talked to him. If there's a defence to be made, we'll know then.'

Hazel nodded numbly. At length, embarrassed, she said, 'Gabriel – can I stay here for a bit? I'm not sure when I'll be able to go back to Railway Street. And anyway, I don't really want to be alone.'

Ash's jaw dropped as if she'd just said something very stupid. 'Of *course* you're staying here!'

Hazel had a clear mental picture of Ash's family solicitor. She imagined he had been inherited, along with the fine, run-down house and eighteen-year-old car, from Ash's mother, was of much the same generation, and wore a small moustache and a homburg hat.

She was wrong.

Dick Gervais was younger than Ash, better looking, and much better dressed. He did sport a moustache, but it was a generous, even dashing, affair as blond as his hair. He arrived at the house mid-afternoon and sat down with them at the kitchen table.

His expression was grim. 'The boy's in trouble, Gabriel.'

'How does he say it happened?'

'He says he was in bed, asleep, when something woke him. He listened and heard someone downstairs. He wondered if Ms Best had changed her mind and come home. But the hall light wasn't on, which he thought was odd.'

'His door was open?' interjected Ash.

'No. When the light's on, he can see it through the gap underneath. He went out onto the landing, and listened some more. He could hear somebody moving downstairs, and he was pretty sure by this time' – to Hazel – 'that it wasn't you. No lights, and a man's footsteps on the kitchen lino.

'The cricket bat was under his bed – he doesn't know why. He went back for it, to defend himself if needs be, and tiptoed downstairs. He says he was going to call the police – that he doesn't have a mobile phone and the land-line's in the hall.'

Hazel nodded. 'That's true.'

Dick Gervais elevated an eyebrow. 'He really doesn't have a mobile?'

Hazel bristled slightly. 'Three months ago he didn't have a bed. *I* bought his bed. The phone can wait until he can buy one for himself.'

246

The solicitor continued. 'He says he got to the phone while the intruder was in the kitchen. But when he lifted it to dial, the click must have warned the guy because he came through the door shoulder first and knocked Desmond the length of the hall. He still had no idea who it was, he says. They struggled, with Desmond getting the worst of it. Then, still in the dark, his hand found the bat. He swung at the guy on top of him, landing a blow around shoulder level, and the guy yelled, then renewed his attack.

'Desmond swung again – he says he was still flat on the floor – and hit the guy's head, and this time he went down and stayed down. Desmond got out from under him and switched the light on. He says that was the first he knew that it was Oliver Ford.'

They sat back in their chairs and avoided one another's eyes for a moment. Then Hazel said, carefully, 'Well, that sounds pretty plausible.'

'It sounds possible,' amended Gervais. 'I think plausible may be pushing the envelope. I'm not sure how plausible Detective Inspector Gorman found it. He was asking a lot of questions he wasn't getting answers to.' He looked directly at Ash. 'He wanted to know why the boy phoned you instead of either the police or an ambulance.'

'What did Saturday say?' asked Hazel.

'He said he panicked. He knew he was in trouble, he wanted someone there who was on his side.' Gervais looked at Ash. 'How long did it take you to get there?'

'Ten minutes, maybe a little over.'

'If Ford dies, that ten minutes may be the difference between a plea of self-defence and a conviction for manslaughter.'

'The man was an intruder in someone else's house in the middle of the night,' Ash said sharply. 'He came unannounced, let himself in with Hazel's keys, and prowled round her house in the dark. He expected to find Hazel there, and since Saturday works nights he probably expected to find her alone. Never mind what Saturday was thinking. Shouldn't we be asking what *Ford* had in mind?'

Hazel paled. 'No. Oliver wouldn't do that.'

'Why do you think he went there? To apologise, to see if you were all right? At one o'clock in the morning? Hazel, he came to your house in the middle of the night to force himself on you. To show you that it wasn't your decision when your relationship ended. You walked out on him, and I'm pretty sure that women aren't supposed to walk out on Oliver Ford.'

'No,' she said again, insistently. 'Gabriel – you're wrong. I know him. He may be a far from perfect human being, but he wouldn't do that. However it ended, we were genuinely fond of each other. He isn't a psychopath! I lived with him, for pity's sake: if he'd been capable of *that*, I'd have known.'

'Two days ago you thought everything between you was fine,' Ash said pointedly. 'Isn't that what you told me? Then you realised that a relationship you were prepared to invest years of your life in wasn't worth an hour of his time to Oliver Ford. You were wrong about him,

248

Hazel. You were wrong then, and you're wrong now.'

'I *was* wrong about him,' she conceded fiercely. 'But not that wrong. I was in love, or thought I was, and maybe that blinded me to his faults. But don't tell me I was in love with a rapist, because I would have known. *I would have known.*'

'Can't you see, this is what he does? He's so used to people dancing attendance on him that he thinks he has a God-given right to have what he wants, when he wants it. And he wasn't going to take no for an answer from you.'

Dick Gervais interrupted the developing row. 'You may very well be right, Gabriel. But suspicions aren't enough. Even if he recovers, Ford's not going to say something that will exonerate Saturday and bring the police to his own door. If he doesn't recover, or doesn't remember, we can only speculate. The plain fact is that it was Ford who got hurt, and it was Saturday swinging the cricket bat.'

Hazel swallowed. 'What about Oliver? Is there any word from the hospital?'

'He has a significant head injury. As with most head injuries, the doctors will only know *how* significant when they wake him up and ask him.'

'Could I – should I – try to see him? Will they let me?' Her voice cracked. 'I don't know what to do. I don't know what to *feel*. I thought I loved him. Forty-eight hours ago I thought we might spend our lives together. Then suddenly it was over; and now maybe he's going to die, and I don't know how to feel about that.'

Already Ash was ashamed of his uncharacteristic impatience. 'You're bound to feel confused. You couldn't have seen any of this coming. And you couldn't have prevented it if you had.'

'But that isn't true, is it?' she countered fretfully. 'Saturday and Oliver Ford would never have met except through me. They move in different worlds. Now Oliver's fighting for his life, and Saturday's facing prison, and whatever you say it *was* avoidable. If I hadn't got involved with Oliver, it would never have happened. But I enjoyed what he had to offer – just not enough to pay what he wanted for it. I wasn't content to be a decoration on his sleeve, which is what he thought he was buying.'

She dashed away mortified tears with the back of her wrist. 'Well, maybe he was entitled to think that. Maybe it was me who misread the situation. I wanted to have it both ways: to enjoy the attentions of a rich and famous man, but still be treated as an equal. And maybe that wasn't fair. It wasn't him being unreasonable – it was me. Even before I got him hurt, I short-changed him.'

Ash tried to answer her, but Hazel rushed on, unheeding in her distress. 'And what about Saturday? He wouldn't have hit Oliver with a cricket bat in any other circumstances. Whatever his motives, it's my fault he found himself in a situation he didn't know how to deal with. This is my doing, Gabriel. I've injured them both, and I don't think I can bear it.'

By then she was crying openly: not a ladylike sniffle into a lace hanky, but a great stormy tempest of tears that coursed in untidy rivulets down her hot cheeks and round the ragged corners of her lips. There was no dignity in it. Emotion was tearing her apart, and that was how she looked: like someone suffering torture.

Ash went quietly to her and, stooping, folded her shaking frame against his breast. With nothing to say that would make things better, he said nothing, just held her and waited for the storm to pass.

Gervais watched the pair of them compassionately. He was no stranger to emotional outbursts, regularly had to take a time out while his clients composed themselves. He wished he could make everything all right, and – as so often – wasn't at all sure he would be able to. Sometimes the best he could do was help them to find the least painful route through the gauntlet.

At length he cleared his throat and moved onto the firmer ground of practical advice. 'As far as visiting Mr Ford, it would be better not to. It wouldn't do any good while he's still unconscious and it might conceivably do harm.'

It wasn't Oliver Ford's condition that concerned Ash. 'Can I see Saturday?'

'Not at the moment. You're not family, you're not part of his legal team, and you *are* a potential witness. Later it may be possible, but not yet.'

'How is he? Is he coping?'

The solicitor looked at Ash as if he was mad. 'Of course he isn't coping. He's scared to death. He's a seventeen-year-old boy facing the possibility of life imprisonment. He has no idea what the future holds for him, only that he's in a whole heap of trouble and he thinks he's got to face it alone.'

'I hope you put him straight on that,' said Ash gruffly.

'Of course I did. I told him I was there because you'd sent me, that we'd both be there for him for as long as he needed us, and that however difficult things got, we would somehow find a way through them. And now I'm telling you – both of you – the same thing.'

'Thank you,' said Gabriel Ash.

Twenty-Nine

Superintendent Maybourne served coffee in small china cups. Detective Inspector Gorman tried not to break the handle off with his thick blunt fingers. The coffee, too, was not what he was accustomed to. He suspected it was foreign and expensive, whereas what he really liked was supermarket instant served in a pint mug.

But for all her airs and graces, Gorman was developing both respect and regard for Superintendent Maybourne. The crystalline accent and perfect manners were no doubt invaluable at Home Office soirées, but immediately under the polished surface was a copper. Perhaps not an old-fashioned, beat-pounding, beer-swilling, collar-feeling sort of copper, but someone with all of a copper's instincts allied to a keen grasp of the modern world. Sometimes Dave Gorman thought he'd been born twenty years too late, might have felt more at home in that simpler time of blaggers and rozzers. But Grace Maybourne had been born at exactly the right time, and knew instinctively how to reconcile the competing demands on a modern police service.

She pressed him to a small iced fancy. The fact that they were both still working on a Sunday afternoon was excuse enough for a little indulgence. 'I suppose the only real issue is, is the boy telling the truth? Did these events transpire essentially as he says they did? Was Oliver Ford the victim of his own misjudgement in entering someone else's house, unannounced, in the middle of the night?'

The small china cup came with a small china saucer. Even the small iced fancy was too large to sit comfortably on the edge of the small china saucer, so Gorman had to balance the saucer on his knee while holding the cup in one hand and the cake in the other. It left him incapable of even the most careful gesture.

Trying not to spray crumbs he mumbled, 'He's lying. I don't know yet what he's lying about, but I'm pretty damn sure that what he's telling us isn't the pure unvarnished truth.'

'Yet it seems clear that he didn't instigate this meeting.' She saw Gorman mentally translating and hid a smile. 'Ford came to his house, not the other way round.'

Another determined assault on it and at least the cake was gone, leaving him only the bitter coffee to struggle with. 'Ford went to Railway

Street looking for Hazel Best. He didn't phone first or he'd have known she wasn't there. He just rolled up in the middle of the night and let himself in with her keys.'

'Which does not seem an entirely reasonable thing to do,' said Maybourne. 'At the very least he risked frightening her.'

They both considered that for a moment before dismissing the idea.

'They'd been living together,' Gorman pointed out. 'Perhaps he didn't think he needed an appointment.'

'But the relationship was over. It ended in acrimony and possibly violence – Hazel isn't sure that Ford meant to hurt her, but he did. Surely, from that point onwards, a reasonable person would not feel entitled to treat a former partner's property as his own. If he was prepared to enter her house uninvited . . .' She didn't finish the sentence, but the thought hung in the air between them.

Gorman gave a lugubrious sniff. He didn't hold much of a candle for either Ford or Saturday, but one of them was in the hospital and the other seemed to be responsible, and somehow he had to work out what had happened. 'Or maybe Ford didn't let himself in. Maybe he knocked and Desmond let him in.'

'In the middle of the night?'

'He works till late at a filling station, doesn't get home till midnight. And Ford works in television. Maybe both of them consider one a.m. the early evening.'

Superintendent Maybourne refreshed both their cups. Her brow was creased with thought.

'Why would Ford go inside if Hazel wasn't there? Why would Desmond ask him in?'

'The boy might ask him in,' said Gorman slowly, 'if he saw a chance to get his own back for that slap. Instead of saying Hazel wasn't there, he might have asked Ford to wait downstairs while he woke her. What he was actually doing, of course, was fetching the cricket bat. Only instead of waiting, Ford got impatient or suspicious and went to see what Desmond was up to. They met at the foot of the stairs, where Desmond swung fast enough to take Ford down.'

They regarded one another in silence for a while, playing the scenario over in their minds. It was at least as plausible as the account Saturday had given.

Finally Maybourne murmured, 'If you're right, that's premeditation. Not self-defence but attempted murder.'

'I know.' Gorman gave up on the horrible coffee and put the cup and saucer on the superintendent's desk.

'You're happy with that?'

'Of course I'm not! He's a seventeen-year-old kid: I don't want to charge him with something that'll put a blight on the rest of his life. But I think that version makes more sense than the one he's giving us. Oliver Ford may be many things, not all of them admirable, but are we really going to say that he went there with the intention of committing rape? The man's a national institution!'

'Does that preclude him from being a rapist?' asked Maybourne coolly.

Gorman shook his head. 'No. If history's any guide, a national institution is more likely to be a self-centred, self-indulgent psychopath than the man on the Clapham omnibus. But you can't level an accusation like that against someone – anyone, but most of all someone with expensive lawyers – just because it's possible. His actions may have been nothing worse than thoughtless. All we know for sure is that Oliver Ford and Saul Desmond fought, and Desmond smashed Ford's head in with a cricket bat.'

'What do we know about this boy?' asked the superintendent. 'What sort of form has he got?'

Gorman gave a prop-forward sort of shrug. 'Petty theft. Nothing violent, so far as we're aware. He was homeless until Hazel took him in.'

'Yes. Why did she do that?'

Of course, Superintendent Maybourne hadn't come to Norbold until after Superintendent Fountain vacated the position. 'Gabriel Ash was getting himself roughed up by the local yoof. Desmond helped him out. Hazel took an interest in him after that.'

'She must have thought he was worth helping.'

'A lot of the time Hazel's right about things. But not always. I'd stake a week's wages that boy's lying to us. About what happened, or how it happened, or why it happened.'

'And why he didn't get help for Ford as soon as he realised what he'd done.'

Gorman nodded. 'He's seventeen, not seven. He knows that when somebody's bleeding on your lino, you call an ambulance. You do *not* phone a friend.'

'I think it's just as well,' murmured Superintendent Maybourne, 'that Oliver Ford isn't the only one who can afford expensive lawyers.'

After tea, Ash and Patience rounded up the boys for a walk to the park. It was something they'd started doing when Ash first brought his sons home, back in August when the evenings were still long. Now it was November and it was dark by tea-time. But the weather remained mild, there were street lamps all the way to the park, and the boys brought flashlights and enjoyed the spookiness of their familiar playground turned strange by the setting of the sun.

Patience played a kind of vampire hide-and-seek with them, lurking in the black shrubbery then springing out at them, to the accompaniment of delighted shrieks. She cast Ash a mildly embarrassed look and he could have sworn she shrugged.

At the pond, transformed by night to a sea whose far shore was invisible, Guy bemoaned the fact that he hadn't brought a boat to sail. (Ash was in the process of making them a proper pond-yacht, with two masts and a bowsprit and self-steering, but it was taking longer than he'd anticipated and in the meantime they were playing with something mass-produced and shop-bought but, and this was important, ready to sail.)

Gilbert was typically dismissive. 'You'd lose it in the dark.'

'I'd keep my torch on it.' Guy demonstrated.

257

'And when it went further than the torch could reach?' Gilbert showed how the pool of light grew paler with distance until there was nothing left.

The younger brother was undeterred. 'I'd get in and fetch it.'

'You'd freeze!' hooted Gilbert. 'That water's freezing.'

'No it isn't.' Guy, ever practical, demonstrated that too by the simple expedient of thrusting his arm into it, windcheater and all, up to the elbow.

Ash snatched him back before any more of him disappeared. But actually Guy was right. He was wet but not chilled. Ash made some ineffectual gestures with his handkerchief and then gave up. 'Tell me if you're getting cold.'

'I'm not cold,' said Guy stoutly.

Ash grinned. 'Tough guy.' The little boy beamed.

They walked home then. Ash put his younger son into a hot bath and hung his clothes over a radiator, and then he got them both off to bed. Frankie had gone out with friends for the evening, and with her unerring instinct for kindness had invited Hazel along, so the house was quiet now. Ash sat in his study, nursing a mug of coffee and his dog's head, his deep-set eyes unfocused with thought.

Then he phoned Detective Inspector Gorman.

Dave Gorman had finally shut up shop and taken his girlfriend out for a meal. She'd been his girlfriend for so long that he really should have taken the next step by now. But perhaps a looser arrangement suited them both, because she dropped no hints about marriage and tolerated his long hours and interrupted weekends with a degree of equanimity unusual in police spouses. When his phone rang, she just raised an eyebrow and indicated that he should take the call.

'It's Ash,' said Ash.

'I *know*,' snapped Gorman. 'What do you want?'

Ash sounded puzzled. 'How did you know?'

Gorman breathed at his phone much as the dragon must have breathed at St George. 'Because when someone I know phones me, their name comes up on the screen. *The same way it does on yours, Gabriel, if you took the trouble to look.* I'm in the middle of dinner here – what do you want?'

'You've got my number in your phone?' He sounded quite touched.

'Of course I have. Something weird happens in Norbold, there's always a good chance you're involved. Gabriel, I'm with someone. *What do you want?*'

Ash refocused on what he'd spent the last hour thinking about. 'When I found Ford in the hall at Railway Street, he was wearing gloves.'

'Yes. So?'

'Why? It isn't cold. He didn't walk from Purley Woods – he drove and parked at Hazel's door. I'm not wearing gloves yet, and I'm guessing you're not. Why was Ford?'

'I bet,' Gorman said heavily, 'if I'm patient, you'll tell me.'

'For the same reason all criminals wear gloves: to avoid leaving fingerprints. He wasn't returning Hazel's keys, and he wasn't there to apologise

259

and ask for another chance. He was there to take his revenge on her. He reckoned that if there was no forensic evidence it would be his word against hers, and most people would take his.'

'If you're talking about rape' – Gorman dropped his voice discreetly; still his companion and half the restaurant stared at him – 'fingerprints aren't the only evidence.'

'They'd been living together,' Ash reminded him. 'Anything else could be explained away. But fresh fingerprints would prove he was in her house after they'd broken up. Everything else could be open to interpretation, but fresh fingerprints would put him somewhere he'd no business being. Inspector – he had only one reason for going to Railway Street, and he knew what he intended to do there before he left home. He brought his gloves with him.'

Across the table, the DI's long-suffering girl-friend had finally had enough. She folded her napkin and went to rise. Gorman waved her back, his broad face twisted with apology. 'Gabriel, I can't talk about it right now. Call me tomorrow. But I'll be honest with you: a pair of gloves isn't going to make the Crown Prosecution Service throw in the towel. If you want to get that boy off the hook, it'll take something that Ford's lawyers can't explain away. Something that marks him, not Desmond, as the aggressor. Without that, I think the kid's going down.'

Thirty

Hazel spent much of the next morning in her room, sewing. Keen to contribute to the running of the household while she remained at Highfield Road, she had taken over the task of keeping the Ash boys decently clad. This could involve anything from replacing a button to stitching up a torn pocket to patching the knees of trousers which, against repeated injunctions, had once again taken part in a game of football (Guy) or climbed a tree (Gilbert).

She came downstairs around eleven and, finding Ash staring wordlessly into the kitchen range, made coffee and toast. 'You look deep in thought.'

He sighed. 'I'm worried.'

'About Saturday.' It wasn't a question.

'Dave Gorman's convinced he's lying.'

Hazel pulled a chair closer to the range. 'What about? I don't see how else it could have happened. It's typical of Oliver that he couldn't wait until morning to talk to me. He let himself into the house in the middle of the night. Saturday thought he was a burglar, they fought and Oliver got the worst of it.'

Ash didn't want to argue with her again about the reason for Ford's visit to Railway Street. After everything that had happened, everything Ford had done, there were still depths that she

261

didn't believe him capable of plumbing. In one way it didn't matter. The evidence that would give Saturday the chance of a future would also prove that Hazel was wrong about Ford. Ash was painfully aware that he could only help one of his friends by crushing the other.

In another way it mattered very much, because it cast light on the kind of man Oliver Ford really was, and therefore the situation in which Saturday had found himself that night. Ash might have left Hazel the small comfort of believing that Ford was just a bit of a bully, if that hadn't tacitly loaded the blame for his current condition onto their young friend. 'Have you got your phone on you?'

She took it out. 'No one's called me.'

'You understand these things better than I do. Is there a way he could have stopped calls from reaching you?'

'That was the woods,' explained Hazel. 'There are lots of places, particularly out in the country, where you can't get a signal.'

Ash persisted. 'Have you heard from anyone since you got back to Norbold?'

She was still looking bewildered. 'Who'd call me? You're right here, and Oliver's in a coma, and there's no one else . . .' But she let the sentence die away. Of course there was. There was her father. There was Meadowvale – she'd been waiting to hear when she could return to work. There were all the people trying to sell her double-glazing. 'Wait.'

It didn't take her three minutes. Then she threw the phone down on the kitchen table, and turned back to Ash, her face grey. 'Well,' she managed, 'it looks as if he knows more about how things work than he let on.'

'He cut you off from anyone you could have turned to for help,' said Ash quietly. If he felt any sense of triumph, he kept it to himself. 'He disabled your car, then took it into town while you were out walking; and he disabled your phone so Diego couldn't let you know when the car was fixed. No one from Meadowvale could contact you, and neither could I. He made a prison for you out in those woods, and he thought he could keep you there as long as it amused him. When you walked out, he was angry enough to do anything.'

It was impossible for her to go on thinking anything else. 'I've been so *stupid*,' she whispered. 'I believed – I honestly believed – that, unlikely a couple as we made, we were good together. I enjoyed being with him; I thought he liked being with me.'

'He obviously did,' murmured Ash. 'On his own terms.'

'He thought he'd bought me. But was that his fault, or mine?'

'His,' said Ash immediately. 'Slavery has been illegal in Britain for two hundred years.'

Hazel stared into the range, finally comprehending the enormity of the danger she had been in. When she found her voice it was thick with grief and anger. 'Dear God, Gabriel, how could I be so *wrong* about him? He never loved me. He just wanted my head on his wall. A trophy. A damned fish that he'd hooked.'

Ash felt her suffering as if it were his own. 'I'm sorry.'

'You never trusted him, did you? Even Saturday saw through him. Why didn't I? Why did I let him treat me like that? I'm not a giddy teenager drooling over her first boyfriend, I'm a professional woman in her late twenties. A police officer, for God's sake! I know about domestic violence. I know about men who intimidate women, sometimes without laying a hand on them.

'For years I've quietly despised those women for not doing something about it. For saying it wasn't true, or it was a mistake, or he only did it because he was drunk or when she made him angry. For loving him anyway. For accepting pain and humiliation as the price of not being alone.' Hazel vented a shaky laugh. 'And now I'm one of those women. That'll hurt for longer than the eye will.'

If he sympathised again, Ash thought she would burst into tears. 'I'm just glad you came home with me that night, instead of staying at Railway Street.'

Hazel nodded slowly. 'You're right about that, too, aren't you? He wasn't there to talk. His pride was hurt, and he wanted to hurt me back. If I hadn't got away from him . . .' Which reminded her of a question she still hadn't had an answer to. 'How did you find me? With my phone out of action I never got round to sending you the Purley address. How come you turned up there? How did you know I needed you, and how did you know where to come?'

'Ford isn't the only one who knows how things

work,' said Ash wryly. 'Saturday ran a trace on Ford's phone. I was worried about you, wanted to check that you were OK. I thought you might have got involved in something you shouldn't have. I never for a moment thought I'd find you bleeding on the driveway.'

'I genuinely thought that was an accident,' Hazel said, shaking her head now at her own naivety. 'But it wasn't, was it? It was part of the pattern. He punishes people who cross him. Who won't go along with his Ford-centric view of the world.'

The situation was far from resolved. But Ash felt it like a weight off his shoulders, that she finally understood how little Ford deserved her lingering loyalty. He had his clear-eyed friend back again, and together they could concentrate on helping Saturday.

'All right,' he said. 'So it's pretty clear that Ford deserved to be brained with a cricket bat. Unfortunately, that doesn't give Saturday carte blanche for doing it. The only way he's walking away from this is if he's telling the God-honest truth – that he went downstairs to call the police, and took the bat to protect himself. I still don't understand what it was doing under his bed.'

That was easy. 'He's a teenage boy!' said Hazel. '*Everything* you can't find is under a teenage boy's bed. Pots, crockery, clothes, books. Anything that will fit, and some things that won't. The underneath of a teenage boy's bed is a combination of wardrobe, chest of drawers, bookshelf, filing cabinet and rubbish bin. Wait till yours are a bit older and you'll see what I mean.'

Ash's grin faded. 'Are you regretting now that you took him in?'

Hazel shook her coppery head. 'He was worth taking a chance on. Even if he's to blame for what happened, even if he has to pay for it, I'll always be glad I gave him that chance. He might have been able to use it.'

'He still might,' said Ash. 'Don't give up on him yet.'

Their mugs were empty. He got up to refill them. Frankie, concerned at the amount of coffee he was getting through each week, had tried to ration him, but none of the alternatives – soft drinks, tea, cocoa – lubricated his thinking muscles in the same way. He was thinking now, and didn't like what he was coming up with.

'Hazel, before this is over you're going to find yourself under attack. People who can't possibly know what happened, who have no conceivable stake in the outcome except that they know Ford's face from the television, are going to take sides. And some of them will back the little guy and more will support Ford, but both lots will have it in for you. You'll be accused of exploiting Ford's friendship, and of using Saturday to get your revenge when Ford tired of your demands and sent you away.'

'Sent me ...?' squawked Hazel in astonishment.

'These are not rational people,' said Ash apologetically. 'They'll hear only what they want to hear; they'll twist the facts until they scream for mercy in order to tell a story they want to believe. Ford is a celebrity. That warps the way people think. They start feeling that, because they know someone's face, he's a kind of friend. It's absurd, but our emotions predate the invention of television. A primitive part of their brains thinks that someone they see in their own living rooms must be a friend, and that you owe it to your friends to support them. And if Ford's the good guy, Saturday – and you – must be the bad guys. Don't be too shocked to find yourself in the fall-out zone.'

'People do get silly about celebrities. And I should know,' said Hazel grimly. 'I wouldn't have made a fool of myself like that over a grocer, or a landscape gardener. I was flattered by his attentions, and not just because I liked him but because of who he is. I can't deny it – it's the only thing that explains how I behaved. As if different rules apply when you're dealing with someone famous.

'It's not healthy. No one should be given the idea they're that special. It's . . . corrosive. Time and again, last year's poster-boy turns into this year's mug-shot because they start believing the everyday rules and conventions we all live by don't apply to them.'

'They start believing in their own myth,' agreed Ash. 'They start to believe they can do anything they want. *Have* anything they want.'

Hazel nodded slowly. 'Oliver seemed to think that the limits and frustrations that restrict other people shouldn't apply to him.'

'Like others before him,' said Ash, 'he believed that his popularity rendered him invulnerable. That he could take what he wanted and no one could stop him. He wanted you, and he wasn't going to take no for an answer. And that's his fault, of course it is. But everyone who subscribes to the culture of the celebrity – following what they do and say with religious zeal, as if being avid self-publicists was enough to make their activities important – bears some responsibility too. They create monsters: they can't pretend it's nothing to do with them when those monsters run amok.'

Hazel gave a weary sigh. 'And now they're going to find, once again, that one of their idols has feet of clay right up to his armpits. I still don't see why they'd blame me.'

'If we can prove that Ford was the author of his own misfortune, they'll turn against him. But while there's still a chance that he was an innocent victim, they'll blame you for introducing Ford to the juvenile delinquent who beat his head in. They'll be vocal, and vitriolic, and some of them will be threatening.

'The media, too, will be deeply interested in what's passed between you,' he added. 'I'm surprised we haven't had them at the front door yet. Gorman must be sitting on some of the details, but he won't be able to do that for much longer. You need to think now, before it all kicks off, how you're going to handle it.'

Hazel felt the burden of Ash's concerns settle on her. She had blamed herself for what happened at Railway Street, but she hadn't really expected anyone else to blame her. She saw now that was naive. Of course it was going to get unpleasant. It would get even more unpleasant when she stood up for her lover's assailant, and made dreadful allegations about the injured man.

'It doesn't have to matter,' she rallied fiercely. 'Saturday's whole future is at stake. He needs me to say what I know, and what I think, and anyone who doesn't like it can do the other thing. What else am I going to do – skulk behind the sofa while Oliver's fan club bays for Saturday's blood? They think Oliver Ford is worthy of their adulation, do they? Let's see if they still think that when I've had my say!'

Ash's heart was so full that for a moment he hardly trusted himself to speak. He managed only by concentrating on practicalities. 'One thing's for sure – you can't go back to Railway Street until all this is settled.'

'That could be months! I'm not giving up my house on the off-chance that some Ford apologist might shout rude words through my letterbox. It's very kind of you, Gabriel, and maybe I'll impose on you for a few more days. But then I'm going home, and if there's trouble I'll deal with it. I just about managed to escape one gilded cage. I'm sure as hell not locking *myself* up where the world can't get at me!'

Her determination filled him with quiet terror. 'A few more days?'

'At the most.'

Ash drew a deep breath. 'Then you'd better collect your car. And I'd better . . .' He let the sentence fade, his eyes slipping out of focus.

Eventually Hazel prompted him. 'You'd better what?'

'This isn't the first time someone's tried to

269

take Oliver Ford's head off. Once could be a misunderstanding: twice is starting to look like a pattern. I need to talk to Rachid Iqbal again. I need to find out exactly why he wanted Ford dead.'

Thirty-One

He began with DI Gorman. But he didn't expect to learn much at Meadowvale, and so it proved. 'CTC collected him from the hospital when the doctors said he could travel,' said Gorman. 'That's a week ago. I don't know where he is now. I'm not sure who you'd need to ask.'

Ash didn't know anyone at Counter Terrorism Command, but he knew someone who would.

He took the train, and he didn't phone ahead. It might be a wasted journey, but he thought it would be harder for Philip Welbeck to refuse him a favour – another one – face to face than on the phone.

He had, of course, no right to ask. There had been a time, years ago, when Gabriel Ash had been a valuable member of Welbeck's team in the offices with no name-plate round the back of Whitehall. His title had been Security Analyst, and his job had consisted largely of reading reports, from all manner of official and unofficial sources, collating the information they contained, and making assessments on which government policy could be based. It wasn't a glamorous or exciting job, but he was good at it for five years. So good that it cost him his family and perhaps his sanity.

He'd been well taken care of, both financially and medically. The therapist Laura Fry who had helped him beat back the madness and was still a sheet anchor in stormy weather was employed by Welbeck. And only this summer Welbeck had pulled enough strings to furnish a good-sized orchestra to help Ash get his family back. He probably thought – was entitled to think – he'd repaid everything Ash was owed.

But Ash couldn't afford to keep count. He needed another favour, he needed it now, so he got on the London train and spent the journey rehearsing his arguments.

Welbeck was in his office. With no time to arrange a prior engagement, he greeted Ash affably. 'Gabriel, what a nice surprise! You're looking well. How are the boys?'

Ash murmured that they were fine, and so was he.

'I don't suppose . . . No, you'd have said if you had.'

'What?'

'Heard anything from your wife.' Welbeck waited.

Gabriel Ash had never lied to his superior, neither during his time in these offices nor since. Welbeck knew what Cathy Ash had done, and why she'd done it. He knew that she was implicated in men's deaths.

But he also knew Ash, and suspected that if the woman he'd loved had turned up again in the last three months, out of money, out of friends and out of places to hide, Ash would have helped her.

But Ash met his gaze without flinching. 'Nothing. I don't know where she is.'

Welbeck was satisfied. 'So, to what do I owe the pleasure of your visit?'

'I need to talk to Rachid Iqbal.'

'Who?'

This was disingenuous. Philip Welbeck never forgot a name. He never forgot a face. He never forgot a fact.

Ash didn't dignify the ploy with a response. He knew it was a delaying tactic, that in the few seconds it had earned him, Welbeck had pulled up a mental file on the museum incident and all its participants and was now listing in order of likelihood the reasons for Ash's request.

'I want to know why he tried to kill Oliver Ford.'

'We asked him,' said Welbeck smoothly. 'I say we – I mean, of course, CTC. He wouldn't tell us.'

'He might tell me.'

'Why?'

'Because he came close to telling me before. He knew my friend was in danger. He didn't want any harm to come to her.'

'And did it?'

'No. At least, not much. But it was a close-run thing. Now Ford is in hospital, and another friend is accused of trying to kill him.' In a few sentences Ash sketched in as much of the background as was necessary for Welbeck to understand the situation.

A sly little half-smile gathering the corners of his eyes suggested that very little of this was news to Welbeck. Whatever information he had must have come from his own sources: thirty-six hours after the event, the media still hadn't learned the details of Ford's incapacity.

'You knew?' said Ash.

The smile broadened. 'Gabriel, dear boy, it's my job to know. Everything. Had you forgotten? And it's my abiding delight to know everything that touches you.' Welbeck had the habit of addressing Ash as an older man addresses a younger, although they were contemporaries. It also amused him to speak like a character from Dickens.

'Can you arrange it?'

Welbeck considered for a moment longer. For a man who had been off the staff for four years, Gabriel Ash was consuming a lot of resources. On the other hand . . . Philip Welbeck had made a career out of keeping his options open. 'I imagine I could.'

'Will you?'

'Will you share with me whatever he tells you?'

There was no reason to refuse. Iqbal would assume as much: he wouldn't tell Ash anything he didn't want CTC to learn. 'Yes.'

'Let me make a phone-call.'

By now Iqbal had been in the hands of CTC for a week. Ash expected him to look worse than when last they met, when Iqbal was still recovering in Norbold General Infirmary. But in fact the young man had put on a little weight. The dark rings under his eyes were no longer so prominent, and the burns on his face had subsided much as Hazel's had done. The clothes he was wearing were better than the ones he had been arrested in.

He recognised Ash immediately, and a smile flickered through his eyes before he suppressed it. He had spent a month giving nothing away: he wasn't going to break the habit without good reason. 'Mr Ash.'

'Mr Iqbal.'

The smile ventured closer to the surface. Ash imagined that, although he might be getting three square meals a day, a good night's sleep and continuing medical attention, Rachid Iqbal was seldom addressed so politely.

But then a shadow fell across the young man's eyes. 'Mr Ash – your friend. The police lady. Is she . . .?'

'She's well. Thank you.'

'You know this? You have spoken to her?'

'She's staying at my house for a few days. There was . . . an incident.'

'Ah.' The long breath expressed, better than words would have done, Iqbal's profound lack of surprise. 'He hurt her? Mr Oliver Ford?'

'No,' said Ash. 'At least, not seriously. But I think he might have done if I hadn't got her away from him when I did. He was holding her against her will.' That wasn't quite right either, but it was as close as he could get without writing an essay on the subject. 'I think, if she'd stayed with him much longer, he would have hurt her.

'And I think, Mr Iqbal, he did something

274

similar once before. To a young woman who mattered to you – a friend, or perhaps a sister or a cousin. Someone you'd have given your right arm to protect.'

It was out before he could stop it. It was just a figure of speech, part of the common lexicon of expressions that we all use as shorthand for feelings that would otherwise need spelling out. But on the table between them was the empty cuff of Rachid Iqbal's new shirt, and Ash was mortified to the depths of his soul by what he'd said. The colour rose dark in his skin, an apology stammered on his tongue, and he didn't know where to look.

His misery was interrupted by possibly the last sound he would have expected to hear here, in this windowless room, sitting at a Formica table bolted to the floor, observed by a security camera in the cornice – the soft, infinitely human sound of a chuckle. Ash didn't believe it, thought perhaps the young man was sobbing. But when he finally dared to look, Rachid Iqbal was indeed laughing gently at him.

'I'm so sorry,' mumbled Ash.

'It is all right,' Iqbal assured him. 'Really. You are precisely right. I would have given my right arm to protect her. And when I failed, I came to England and gave my right arm to avenge her.'

For a moment Ash said nothing more. Then, because it seemed that Iqbal might finally be ready to talk, he said, 'What happened?'

Her name was Safora, and Rachid Iqbal had loved her all his life. She was his sister. She was more than that. They had lost their parents during one of Syria's periodic upheavals – literally, they had gone out one evening, leaving the children with their grandmother, and never returned. Rachid assumed they'd fallen foul of militias or insurgents, or perhaps a band of robbers, but anyway he never saw or heard from them again. The grandmother died soon afterwards, leaving Safora at the age of fourteen to raise her ten-year-old brother.

Despite her youth, she was a girl of firm opinions – rather firmer, if truth be told, than was considered modest in a country which, when it wasn't blowing itself inside out, was essentially conservative. One opinion she formulated early on was that Syria was no country for a pair of orphans, and she set about finding a better one.

Rachid celebrated his twelfth birthday in a refugee camp on the Turkish border. It wasn't a lot safer than the streets of Damascus, but Safora had a plan. She made herself useful to a French medical team working in the camps. Rachid had heard of girls who made themselves useful to foreigners, but Safora was not like them. She worked long hours tirelessly and with good humour, fetching and carrying and cooking and washing clothes and boiling bandages. After a while the nurses let her help with their work, and taught her to speak French, and said they didn't know how they would manage without her; and when the team moved to a camp in Turkey, they arranged to take Safora with them. Safora arranged to take Rachid. He celebrated his fourteenth birthday in a UN compound outside Ankara, and his fifteenth in Istanbul where Safora was making herself useful to a team of European historians working in the great basilica that shared her name.

They had come eight hundred miles from where they started, and now they were on the edge of Europe where Safora was certain they could make a good life for themselves. In addition to French, she had now acquired a working familiarity with German and English, and was well liked as the girl who fetched and carried and washed clothes and was a safe pair of hands to clean an intricate carving or wrap a pot.

She found them two rooms in the basement of a Cypriot family's house. She enrolled Rachid at a school, and in the evenings she would tell him of the future she had planned for them. How they would go to Paris, and he would go to university, and she would get a job as a translator with the UN, and never have to fetch and carry and wash clothes – except her own and Rachid's – ever again.

Oliver Ford was one of the scholars working in the Hagia Sophia museum, on texts relating to the Crusades of the eleventh to fifteenth centuries. The texts were very old and very fragile, and an assistant with small, delicate hands was a great help to the team studying them. Safora was willing and careful, and could by now take instruction in all the main European languages, and Oliver Ford said he didn't know how he'd have managed without her.

In retrospect, Iqbal thought he had been slow to realise that his sister's relationship to the man she worked for was changing. Perhaps he saw a little less of her, but he was pleased that she was well thought of and her services were in demand. Perhaps they enjoyed a rather better standard of living than previously – but that was why Safora worked such long hours, so that she could look after her brother and put money aside for Paris.

He finally understood the extent to which things had changed when she came home one day in clothes she hadn't been wearing when she left for work. Fine western clothes, and leather shoes with heels, and a single strand of pearls so simple they had to be precious.

Rachid was too young to be a man of the world, but he'd seen a fair bit of it, good and bad, in the last few years, and he knew that even Safora could not have worked that hard, and the sudden acquisition of wealth by an unmarried woman was always a danger sign. He demanded an explanation.

But instead of blushing guiltily, she had turned on him a face aglow with happiness. 'Rachid, my brother – I am to be married!'

There was no doubt that it was the answer to the Iqbals' situation. Marriage to an English academic would change a girl of no family, no status, no home to speak of and only such wealth as she had been able to earn by her own labours, into a woman of substance. It would enable her to help the only other person in the world she cared about.

But Rachid looked at her, and listened to what she had to say, and did not believe that mere practicality was her motive. He believed that Safora was in love. No sense of foreboding cast its shadow over her joy.

And he? He was happy for her. She had found someone who wanted her, and whom she wanted in return; a man capable of giving her the kind of life that people like the Iqbals could usually only dream about. Perhaps she would take her brother to Europe after all. Even if that proved impossible, a good marriage would relieve him of the responsibilities an Arab man owes to the unmarried women of his family. He would not have seen her enter a duty marriage in order to make his life easier, but certainly his options would be wider if he entered manhood unencumbered by an unmarried sister.

Although he was only fifteen, Rachid expected Oliver Ford to seek an interview with him in order to formally ask for his sister's hand and settle the arrangements. Safora assured him the Englishman would visit shortly. But somehow it never happened. Of course, Oliver Ford was an important man and a busy one, and Rachid Iqbal was a fifteen-year-old boy who attended school for part of every day and also now worked in a small leather-tanning establishment. It proved difficult to find a time when both were free. Safora assured her brother that all was proceeding as it should, that Oliver Ford was as anxious as she to formalise arrangements for the wedding, and next week he would visit Rachid at home; or, failing that, the week afterwards. But he never did.

Then the happy couple left Istanbul, for a few

days that turned into several weeks. Rachid never thought his sister had been kidnapped. He was sufficiently acquainted with the world by now to know that there were parts of it where marriage was seen not as the start of a relationship between a man and a woman but more as an afterthought, to be squeezed in (preferably though not necessarily) before the birth of the first child.

This was not how things were done in Syria, or even in Turkey, and Rachid was not comfortable with the situation. He might have remonstrated with his sister about the gossip she was fuelling, if he had been able to talk to her. But all he got were postcards of various monuments to the Ottoman empire.

Safora returned five weeks later. She came home late at night, and did not light the lamps, and woke Rachid with a hand over his mouth. His first thought was that he was being robbed. There were people here with even less than he had, though usually they did not smell so sweetly.

'Safora?'

Outlined against the uncurtained window, he saw her nod.

'What's the matter? Put the light on, I can hardly see you.'

But she didn't. 'Forgive me for waking you, brother. But I need your help.'

He was wide awake now, sitting bolt upright on his bed. 'What has happened?'

Again she evaded the question. 'I need money. Whatever you can spare. I have to get away from here.'

'But you've only just come back!' Rachid

frowned. 'Safora, you have to tell me. What has happened?' And he reached for the light.

What shocked him most of all was not her split lip. It was not her black eye. It was the fact that the bruises despoiling her face were of different hues, because some of them were only hours old, and some of them were days old, and some of them had faded almost to nothing. His beautiful sister had been struck, repeatedly, forcefully, and on numerous occasions.

Rachid stood up, gathering the sheet about his modesty. With restraint beyond his years he said quietly, 'Tell me where to find him, and I will kill him.'

Safora managed a little broken laugh at that. 'Rachid! You cannot touch him. Men like him take what they want and cannot be made to pay the price. We are here on sufferance: remember that. If there is trouble, we are the ones – you and I – who will be made to pay. Mr Oliver Ford is an important man with many friends. We have no friends except one another.

'He will come here,' she said with absolute conviction. 'He will come looking for me. I cannot be here. Have you any money, for I have none?'

'Such money as we have is yours,' Rachid said simply. 'You earned it. If there is not enough, I will sell my schoolbooks. If *that* is not enough, I will sell my shoes. Where will you go? Back home?' It had been years since he'd referred to Damascus as home.

His sister shook her head. 'There is nothing for us back there. Also, he would find me. I will go somewhere I have never been, and when I find it I will tell only you.'

Rachid was working his way systematically around the room, turning out coins and small notes from drawers, boxes and pockets – anywhere he might have left funds for an unexpected emergency. He would never have greater need of them than now.

In the end there was more than he had thought. Still he doubted it would be enough to take his sister somewhere safe; but if it wasn't she was careful to keep the fact from him. Tears glittered on her bruised cheeks. 'Thank you, my brother. I do not know when I shall be able to repay you.'

'You repaid me years ago,' said Rachid.

She kissed him, and she left.

'I never saw her again,' whispered Rachid Iqbal. His dark head was bowed; a tear glistened like a diamond stud in the crease of his nose.

Gabriel Ash had sat with him, transfixed, all through the long telling, his heart aching for the young man's tragedy. Later he would be appalled by how close Hazel had come to sharing Safora Iqbal's fate, but for this one moment he had entirely forgotten the events that had brought him here. The account of the abused girl, and the boy left to manage his grief alone, filled his mind entirely.

'You don't know what became of her?'

But there was something in the way Iqbal glanced at him, a hunted quality that he hid by immediately dropping his eyes, that suggested the bitter tale was not yet told to its end.

282

Ash leaned closer. 'You do? Rachid, if you know where she is, I can help her. She may need money. She may need something else I can help with.'

But Iqbal shook his head. 'There is nothing she needs.'

Ash's eyes slid shut over his sorrow. 'She's dead?' Iqbal nodded. 'Was it Ford? Did he find her? Rachid – did Oliver Ford track your sister down and kill her?'

Iqbal drew in a long breath. These were deeply personal matters he was speaking of, and he wasn't entirely sure why he was sharing them with this tall stooping stranger when he had refused to explain to the policemen who had had every right to ask. He thought it was because Ash knew how it felt to lose someone he cared about to Oliver Ford. Neither of them could help Safora now, but perhaps they could help Ash's friend, the kind girl with the yellow hair.

'No,' he said at length. 'He didn't find her. And yes, he killed her. In every way that matters, he was responsible for my sister's death.'

Before Ash worked in national security, he worked in insurance, specifically in insurance investigation. It wasn't an obvious career path, but in fact many of the skills were the same. The ability to listen not only to what people were saying but also to what they weren't saying. The ability to spot the inconsistencies. The ability to play percentages: to know instinctively when something was odd enough to be true, and when it was just too odd – or just too obvious – to be believed.

All he knew of Rachid Iqbal and his sister was what Iqbal had told him. Except that he also knew something of the culture they came from, and more than he cared to about Oliver Ford. There were enough numbers drifting round for them to start adding up.

There was no tactful way of asking, but he needed to know. Saturday's future depended on him getting to the truth of this matter. 'Forgive me,' he murmured. 'But, was it suicide?'

The silence stretched for so long that Ash began to wonder if Iqbal didn't know the word – if it would be necessary to explain its meaning. But then the boy dipped his head again and said, barely loud enough to be heard, 'Yes.'

It might have been the full story. That, broken by abuse and disappointment, crippled by the loss of her honour, and terrified of being discovered by her tormentor, the girl had given herself up to the only peace she could now conceive of. And yet . . .

This was a strong girl. She had survived a civil war, the loss of both parents and the breakdown of her society, and she'd got herself and her brother to a place of safety. By means of nothing but guts and hard work she had created for them a life worth having. *Was* this someone who would cash in her chips early? Or was she someone who would draw the last card and stake everything she had on it? If Ford never caught up with her, what would have made *this* girl, this strong determined girl, despair of any kind of a future?

Ash bit his lip. 'Was she pregnant? Was that

284

the last straw that made her turn her back on the world?'

Across the table Iqbal snapped upright. This was not a thing that anyone from his culture would have asked. Yet he still felt that the big man meant well. That he would have kept his word if something as simple and as difficult to obtain as money could have made things better for his sister.

So he swallowed his anger, and only said, a little curtly, 'No, Mr Ash. She was betrayed. But that at least was spared her.'

Bewildered, Ash shook his head. 'Then I don't understand. She'd been hurt. She'd been humiliated. But she got away from the man responsible, and you say he never found her. You gave her some money to start a new life. I know she was capable of doing that: she'd already done it once. Why didn't she do it again?'

'Because . . .' The time had come to tell it. It was necessary to explain what Safora had done; if he didn't, her desperate attempt to salvage some honour from the situation would never be understood. If he didn't, Oliver Ford would have got away with what he did to them.

Even so, it took two goes for Rachid Iqbal to begin the final chapter of his tale. 'Because Ford did not catch up with Safora. He caught up with me.'

Thirty-Two

Detective Inspector Gorman's eyebrows jutted alarmingly. 'You want to do *what?*'

'I want to talk to Saturday,' said Ash. 'And I want to do it with no one else in the room.'

'That isn't possible.'

'I need you to make it possible,' Ash said calmly.

'He's a juvenile. *I* can't interview him without an appropriate adult being present.'

'I'm not a policeman,' Ash pointed out, 'I'm his friend. Actually, I'm yours too. Find a way to do this. I promise you won't regret it.'

Gorman narrowed one eye at him. 'You know what happened.'

Ash nodded. 'I think so. And I think Saturday will confirm it. But only if there's no one else there.'

The DI shook his head. 'I can't. You know I can't. You know how little discretion I have when it comes to processing a suspect. Even an adult suspect: multiply that by five for a juvenile. I imagine you're familiar with the Police & Criminal Evidence Act.' He gave a suspicious sniff. 'Of course you are – you probably wrote it.'

Seven months ago, along with virtually everyone at Meadowvale – virtually everyone in Norbold – Gorman had thought Gabriel Ash an idiot. Somewhere between then and now he'd gone to the other extreme and started crediting him with powers verging on the supernatural.

Ash sighed. 'No, that was the week I was reconciling general relativity with quantum mechanics. Dave' – they'd been through too much together to preserve the formalities – 'I'm trying to help here. I think I can help you *and* Saturday. I think I can prevent a miscarriage of justice. But I need a bit of latitude, because if we play it by the book, the bad guys are going to win.

'What have you got to lose? The worst that can happen is that I'm wrong, in which case nothing changes. But if I'm right, it's important that I get him to tell us what happened. Everything that happened.'

'Which is?' Gorman waited.

Ash regarded him steadily. 'Let me talk to him.'

There was nothing refined about Dave Gorman. He looked as if he'd been chiselled out of a mountainside by a sculptor with a really big hammer and no patience, and his thought processes were more direct than subtle. Catch him at a bad time – early in the morning, or late at night, or any time when the coffee machine in the corridor wasn't working – and he could look positively simian, as if he hadn't quite figured out what the opposable thumbs were for and why he felt the urge to bang rocks together.

But he wasn't stupid. He'd won his promotions by hard work rather than brilliance, but he'd developed good instincts and just occasionally he was prepared to stake more than he could afford to lose on his judgement.

He felt the prickle along his spine that suggested this was one of those occasions. 'Can I listen in?'

'Yes,' Ash said immediately. 'I think you should.'

'Will you tell him that I'm listening in?'

'Good grief, no.'

Gorman went on looking at him, his expression unreadable. Then he reached for his phone.

Saul Desmond, known as Saturday, was seventeen. You had to know that because it wasn't easy to guess. Sometimes he looked about twelve. And sometimes he looked like a little worn-out old man.

In a rare moment of sensitivity, Gorman had opened up the special suite at Meadowvale. Furnished somewhere between an office and a sitting room, it was designed to provide a less intimidating backdrop than the interview rooms for dealing with matters of a difficult and personal nature. He thought it might encourage the youth to relax, and that relaxing might encourage him to talk.

Also, he thought it might help if this went pear-shaped and he ended up trying to explain to the assistant chief constable. It wasn't an interview: that was the thing to hold onto. It was a friendly meeting between the youth and a concerned adult who was looking out for him. An Almost-Appropriate Adult.

Who just happened to have spent time in a mental institution.

Ash, who'd arrived first, looked up when the

door opened and Gorman steered Saturday inside. He tried not to wince. This was one of those days when the boy looked old and tired and scared. He went where the DI pointed him, took the chair indicated and sat, hunched up, waiting to be told what to do next. He'd registered Ash's presence in the first second, but he didn't look at him again, as if afraid that any show of hope might be punished.

Ash too was trying not to let his feelings show. He nodded a greeting, and filled two mugs from the electric kettle on the counter, and brought them over to the low table between the comfortable chairs. The one he pushed towards Saturday, the one with three spoonfuls of sugar in it, was inscribed with the legend: *It is better to light a candle than to curse the darkness.* The other said, *World's best grandma.*

Two mugs. This was not lost on Saturday. He cast a furtive glance at Gorman, but the DI was already heading for the door.

'I'll try not to disturb you,' he said as he went. 'Unless we're desperate for the suite.'

When they were alone, Saturday loosened up visibly. A decade fell off his face, and he glanced round the room appreciatively. 'This is nice.' He looked at Ash. 'You been pulling strings again?'

Ash shrugged. 'He owed me a favour. At least, I told him he did. I wanted somewhere we could talk. The interview rooms are about as comfortable as a tin box.'

'There's a room at the Young Offenders' Institution.' From Saturday's ironic tone, Ash guessed the residents called it something else.

'I wasn't sure I could see you alone there.' He gave a rueful grin. 'No strings to pull. No one there who might owe me even a very small favour.'

Saturday took a gulp of his coffee. 'What do you want to talk about?'

Ash blinked at him. 'Oh, I thought we could discuss the weather, and the price of fish, and the way the dollar exchange rate causes fluctuations in the housing market. Saturday, I want to talk about you! About how we're going to bring you home.'

Saturday gave a cautious nod. 'I'm up for that.'

'The first step is where you tell the truth.'

Saturday raised one thin eyebrow at him. 'Again?'

Ash hung onto his patience. 'No, not that truth. The other truth. The way Oliver Ford really got his head beaten in.'

Saturday looked away. 'I told the cops.'

'I know what you told the' – slang still came as naturally to him as the ability to tap-dance – 'police. And I know, and they know, and you know, that's not what happened.'

'How do you know?' said Saturday defensively. 'It could have.'

'It could have,' Ash conceded. 'But it didn't. Did it? Saturday, I am not your enemy. The people out there' – he gestured towards the door – 'are not your enemies. We're all just trying to make sense of this, and if there's a way that you walk away from it undamaged, we want to be sure of finding it. But we need – *I* need – you to be honest and frank. Tell me what happened.'

290

Saturday shrugged narrow shoulders. They were his own clothes – Hazel had bagged up some things for him – but the stress of the last week had stripped pounds from him and his shirt fitted only where it touched. He looked like a boy who'd been dressed in his father's clothes for a family funeral.

The story he told was exactly the one he'd told to DI Gorman.

Ash wasn't surprised. Saturday had spent a long time living on the streets. He'd lost the habit of trust.

Expressionless, Ash nodded and went back to the counter. 'Top up?' He added more coffee to both mugs and pressed the button on the kettle.

While he was waiting for it to boil, he let his eye travel appreciatively around the room. 'They've made a nice job of this, haven't they? A big improvement on the scruffy little room they used to use. It must make such a difference when it's needed for its designated purpose.'

His story told, and so far as he could judge accepted, Saturday relaxed enough to lean back in his comfortable chair. He thought interior decoration was a safe enough topic for discussion. 'What is its designated purpose?'

'It's the rape suite,' said Ash.

In the moment he said it he knew, from the way the boy's whole body stiffened, that he'd been right. The heart lurched within him. This was what he wanted, what made it a formality to get Saturday released and the charges against him withdrawn. At the same time, Ash almost wished he'd been wrong. If the stakes hadn't been

291

so high he'd have been tempted to let the boy nurse his pain in decent privacy. But the stakes were about as high as they could be, and Ash wasn't going to let Saturday squander years of his life rather than face up to what had happened to him.

And the job wasn't done yet. Ash took his time over the coffee, pouring the boiling water carefully, adding the milk a dribble at a time. He wanted to give Saturday time to accept the fact that he knew before they faced one another again.

When he'd done as much to a pint of instant coffee as was humanly possible, he returned to the table and put the *Light a candle* mug in front of Saturday. Ash gave an amiable smile as he sat down, but he said nothing. He didn't intend to be the next one to speak. He studied the décor some more, and sipped his coffee, and waited for Saturday to respond.

For perhaps a minute, which is longer than it sounds when there are only two people in a room and the atmosphere is suddenly electric, the boy seemed determined not to. Ash needed no imagination at all to visualise the thoughts in Saturday's head chasing one another's tails like a demented carousel.

This wasn't something he wanted to talk about. He'd taken the decision not to talk about it, and had stuck with that decision even when it seemed he might pay for it with years of his life. But Ash knew. He must know – God alone knew how, but this was what he did and he'd done it again. The lies Saturday had told, the story he'd worked out so carefully, hadn't fooled

292

him. And silence, he was beginning to feel as the minute ticked away, wasn't a long-term solution. All that was left was the truth.

When it finally came, his voice was so low that if Ash hadn't known what he was saying, he wouldn't have been able to hear it. 'How long have you known?'

Gabriel Ash looked at his watch. 'About fourteen hours.'

'*How* did you know?'

'I found someone else Ford did the same thing to. And for the same reason – to avenge himself on a woman who rejected him.'

Saturday didn't want to ask. But he needed to know. 'Another . . . Another guy?'

'A fifteen-year-old boy. His sister thought Ford meant to marry her. When she realised that what he really wanted was to own her, she got away from him and went where she thought he couldn't follow.'

Saturday's voice was a whisper. 'She was wrong about that?'

'No, she was right. But Ford didn't need to find her in order to punish her. He raped her brother. The guilt she felt overwhelmed her, and she killed herself.'

Saturday hadn't a lot of colour at the best of times. Now his face was grey. 'He told you this? The brother?'

'Yes, he did. He's a little older now. He blamed her, for a while, but he doesn't any more. He knows who was to blame.'

'He wanted to own her,' Saturday repeated softly. 'That's what he was doing to Hazel, isn't

293

it? Taking control of her. Making her into what he wanted. Like she was a pet.'

'Yes.'

'If we hadn't brought her home . . .'

Ash nodded sombrely. 'She'd have been badly hurt. Instead of which, you were.'

Saturday thought about that. About how much he owed to Hazel Best. About what he'd have been willing to do to protect her. About how she would feel when she learned what her escape had cost him. His eyes flared wildly, like a horse shown the whip. 'Hazel must never, *never* know about this.'

But that wasn't realistic. 'Saturday, she has to know. Mr Gorman has to know. He knows Ford didn't get his injuries the way you said. He thinks you launched an unprovoked attack on him. He has to be told it was the other way round.'

Saturday stared at the floor. In the stubborn whine of his voice was the suspicion of tears. 'I don't want people to *know*.'

Ash reached across the table and took the boy by both hands. This was something he would not have done three months ago. But comforting upset and angry boys was now part of his repertoire, and he'd learned that physical contact was not something to be feared, that nothing calmed and reassured like the touch of a sympathetic hand. 'And I don't want you going to prison when you don't deserve to. Hazel won't want that either. She's been desperately worried about you.'

'She'll blame herself . . .'

'Perhaps she will. But she'll know, when she

thinks it through, that the guilt is Ford's alone. She wouldn't want you to spend another minute under suspicion to protect her from the truth.'

Saturday's thin muscles clenched as if he meant to pull his hands away. But he didn't. 'If you want the truth – the God-honest truth – I did go after the bastard with that cricket bat. He was finished, he was leaving. I could have let him leave. But I wanted to hurt him. I wanted to kill him,' he said thickly.

'Of course you did. You'd been brutalised by a man who came into your home in the middle of the night. No one – not Mr Gorman, not the Crown Prosecution Service – is going to hold you responsible for what you did in the moments following that.'

'They'll let me go? You can make them let me go?' The desperate hope in his young voice was heart-breaking.

'I won't have to make them do anything. Tell them what happened. Exactly what happened. No one will think that the public interest will be served by persecuting you. They *will* prosecute Ford, if he recovers sufficiently.'

'But then everyone will know,' muttered the boy unhappily.

Ash shook his head decisively. 'Apart from me and Hazel, no one you know will ever hear that you were involved. Rape victims have a statutory right to anonymity. The only people who will know are those who have to know, and they'll be on your side.'

Saturday was staring into the depths of his mug as if he might find some answers there. He said nothing for so long that Ash wondered if the conversation was over. But it wasn't.

'I should have been able to stop him,' mumbled Saturday. 'I keep thinking, I should have been able to stop him. It's not like he's a commando or something. He's a talking head, for God's sake – a TV celeb. I should have been able to fight him off.'

'No, you shouldn't,' said Ash firmly. 'He had all the advantages. He's bigger than you, he's older than you, he's stronger than you, and he hadn't been asleep five minutes earlier. He came to the house knowing what he was going to do. He'd done it before. He was prepared, and you weren't.

'Saturday, however strong you are, there's always someone stronger. When you're young, or if you're a woman, half the human race is likely to be stronger than you. Mostly it doesn't matter. The vast majority of people won't use violence to take what they want. It's a defining characteristic of civilisation. People like Ford are an aberration. They don't understand that they can't just do what they want – that other people's rights are important.

'You couldn't have anticipated what he was going to do, and if you had you couldn't have stopped him. If he'd come after me, I probably couldn't have stopped him either. The advantage that a psychopath has is that there's no internal voice telling him to think about what he's doing, about the effect he's having on his victim. But it's that emotional blindness that trips him up in the end. Someone turns out to be braver, or tougher, or more resilient, than he ever imagined they could be. This time it was you.'

The boy gave a moist sniff. 'I don't *feel* very brave.'

'Well, you should.' The coffee had gone cold. Ash finished it with a grimace. 'I'll get Mr Gorman to come in, shall I? So you can tell him everything that happened.'

It was almost a bridge too far. He was still a seventeen-year-old boy who'd been so traumatised that he'd preferred to take whatever the legal system might throw at him rather than admit how he'd been abused. Ash was different: Ash was a friend, and anyway – somehow – he already knew. Saturday didn't think he could find the strength to talk about it to the policeman. 'I don't want to,' he whined.

'I know,' Ash said. 'But you have to. It's important. It's important to Mr Gorman, because if Ford recovers, the police need to get him behind bars before somebody else stands up to him. But it's also important to you. You have nothing to be ashamed of, and you shouldn't be hiding as if you had. You were assaulted, the same as if he'd beaten you with his fists. Rape isn't an act of sex, it's an act of violence. But you are not a helpless victim. You can make him pay for what he did.'

A sudden thought occurred to him, and he reached over and turned Saturday's mug in the compass of his hands. 'See that?'

Saturday read the legend. He looked up, puzzled, and the savage grin on Ash's face took him entirely by surprise. 'So?'

'It is better to light a candle than to curse the darkness. Do you know what's even better?' The boy shook his head. 'Lighting a flame-thrower.'

Thirty-Three

The tears that Ash and Saturday had somehow got through their discourse without shedding were coursing freely on Hazel's cheeks before the story was told.

It was Ash telling it. He'd asked if Saturday wanted to, but the boy couldn't face it. Nor had he wanted to be present. He'd pleaded exhaustion and gone to bed, leaving Hazel and Ash, and Patience, in the living room of the little house in Railway Street.

When he'd finished Ash went through to the kitchen, to tackle a stack of washing up that had hung around long enough for new life-forms to evolve in the crusty remains. Hazel stayed where she was, trying to get her head around what he'd said.

Twenty minutes later, pots disposed of, Ash returned to find Hazel's eyes red and her damp hankie spread on her knee, but her distress finally under control. When she spoke, her voice only cracked a little.

Her first question was the obvious one. 'Why didn't he *say*?'

Ash sat down beside her. 'He felt humiliated. He didn't want anyone to know what Ford had done to him. He was happier for people to think he'd attacked Ford than for them to know that Ford had raped him.'

'That is so . . .' Hazel began the sentence in outraged exasperation. But halfway through she found herself empathising with the boy's dilemma. He hadn't been the first to face it, nor the first to react as he had. Everyone in law enforcement knows that rape is the great under-reported crime. What no one knows is the extent to which it is under-reported.

'. . . Completely understandable,' she finished lamely. 'Isn't it? What teenage boy inching towards manhood wants to tell people he's been violated by another man? He saw a way out – an alternative version that was almost true, that only left out one significant detail. He thought it would put him in the clear without having to say what really happened.'

Ash said nothing. Patience looked the other way.

Hazel had known both of them long enough now to know that there was something she was missing. That Ash was hoping she'd put the pieces together without his help. The only reason for him to stay silent instead of explaining was that he didn't want to hurt her any more.

Once she'd got that far, it was only a matter of moments before she completed the jigsaw. Ash saw the last piece fall into place. Her expression froze. For a painfully long time, the only movement she was capable of was in her eyes, which stretched with shock and hollowed with grief and then filled afresh with the tears she thought she'd mastered.

'It wasn't *people* he wanted to hide the truth from – it was me. He didn't want me to know how much my lack of judgement had cost him. He was willing to go to prison to keep me from knowing that my lover raped him to punish me!'

Finally Ash nodded. 'Yes.'

'Gabriel – I can't bear it.'

'Yes, you can,' he said; and there was no unkindness in his voice, only certainty. 'Saturday can, and so can you. You have to. Or – dead or alive – Ford has won.' Patience stretched her long head across his knees. He stroked her ears while he marshalled what he wanted to say.

'If Oliver Ford recovers from his injuries, he'll stand trial for what he did to Saturday. He'll be convicted, and he'll do time. But he won't just be paying for Saturday – he'll be paying for you, for Rachid Iqbal and for his sister Safora. And maybe others that we don't know about and never will. And when it's all over you, and me, and Saturday, are going to take the ultimate revenge, which is to get on with our lives as if he never existed.'

It wasn't a big room, nothing larger than a two-seater sofa would fit along the longest wall. It was seriously snug with Hazel, Ash and Patience crammed onto it together. But the warm proximity of her best friends was a comfort to Hazel, and not for the world would she have tried to move.

'I don't understand,' she ventured at last. 'I don't understand *why*. I mean, I *know* Oliver likes women. So why Saturday?'

Ash sighed. 'I told Saturday – I shouldn't really

have to tell you. Rape is not about sex. It's about power. It's about grinding someone's face into the dirt because they're not strong enough to stop you. Ford knew he was stronger than Saturday. He also knew that he probably wouldn't report the attack; and, even if he did, no one would take the word of a criminal-fringe street kid over that of a respected academic and television personality. Except you. Saturday is your friend, and you'd believe him, and you'd blame yourself.'

'He hated me that much?'

Ash thought about that. 'I'm not sure hate is the right word. It suggests a range of emotions that may be quite foreign to him. Psychopaths have limited emotions of their own and struggle to understand anyone else's. They act them out – some of them do it very convincingly – but they don't really feel them. I don't think he hated you any more than he was in love with you. I doubt if he was capable of feeling what normal people mean by those words. The only emotions that resonated with him were the egocentric ones of self-importance, acquisitiveness, and resentment when his desires were thwarted. He always and only thought of himself. He felt he was entitled to have what he wanted, to do whatever was necessary to get it, and to punish anyone who tried to thwart him. He was a deeply dangerous man.'

'Do you suppose he'll recover?'

'He may well recover from the head injury. No one recovers from a personality disorder. Some people learn to manage them. What we

301

know of Ford's history suggests he isn't one of them.'

Later, after Ash and Patience had gone home, Hazel went upstairs. No light showed under Saturday's door; still, on an impulse she could neither have explained nor ignored, she went into his room and sat quietly on the end of his bed. The boy didn't stir.

'It's quite possible,' she whispered, 'that you are indeed asleep. After all, it's' – she pressed the backlight on her watch – 'good grief, it's quarter to three! And God knows you need a decent night's rest, so I'm not going to wake you. But just in case you can hear me, I want you to know how sorry I am for everything that's happened. And how angry I am, and also how touched, that you put my feelings ahead of your own best interests. If Gabriel hadn't figured it out, God knows how things would have turned out.

'But I will never, ever forget what you were willing to do for me. And one day I'll find the courage to say all this again, with the light on.'

Then she went to bed.

The following day DI Gorman got the call he'd been waiting for. 'Show him up.' If there'd been anyone in his office just then they'd have noticed his odd, almost predatory smile.

He was slightly put off his stride by the fact that Nicky Purbright wasn't a he but a she. It made no difference. She was Oliver Ford's London solicitor, and Dave Gorman had been looking forward to this interview.

On reflection, he decided she was exactly what he should have expected: young enough to be striking, old enough to be experienced, wearing a sharp suit and her hair up in a stately pleat. They greeted one another courteously – Gorman had long outgrown the inclination to blame legal representatives for their clients' offences – and sat down.

Ms Purbright began. 'Mr Ford is sorry he can't be here himself. He'll be in hospital for some time yet, and his doctors are limiting the number of visitors he's allowed and how long they spend with him. But he feels it's important to get things moving. As soon as he's able to give a written statement, he will do. In the meantime he wants me to assure you that he will be happy to give evidence about the assault on him. He doesn't want you to worry that, when the case comes to court in six months or a year, he'll decide the publicity might be detrimental to his career and want to let the matter drop.'

'Ah,' said Dave Gorman.

A tiny frown troubled Ms Purbright's alabaster brow. 'I'm assuming you'll go for attempted murder rather than GBH. The severity of the attack seems to indicate that was the young man's intention. And in fact, he almost succeeded. Mr Ford was in a coma for four days. He could have died. He could have suffered significant brain damage. It was only after he woke up that there was any confidence about his making a good recovery.'

'Well now,' said Dave Gorman judiciously. 'The final decision, of course, lies with the CPS.

303

But the evidence I have before me doesn't seem to support attempted murder. It doesn't seem to support assault occasioning grievous bodily harm. In fact, Ms Purbright, I don't anticipate bringing any charges at all against Saul Desmond.

'Your client, on the other hand, will be interviewed as soon as he's fit about Mr Desmond's allegation that Mr Ford entered his house in the middle of the night and raped him.'

Of necessity, solicitors learn to keep their thought-processes off their faces. Nothing should be seen to surprise them: nothing their client says, nothing which is said about their client. Ms Purbright hardly blinked. But Gorman was sure that it was the first she'd heard about this. 'I feel confident that my client will deny any such allegation.'

Gorman nodded cheerfully. 'Oh, so do I. I was a bit taken aback myself. After all, on the one hand there's Oliver Ford, an important academic, a face everyone knows from their television screen; and on the other there's a seventeen-year-old kid who was homeless until four months ago, who's only recently got his first job stacking shelves in a garage shop, and who never mentioned any of this when we responded to the original call-out. I mean, it's not difficult to decide who's the most credible, is it?'

'No,' murmured the solicitor cautiously.

'So of course I went looking for evidence. And funnily enough, even though we thought we were investigating Desmond's attack on Mr Ford, the material gathered by the scenes of crime officer, together with the clothes both of them were

304

wearing, turned out to be exactly the evidential materials we *would* have bagged if Desmond had made his allegation right away. Wasn't that lucky?'

Something in his tone warned Ms Purbright that it may have been lucky for someone but possibly not her client. She made no response.

Gorman waited just long enough to make her uncomfortable, then carried on. 'You'll never guess what forensics found when they turned their microscopes on what that kid probably describes as his pyjamas. Blood from the injuries to Oliver Ford's head, certainly. But also Oliver Ford's bodily fluids in places where Oliver Ford's bodily fluids had no business being.

'So, Ms Purbright,' he concluded happily, 'we're singing from the same hymn-sheet here. I'm ready to discuss these matters with your client just as soon as his doctors give us the OK. I'll be most interested to hear how he's going to explain that.'

Again, Ms Purbright said nothing. But what she was thinking was, You and me both.

It wasn't the kind of success you celebrate. All the same, Ash thought that once the dust had settled he'd take his friends out for a meal, see if they couldn't re-establish normal, casual, uncharged relations over the sticky toffee pudding. Or maybe get Frankie to make up a picnic and take the boys as well. There was a shop opposite the park where he could buy a kite. A bit of running round and shouting would do Saturday the world of good.

But it never happened. Three days after he'd secured Saturday's freedom, Ash was putting his sons to bed – to the nightly complaint from Gilbert that he was two years older and shouldn't have to go to bed at the same time as Guy – when the calm he'd just about established was fractured by hammering at the front door.

He left Frankie to answer it, continued reading *Treasure Island*. The boys seemed to consider it a satisfactory bedtime story, although Ash found himself shivering at the tap-tap-tapping approach of Blind Pew.

But Hazel's voice – more particularly the distress in Hazel's voice – came up the stairs to him, and he brought the chapter to an abrupt finish and went down.

'He's gone! Gabriel, he's gone.' Her hair – shaggy as the sharp cut grew out and skewbald as it reverted from red to her natural blonde – was awry and she was crying.

'Who's gone? Saturday? Gone where?'

'I don't know!' she wailed. 'He's taken his things, and that ghastly rucksack, and picked up his wages from the garage and gone.'

Ash tried to reassure her. 'He can't be far away. He's hardly been out of Norbold in his life. I'll drive, you look. It won't take us half an hour to find him.'

'Do you think I haven't *been* looking? He's gone. The people at the garage saw him hitch a lift on a truck heading for the motorway. They thought it was bound for London.'

Ash was puzzled. 'Why would Saturday go to London? He doesn't know anyone there.'

It infuriated Hazel how dim an intelligent man could be. 'That's the whole point! He wants to go where nobody knows *him*. He wants to disappear. He can't face being here, being with us, after what happened.'

Ash stared at her. 'He told you this?'

'Of course he didn't tell me! If he'd told me he was going, I'd have stopped him. He left me a note. I found it when I got in this evening.' She brought it from the pocket of her jeans and held it out to him. Her hand was shaking.

The note said rather less than Hazel had read into it. Like its author, it was wary, oblique, guarded. If a note can be uncommunicative, it was uncommunicative, giving the minimum amount of information that he'd thought would prevent its recipient from worrying or – since it was addressed to Hazel – calling out the Marines.

'Going away for a bit,' he'd written, in the carefully drawn letters of someone who'd hardly picked up a pen since puberty. 'Get my head straight. Do not worry about me I will be fine. Will get in touch when I know where I am going to be. Tell Mr Gorman sorry. Tell Gabriel sorry. You two. Thanks for everything, Saturday.'

'"You two"?' Perplexed, Ash read it aloud.

'He means, "You too".' Hazel sketched the double O in the air with a finger. 'Gabriel – he's taken his second-best pyjamas. He hasn't a bed to go to, but he's stuffed his pyjamas into that battered old rucksack. We have to find him!'

There were two possible responses. One was to point out that, if the boy had gone to London because he didn't want to be found, their chances

307

of finding him were vanishingly small. The other was to drive around until the impossibility of the task became inescapably clear to her.

Gabriel Ash had no talent for lying. And lying to Hazel about this could only prolong the misery. 'I don't think we can,' he said honestly.

'We have to! Gabriel, you know people – people in London, security people. They can help.'

Ash suspected that the stock of favours he could still call in was all but exhausted. But he'd have tried, for her sake and for Saturday's, if he'd thought there was any point. 'This truck he got a lift with. Are we sure it was heading for London?'

'Not exactly.' Someone in the garage had thought that was what the driver said when Saturday asked where he was bound. Someone else thought he said Dublin. 'But if he wants to lose himself, that's where he'll go. We can catch them on the motorway.'

'Hazel – he's probably there by now. He left the note while you were out specifically so he could get a head start. This truck: were the people at the garage able to describe it?'

'White, with some kind of machinery on the back.'

'A white truck hauling machinery to London, or possibly Dublin, that left hours ago – and you think we can find it? I'm sorry, I know it's not what you want to hear, but we're already too late. He wanted to disappear and that's what he's done.'

'I can't let him go like this!' she cried from

the breaking of her heart. 'This is my fault! It's my fault he was hurt. But for me he'd never have met the bastard who hurt him. And now, because my face would be a daily reminder of that, he's turned his back on the only home he's known for three years and the only people in the world who give a damn about him. Gabriel, help me! Help me to find him. You found your wife, for God's sake, when everyone thought she was dead. You can help me find Saturday.'

He understood where it came from, but still the reference to Cathy turned a knife under Ash's ribs. He bit back the retort that was already in his mouth, reminded himself that Hazel was floundering in a toxic emulsion of grief and guilt, and sinking more than she was swimming.

So instead he said gently, 'I didn't find Cathy – Cathy found me. It only looked as if I'd been clever. You know that, Hazel. You know I have very little to be proud about as far as Cathy's concerned, and it was nothing more than luck, and the bloody-mindedness of my eldest son, that meant I got the boys back.

'Of course I'll help you. Tell me what you want me to do. But I don't think we'll succeed. Saturday spent three years staying under everyone's radar. If he's chosen to melt back into the shadows now, no one is better equipped.'

'You're saying we'll never see him again,' Hazel whispered brokenly. She laid her cheek against Ash's broad chest, and he put his arms around her for the comfort of them both.

'No,' he said, 'that's not what I'm saying. I'm saying, this is what he wants right now. And maybe it's the right thing for him. He wants to be alone for a while, to come to terms with what happened without his friends smothering him with sympathy. He wants to be anonymous. And there's nowhere like London for being anonymous in.

'But it won't be forever. He's growing up. This was a pretty significant event in his life, but it's not the first significant event he's had to deal with. He managed before, and he'll manage now. They have shelves to stack in London, too. He'll get a job, he'll rent a room, and he'll be OK for as long as he feels he has to stay. And when he feels he doesn't have to stay away any longer, he'll come back.'

Hazel sniffed moistly. 'If he can keep out of trouble.'

'He kept out of trouble for three years,' Ash pointed out. 'The only trouble he ever got into was when he was with us.'

It was true, though hardly calculated to make her feel better. 'What about the case? Saturday's the chief witness: if he doesn't give evidence, will Dave Gorman have to let Oliver go? If that happens,' she advised darkly, 'I may well buy a gun and go after him myself.'

Ash shook his head. 'There's plenty of evidence without Saturday's testimony. The best of it is the forensics. The only possible defence Ford can muster is to say that the sex was consensual – and that makes so little sense in the context of their relationship that his defence team will be reluctant to field it. For one thing, a consensual relationship with a teenage boy would do nearly as much damage to Ford's reputation as being accused of rape.

'For another, there's Rachid Iqbal. He came to England looking for revenge, and you stopped him. If he's offered the chance of another kind of payback, by telling a court how Ford used him exactly as he used Saturday, in almost identical circumstances, he'll take it. You don't need to worry about Oliver Ford, Hazel. You aren't going to bump into him in Sainsbury's any time soon.'

'And you really think Saturday will come back?' She sounded like a child pleading for reassurance, her voice small and muffled by his increasingly damp shirt front.

Ash smiled sombrely into the top of Hazel's head, where a line like a Cold War frontier divided the red ends of her hair from the blonde roots. 'I'm sure of it. When he's had a chance to heal. When the appeal of anonymity has started to wear thin. Or when he needs something, he'll be back.'

He thought about that then and realised he wasn't being fair. Saturday had never taken much from them. A second-hand bed in Hazel's house; a few square meals; some clothes to sleep in that weren't the ones he spent the rest of the time in. What he'd given in return was more significant. For starters, he'd saved Ash's life.

'Or maybe,' he added, 'when we need him.'

THE END